Praise for Stuart M. Kaminsky's MIDNIGHT PASS

"Good dark fun . . . Kaminsky strikes new chords of imagination every time out."
—*Chicago Tribune*

"Unique and witty, this third Fonesca mystery will keep readers on their toes and serve up a few surprises at the conclusion."
—*Romantic Times* (4 stars)

"There are three things we've come to expect from a Kaminsky story: superb plotting, real-world dialogue and character development. He doesn't place a foot wrong in any of these departments in *Midnight Pass*."
—*Sarasota Herald-Tribune*

And for RETRIBUTION

"A polished follow-up to *Vengeance* . . . Kaminsky is such a pro that the pages fly by, and even though Lew is often such a sad sack, it's hard not to root for him."
—*The Chicago Tribune*

"Lew is still a triumph: a Lew Archer type with nerve endings so sensitive that when he's asked, 'anybody dead?' he replies, 'Most of the people who ever lived.'"
—*Kirkus Reviews*

"Kaminsky's gifts for visceral scene-setting, for dialogue that has perfect pitch, and for telling details are much in evidence here."
—*Booklist*

"An excellent hard-boiled novel . . . Kaminsky expertly delivers a sense of foreboding in Sarasota where 'one can spend a day, a week or a lifetime avoiding the mean streets, the dark corners . . . Sarasota is a beautiful bright orange blanket over a layer of darkness. Most people who come here don't look under the blanket."
—*The Sun-Sentinel*

D1197888

BY STUART M. KAMINSKY

Lew Fonesca Mysteries

Vengeance
Retribution
Midnight Pass

Abe Lieberman Mysteries

Lieberman's Folly
Lieberman's Choice
Lieberman's Day
Lieberman's Thief
Lieberman's Law
The Big Silence
Not Quite Kosher

Toby Peters Mysteries

Bullet for a Star
Murder on the Yellow Brick Road
You Bet Your Life
The Howard Hughes Affair
Never Cross a Vampire
High Midnight
Catch a Falling Clown
He Done Her Wrong
The Fala Factor
Down for the Count
The Man Who Shot Lewis Vance
Smart Moves
Think Fast, Mr. Peters
Buried Caesars
Poor Butterfly
The Melting Clock
The Devil Met a Lady
Tomorrow Is Another Day
Dancing in the Dark
A Fatal Glass of Beer
A Few Minutes Past Midnight
To Catch a Spy
Mildred Pierced

Porfiry Rostnikov Novels

Death of a Dissident
Black Knight in Red Square
Red Chameleon
A Cold, Red Sunrise
A Fine Red Rain
Rostnikov's Vacation
The Man Who Walked Like a Bear
Death of a Russian Priest
Hard Currency
Blood and Rubles
Tarnished Icons
The Dog Who Bit a Policeman
Fall of a Cosmonaut
Murder on the Trans-Siberian Express

Nonseries Novels

When the Dark Man Calls
Exercise in Terror

Short Story Collections

Opening Shots
Hidden and Other Stories

Biographies

Don Siegel: Director
Clint Eastwood
John Huston, Maker of Magic
Coop: The Life and Legend of Gary Cooper

Other Nonfiction

American Film Genres
American Television Genres
(with Jeffrey Mahan)
Basic Filmmaking
(with Dana Hodgdon)
Writing for Television
(with Mark Walker)

Stuart M. Kaminsky

_M IDNIGHT PASS

A Lew Fonesca Mystery

A Tom Doherty Associates Book
NEW YORK

This is a work of fiction. All the characters and events portrayed in this book are either products of the author's imagination or are used fictitiously.

MIDNIGHT PASS: A LEW FONESCA MYSTERY

Copyright © 2003 by Stuart M. Kaminsky

A Forge Book
Published by Tom Doherty Associates, LLC
175 Fifth Avenue
New York, NY 10010

www.tor.com

Forge® is a registered trademark of Tom Doherty Associates, LLC.

ISBN 0-765-34383-5
EAN 975-0765-34383-3

First Edition: December 2003
First mass market edition: December 2004

Printed in the United States of America

0   9   8   7   6   5   4   3   2   1

This one is most definitely
for Polly Curry.

I did not know what to say to him. I felt so awkward and blundering. I did not know how I could reach him, where I could overtake him and go on hand in hand with him once more.

It is such a secret place, the land of tears.

— Antoine de Saint-Exupéry
The Little Prince

Author's note: There really is a Midnight Pass. There really is a controversy over whether it should be opened. However, this is a work of fiction. The issues I have created differ from those in reality, as does the history of the controversy and some of the history of the Pass itself. The motives of those who have taken sides about whether to open the Pass are very different from and far less dramatic than the motives and people in the story I have invented.

MIDNIGHT PASS

PROLOGUE

THROUGH THE PARTIALLY open door in a treatment room in the E.R. of Sarasota Memorial Hospital, I look out at the cluttered counter of a nursing station.

Small colored sheets of paper are skewered on an upright thin spike. Wire baskets flow over with charts and graphs. A single thin brown folder totters at the edge of the counter, threatening to fall whenever a blue-clad nurse or aide shuffles or hurries by.

On my right in the small, darkened room, the machine next to me gives out a steady, slow series of beeps and a simultaneous series of blips, black dots of sound. The fluorescent lights in the corridor beyond the open door hum. Blips, beeps, and hums. A little night music complete with vocal accompaniment.

"Ron"—a woman's voice, calm, weary—"glucose was two-five-two."

A young man in short-sleeved whites wheels a gurney past the cubicle I'm in. Covered by a thin white blanket, an old man with eyes closed pauses just outside the room for an instant and then is pushed out of sight.

There is a low, calm chatter of voices, and then a heavy white nurse with glasses and close-cropped hair pushes a wheelchair past the door. A pretty young black woman sits in the chair, holding an infant.

"Four months old," the young mother says. "She's got asthma and something wrong with her heart."

The heavy white nurse with glasses and close-cropped hair touches the young woman gently on the shoulder, and they roll by.

The passing parade pauses.

I look around the room. In the band of cold white light that comes through the open door, I see a gray stool and an overflowing ivory-colored trash can with the fingers of a blue rubber glove dangling out, as if someone or something is trying to escape.

There is a box on the wall, a see-through rectangular box with a plastic slot. The word "Danger" is printed in black letters on an orange square on the box and under it, also in black, "Used Needles."

There is a pink plastic tray to vomit in on the small, shining steel table next to the bed. All the discomforts of home.

A new voice, female, beyond the curtain.

"What'd I do with my pen? I've lost two today."

A man in hospital blues, dark haircut almost scalp short, clipboard in his hand, walks slowly by, talking to an older woman in blues with washed-out blond hair.

They glance at me through the parted curtain and walk on. I hear him say, "Dr. Greenspan wants him in op in ten minutes."

The woman says, "Okay."

"Saturday morning," the man's voice comes back.

"Saturday morning," the woman repeats.

I listen to more blips and bleeps. A man moans from somewhere; two female voices giggle. Is there going to be a third? Does Dr. Greenspan know what he is doing or looking for? Who is this Dr. Greenspan?

My back aches. I have a headache.

I wait, listening for the wheels of a gurney moving to the room I am in. I wait to look up at whoever will be pushing it. I imagine a thin-haired, short, well-muscled orderly in blue, his hairy arms, and a wide-band metal wristwatch. I wait for him to cheerfully say, "It's time."

The road from a cold Dairy Queen Blizzard to the hospital emergency room began five days earlier.

Three people had died in those five days. There was a good chance there would be a fourth soon, a fourth who lay in a small triage room, a fourth whose odds were not looking too good.

Sally Porovsky steps into the room and looks down at me.

"How does it look, Lew?" she asks.

I don't have a good answer. I try a smile. It doesn't work. She takes my right hand in both of hers.

It had been bright and sunny and humid and definitely Florida when I got up healthy on Monday. Time generally seems to move slowly for me, but on Monday the clock began to spin.

Here's how it went.

1

NO AMOUNT OF SUNSCREEN will save her," Dave said, shaking his head.

I nodded and looked up at the jogger passing in front of the DQ, headed downtown. She wore shorts and a tank top, a Walkman singing in her ear, a serious look on her pretty face, her sunbleached blond hair bouncing against her back in a long ponytail.

She made a left turn and headed out of sight toward Towles Court, a collection of small shops and homes owned by painters, sculptors, jewelry makers . . . people who had once been successful in business or raising a family and now were retired and wanted to change the label they wore from no one in particular to Artist. Few of the community in Towles Court, mostly women, had illusions about breaking out and getting famous and wealthy. They enjoyed what they now were and what they were doing. They had peace, time, and identity.

I cannot paint, sketch, sculpt, or draw, and I have no urge to try. Unlike the artists of Towles Court in their brightly painted houses, I have as little identity as possible.

Dave owns the Dairy Queen franchise across the parking lot from where I live and work in a walk-up office building with peeling paint and crumbling corners of concrete. The building had begun life as a two-story, 1950s motel and had gradually gone downhill till it was ready for me. I'm not supposed to live in the back room of my office, but the landlord doesn't care as long as I pay my rent on time and don't complain. I don't complain.

Dave looks like a dark, deeply weathered mariner, which he is when he's not handing out Dilly Bars, Blizzards, and burgers. He owns a boat and is out in Sarasota Bay and the Gulf of Mexico whenever possible. The sun has leathered him. The boat has given him muscles and kept him trim.

Dave is about my age, early forties. I like to think that with his face and bleached-out hair he looks older than I do, but I'm dark with a rapidly receding hairline that makes me look every minute of my age.

My name is Lew Fonesca. I live in Sarasota, Florida, where I drove a little over three years ago when my wife was killed in a hit-and-run "accident." "Accident" is in quotes because the police couldn't find out who the driver was. My wife was a lawyer in the Cook County State Attorney's office, where I worked as the head of legal research. She had prosecuted a lot of people, made a lot of them and their relatives angry. Maybe it wasn't an accident, a drunken driver, a panicked kid who had just gotten his or her license, someone on a cell phone not paying attention.

When the funeral was over and I had nothing left to weep, I got in my 1989 Toyota in the cemetery parking lot and started to drive. I headed south, in the general direction of oblivion and the tip of Florida. I had no idea of what I would do when I got there.

Stuart M. Kaminsky

I wasn't sure where "there" was. In those four days, I listened to the voices of conservative talk-show hosts, Don Imus, Rush Limbaugh, Neal Boortz, Michael Savage, and the advocates of the unknown like Art Bell and Whitley Streiber, anybody who was talking. I didn't want music. I wanted company, a voice, anyone speaking whom I didn't have to answer. I listened but I heard nothing.

My car had given out in the DQ parking lot in Sarasota. There was an "Office For Rent" sign on the office building. I sold the car for twenty-five dollars to a couple of kids eating hot dogs and drinking Blizzards and made the first month's rent on the office overlooking the DQ parking lot and heavily traveled Route 301, which was named Washington Street for the stretch through Sarasota.

Now I sat at the white, chipped enamel table with the sun umbrella with Dave talking about the sun and pretty women joggers. Dave was drinking water. I was working on a cheeseburger and a chocolate-cherry Blizzard, my copy of the Sarasota *Herald-Tribune* folded on the table in front of me.

The ultraviolet index, which I could never understand, was close to ten, which meant that if you stepped out into it you'd probably die of skin cancer faster than you would of exposure in the middle of winter at the North Pole. I pulled my Chicago Cubs baseball cap down about an inch.

Earlier that morning I had biked the five blocks to the downtown YMCA, locked up my bike, showed my card, got my things out of my locker, and worked out. Pounding the step machine, fighting the leg weights, pumping, running, stretching muscles, straining arms and legs, pushing. I needed it. Not because I treasured my body but because I could lose myself in the burn, the edge of physical pain, the satisfaction of starting at A and completing stages that took me through to Z, if I decided to go that far. At the end I could feel what I had accomplished or had done to myself. It was finite. It was satisfying. When I was finished working out, I always showered slowly, the water as hot as I could take it, letting it beat into my head and body drowning out voices, light, the world. It never fully exhausted me, though. That would have been an additional benefit. One of the many blessings or curses of Lewis Fonesca was that nothing exhausted me for very long: not working out, not working, not too little sleep or too much sleep.

I had pedaled back past the Hollywood 20 theater, the city and county buildings on Washington, past the small shops and to where I sat now, early burger and Blizzard in hand, newspaper in front of me.

I sat quietly digesting my burger and Dave's observation. Dave drank his water and accidentally spilled a few drops on his white apron.

"My kids are coming Saturday for their annual two weeks," he said. "My ex is going to Guam to study brown tree snakes. What do you do with an eight and ten year old? I'll take them to Busch, Universal, Disney. Saturday I'll take them to First Watch for breakfast. They love it. Another year or two and they'll outgrow it. Maybe."

"Maybe," I said, finishing the burger and giving my full attention to the Blizzard, working at the chocolate that stuck to the side of the cup, careful not to break the red plastic spoon.

"*Das es shicksall giveren,*" he said. "It's fate."

Dave spoke five languages, all picked up when he traveled in Europe for five years when he got out of high school over twenty years ago. Dave was a quick study with not much ambition. I didn't know what "fate" or whose he was talking about.

"You know Christopher Lee speaks Russian and Greek?" he asked.

"No," I said, finishing my drink.

I checked my watch. I had an appointment I wanted to skip but knew I wouldn't.

"And Kobe Bryant speaks French?" Dave said.

I didn't answer.

"Kobe Bryant, the kid on the Lakers. I talked to him once on a plane. In French. Kid had a great accent. Never finished high school."

Dave was like one of the radio voices that had accompanied me when I drove, only Dave sometimes required an answer and deserved attention, which I tried to give.

"You Fonesca?" a deep voice behind me said.

Dave squinted up over my shoulder. I adjusted my baseball cap and turned around.

I recognized him.

"I'm Fonesca," I said.

"Went to your office," the man said, nodding toward the open space on the bench between Dave and me. "Man up there pointed you out."

I looked up at the second-floor landing just outside my office. Digger, a homeless man who used the building's rest room as a frequent refuge, waved down at me. I waved back.

I invited the man to sit. After all, he was a distinguished local figure, a minister, a leader of the local civil rights movement, a high-ranking official in the Florida ACLU, and a member of the County Commission, the only African-American in the city or county government.

The Reverend Fernando Wilkens was in the newspaper and on the local television news almost every day. I almost never watched the news but I did read the *Herald-Tribune*. Well, that's not exactly the truth. I looked at the headlines, checked to see how Sammy Sosa was hitting, and examined the obituaries year-round to see who had died and left a small or large hole in the world.

I knew almost nothing about local politics, but Reverend Wilkens was a hard man to miss.

Wilkens was big man, running toward the chunky side, in tan slacks and a white pullover short-sleeve shirt with a little green alligator on the pocket. He was about fifty, had good teeth, smooth brown skin, an even smoother bass voice, and a winning public smile, which he was not sporting at the moment.

"Can I speak to you privately?" Wilkens said, sitting down without looking at Dave.

"Customer at the window," Dave said, getting up. "Want a Dilly Bar or something?"

"No, thank you," Wilkens said, folding his hands on the table."

Dave shrugged and moved toward the door at the back of the DQ. A young, frazzled-looking woman lugging a heavy baby was at the window. The baby was trying to squirm out of her arms.

"You know who I am?"

"Yes," I said, tapping at the Local section in front of me, which featured an article on the mysterious death of more manatees. Manatees seemed to be constantly dying mysteriously just as red tide seemed to roll in once a season and linger in the warm water and hot sun over the Gulf of Mexico. It gave the Local-section reporters surefire story material and once in a while made the front page.

The doings of both the City Council and the County Board of Commissioners, on the other hand, made the front pages only when there was a controversy so major that at least fifty citizens protested with marches and placards and complaints before the open hearings of the council or board. Few people went to these meetings with any real hope of convincing the council or board of anything. Few people when addressing the council for their allotted three or four minutes even expected their elected officials to listen to them. In the middle of an impassioned speech by an ancient resident, members of the council or board would pass notes on the latest Florida State or University of Florida football or baseball scores, hand-carried to them by a Manatee Community College intern.

Most of these meetings were on television for those who chose to watch, which was few. I sometimes tuned in and found myself dozing unless there was a new issue and lots of complaints such as whether to build another high-rise hotel like the Ritz-Carlton to block out more of the sun and the view of the Gulf.

"There's a commission meeting Friday night," Reverend Wilkens said, soft and deep, as I pushed away my empty plastic cup and glanced up at a couple of shirtless boys with lean bodies and a desire to be killed by the sun. I heard them order large Oreo-cookie Blizzards.

"A commission meeting," I repeated.

Reverend Wilkens nodded.

"There's going to be an open hearing about six items," he said. "The last one is whether to open Midnight Pass."

I nodded, not knowing where this was going.

Midnight Pass was a hot issue every few years in Sarasota County. Cars with bumper stickers reading "Open Midnight Pass" had been common when I first came to town. There were fewer now, but the Pass had become an issue again.

"What do you know about the Midnight Pass controversy?" he asked.

I told him what I thought I knew, which wasn't much and was probably half wrong. There had once been a narrow waterway separating Siesta Key and Casey Key, two of the high-priced islands off the Sarasota coast. The Pass was closed now, creating one long island and cutting off access to the mainland unless a boater went down to the end of the Casey Key and came up the inlet. People on the mainland coast, realtors and land developers, wanted the Pass open so mainland property prices would go up because pleasure and fishing boats could have direct access to the Gulf. People who owned property on the Gulf side of the island wanted it left closed so their property would be worth more because there would be less shoreline with direct access to the Gulf. Then there were two additional groups of people who fought over what would be best ecologically, no Pass or an open Pass. From what I could tell, however, about ninety-nine percent of the population of Sarasota County didn't care either way.

"A bit oversimplified," Reverend Wilkens said with a smile that indicated I was woefully uninformed on the issue but that he was a tolerant and patient man. "Before 1918, Siesta and Casey Key were separated by Little Sarasota Inlet. In 1918, a strong gale broke open Musketeers Pass about halfway down Casey Key and created Bird Keys, a small and a tiny island formed by wash-through sand. In 1921, Little Sarasota Inlet was partially closed by another storm. Property owners finished filling it in."

"Leaving only Musketeers Pass between Casey and the south end of Siesta Key," I said to show I was paying attention.

"That is correct, but without going into more of the Lord's manipulation of the land and elements, let it suffice that Musketeers Pass was renamed Midnight Pass, a fifty-foot inlet separating Casey and the south peninsula of Siesta Key and providing direct access to Little Sarasota Bay and Bird Keys. The Pass began to grow smaller as the keys drifted toward each other or nature just filled it in. In 1983, two homeowners received permission from the state and county and closed what remained of the Pass. Result? Little Sarasota Bay became stagnant, creating a new ecological system."

"And that's bad."

"No," he said, "that is good. Little Sarasota Bay has become a unique plant and animal sanctuary, a relatively tourist-free nature haven. The Lord allowed those homeowners to close that Pass for a reason. They simply finished the work He had begun. If He wants it open, He'll do so without the Corps of Engineers and many millions of dollars the county can ill afford. He parted the Red Sea. I trust he can part a narrow fifty-foot stretch of filled-in land if He so chooses. I wish the Pass to remain closed until the Lord chooses to open it. The Army Corps of Engineers has indicated the cost to reopen will be as much as ten million dollars, and then the cost of keeping God from closing it again after that will be a million or more each year."

He started at me with sincerity and unblinking eyes. He was good, but I could see there was another reason for wanting Midnight Pass left closed lurking behind those deep, brown eyes.

"It will be the last item on the agenda and probably won't come up till after midnight on Friday. I've got the feeling that a few of my fellow board members whose views differ from mine will have lots to say on the earlier items such as tearing up Clark Road again or replacing blighted trees on Palm Avenue. We'll listen to the public and then discuss and vote on Midnight Pass. The vote won't be subject to review unless there's a violation of the state or federal constitution."

Wilkens basically represented Newtown, the African-American ghetto in Sarasota running about four blocks or more in either direction north and south of Martin Luther King Jr. Street. The far south end of what could be called Newtown was within walking distance of downtown. A curious man might have wondered what the Midnight Pass business in another district forty minutes south had to do with Newtown. I wasn't curious.

I was about to say, "What's this got to do with me?" when Fernando Wilkens told me.

He leaned over and whispered, "I've got the votes."

"The votes?"

"To keep the Pass closed," he said. "There are five members on the County Commission. Votes involving contracts for millions of dollars are routinely decided by simple majority."

I nodded to show him that I was paying attention.

"I have your assurance that this is a privileged conversation?" he asked softly, though no one was listening. He looked around to see if we were being watched by anyone. Cars drove by but on a day like this only teens, joggers, and the homeless wandered the streets of Sarasota.

It's privileged. How did you find me?" I asked. "And why?"

I'm not listed in the phone book, either in the white pages or in the yellow pages. I'm a process server with even less ambition than DQ Dave. I work as little as I can, live as cheaply as I can, and have as little to do with people as I can. I checked my watch and glanced at my bicycle leaning against the side of the DQ. If I didn't get going in the next five minutes and pedal hard, I'd be late.

"My lawyer, Fred Tyrell," Wilkens said. "He told me about you."

I nodded. Tyrell was the token black in the downtown law firm of Cameron, Wyznicki, Forbes, and Littlefield. No "Tyrell." Tyrell's job was to take minority clients and even drum them up. Sometimes it worked. Sometimes even the most committed African-American activists wanted a smart white lawyer, preferably a Jewish one. Cameron, Wyznicki, etc., had one of those too, Adam Katz. I think the firm took him in about a decade before I came simply because of his last name. I had done work for both Katz and Tyrell. The partners had their own short list of investigating and process-serving private detectives and process servers, though I got most of my business from another law firm, Tycinker, Oliver, and Schwartz on Palm Avenue.

I nodded again, looked at my empty cup.

I'm what is usually called medium height and probably seen

as being on the thin side, but I pedal to the downtown Y every day, work out for at least an hour three times a week, and have grown hard in a town of white sand beaches and lazy hot days. I grew hard to stay away from my own desire to turn into a vegetable.

"Parenelli will vote with me," said Wilkens.

I nodded a third time. This was no surprise. Parenelli was the closest thing we had to a radical liberal on the council. He was old, crusty, had moved down from Jersey thirty years ago, and would have gladly voted for Eugene V. Debs for governor if Debs were alive and eligible. Sometimes the other council members kept certain issues until late in each session in the hope that Parenelli would be too tired to protest or might even doze off. Parenelli was too crafty an old socialist to let that work. He sat with his thermos of black coffee, did crossword puzzles while he pretended to take notes, and waited for the big vote.

Three commission members always voted together on money issues. They would furiously debate for hours whether they should approve an unbroken or broken yellow line down the middle of the recently widened Tuttle Avenue, and you would never know how that one would go, but on expenditures, they were closer together than the Statler Brothers. That left Wilkens and Parenelli together on social issues. Votes of three to two were common, but it was even more common to have unanimous votes because most issues were without controversy and without interest to even the commission members.

"The way I count it, you're one vote short."

"Trasker," the Reverend Wilkens whispered, leaning even closer to me.

I thought delusion had set in on Wilkens and considered advising him to wear a hat and stay indoors. I had a University of Illinois baseball cap I could offer him, but I didn't think he'd accept the gift or use it.

I even considered inviting him across the parking lot to my barely air-conditioned office and living closet, but decided that whatever confidence he might have in me would be gone with his first view of my professional headquarters.

"William Trasker is one of the block of three," I said.

Wilkens smiled. Nice teeth. Definitely capped.

"William Trasker is dying," he said solemnly, though I had the feeling that Trasker's impending death didn't completely displease him.

"Trasker came to my church office day before day before yesterday," Wilkens went on. "Told me, said there was nothing they could do to him now and that he'd enjoy surprising the commission by voting with me. It was to be a done deal."

"Still two questions," I said, pitching the empty cup toward the white-plastic-lined metal mesh trash basket and sinking it for a solid two points. "First, what did Trasker mean by saying there was nothing 'they' could do to him now? Second, what do you need me for?"

"Trasker wouldn't say much," said Wilkens, "but we were either talking past payoffs or things someone had on him for some of the less than legal deals he might have made for his contracting business. Since Trasker is up to his kneecaps in money, I'd say it was the contracting deals. We've got buildings in this town that crumble after a decade. Trasker's company put up a lot of them, some of them public buildings. It doesn't cost him anything to go out on the side of righteousness. Get him some good headlines and maybe a ticket to heaven, though I think the good Lord will look hard and long at the scales of this man's life before making a decision to let him enter the gates."

"And me?"

"I can't comment on your chances of eternal peace," he said with a smile. "I can tell you what I want from you. William Trasker is missing. I want you to find him, get him to that meeting on Friday so he can vote. If he doesn't show up, we deadlock. If Trasker dies, we have an election fast, and I have no doubt given the constituency and the inclination of both parties, the new member will probably not vote with us. In addition, Parenelli stands a good chance of being defeated himself in the next open election."

"You don't?"

"I'm the token everything with Parenelli gone," said the Reverend Wilkens. "The token black, the token liberal, the token clergyman. I am the exception that supposedly proves fairness. Every hypocrite in the business community will support me, even those who don't live in District One, which I represent."

"How do you know Trasker is missing?"

"I called his office," said Wilkens. "He hasn't come in since he came to see me. I called his home. His wife didn't want to talk, but said Trasker was out of town on a family emergency and she had no idea when he would be coming back. I called the police and they asked me what the crime was?"

"You think he's in town?" I asked.

"I *pray* he's in town," said Wilkens. "He led me to believe that he didn't have very much time and that even coming to the meeting Friday would be against his doctor's recommendation. I find it difficult to believe under the circumstances that he would go out of town for any reason. I want you to find him."

"I'm sorry," I said. "But I can't do it. I can recommend a good private investigator in Bradenton, Wayne Barcomb. He's in the phone book. I've got to go now. I'm late for an appointment."

I started to rise. He put his hand gently on my arm.

"The money we save can be put to good use to support improvements in the African-American community. My dream is a renovated Newtown with decent housing and safe streets. We've started but we've got a long way to go, and I don't want limited resources going to projects that make the rich richer. I'm asking only that you do your best for a few days to find a sick man so he can do one final decent thing."

"I've got some papers to serve and something I've got to do that'll take me out of town for a few days. Today's Monday. If I go out of town tomorrow and Wednesday, that'll give me what's left of today, Thursday, and Friday till midnight. Not much time."

"But it can be done," said Wilkens. "You can do it."

"I don't know."

"How can I persuade you?"

I thought about that for about five seconds.

"Can you get someone's driver's license back for them?" I asked.

"DUI?"

"Yes, more than a couple, but she's clean and sober now. Needs her van because she's taking care of a baby."

"Her baby?"

"Flo's in her sixties," I said. "The baby belongs to an unmarried student at Sarasota High. Girl's mother was murdered by her father. A prominent member of this community, now in jail, gave her heartbreak and a baby."

"Girl is black?"

"Girl is white," I said. "So is Flo."

"Last name of this Flo lady?" Wilkens said.

"Zink. Florence Zink. Lives in the county."

"Are you a Catholic, Mr. Fonesca?"

"A lapsed Episcopalian."

"But I understand your word is good."

"My word is good," I said.

My "word," my few pieces of furniture, a pile of prescreened videotapes, an old television and VCR, and a bicycle were all I had. The only "good" thing in that list was my "word."

"She will not lapse?" he asked. "If she were to and it was discovered that I had helped her get her license . . ."

"She will not lapse," I said.

"It can be done," he said, sitting back. He had done his best and now his eyes were fixed on me, waiting.

"Let's say Flo gets her license back, and I get three hundred dollars flat fee for the job plus the cost of car rental," I said. "I've got a deal with the low-cost place down the street so a three-day won't be much. Give me your card and I'll have them bill you for the car. The other business I have to do will take care of two days on the rental."

"That will be satisfactory," he said, holding out a large right hand and a smile. "Florence Zink?"

"Florence Zink."

We shook and he immediately reached into his pocket and counted out four fifties and five twenties. He handed the money to me along with his card. On the back in dark ink was his home number.

"Want a receipt?" I asked.

"Under the circumstances, I would prefer as little in writing as possible," he said, rising. "For a change, if necessary, Parenelli and I will stall on other issues on the agenda on Friday. Members of my congregation will also be present to speak out at the open forum. I would guess that we can keep the meeting going till at least midnight. I would also guess, if they truly don't know yet, that the block will want to wait for Trasker, assuming he will vote with them. They don't want a deadlock any more than we do."

The Reverend Wilkens stood, shading his eyes and looking toward the sun almost overhead, and then grasped my right hand in both of his. I felt as if I had just been baptized again.

"Find him, Lewis," he said. "I'll pray for you to find him."

He got into a clean, dark green, five- or six-year-old Buick about a dozen yards away in the small parking lot and pulled out, waving at me.

This wasn't going to be easy, but it was probably only a day's work and I had just pocketed three hundred dollars. If I hurried, I could rent a car and get to my appointment on time instead of pedaling and being late.

Adding the three hundred to the five hundred my other client had given me Friday and the two hundred I had saved, the cash in the toe of my other pair of shoes in my office came to a thousand dollars. I was suddenly a rampant capitalist and I had papers for two summonses to serve.

There was a small flush through the broad gray hush of my existence, trying to lure me toward wanting even more, toward a sense of tomorrows to come. I did not want to think about tomorrows to come.

I brought my bike up to my office, locked it inside, and went down the street to the EZ Economy Car Rental Agency, where Fred, large of belly, nearing retirement, constantly eager, stood talking to his partner, Alan, large, forties, hard to convince. They played good agent and bad agent with their customers. I was used to it and suffered it to keep from hurting their feelings.

"Social call?" asked Fred. "Bring us some donuts and coffee from Gwen's so we can sit around and talk about the economy."

"Need a car," I said. I wanted to add that I had an appointment and was in a hurry, but I knew that would lead to delaying mode to make me easier to manipulate.

"How long?" Alan said, as if I had said something that aroused his suspicion.

"Till Saturday afternoon," I said.

"Taking it on the road?" asked Fred with a grin. "Get away. Over to Fort Lauderdale, down to Key West?"

"Orlando," I said.

Alan shook his head as if I had given him the wrong answer.

"Got a good road car," said Fred. "Olds Cutlass Sierra, 'ninety-five. Special rate, two hundred. You get a full tank of gas."

"Something newer," I said.

"The man's talking serious business here, Alan," Fred said, moving away from the desk. Alan was still leaning against it.

"The Nissan," Alan said.

Fred clapped his hands and said, "The Nissan," as if his partner had just discovered a new moon around Jupiter. "Why didn't I think of that?"

Fred told me it was a 'ninety-eight with mileage too good to be real.

"One hundred and forty-five," Alan said.

Fred looked sadly at me and shrugged a what-can-I-do-with-him shrug.

"One hundred," I said.

Fred looked at Alan hopefully.

"One-twenty-five," Alan said. "You return it full of gas."

"Deal," I said. "Bill it to him."

I handed Fred Wilkens's card. He passed it to Alan, who said, "Moving up in the world, Fonesca."

"We'll need a credit card," Fred said apologetically.

"Call him," I said. "He'll give you one."

"Not our policy," said Alan.

"Alan, this is Lew Fonesca, a regular client," Fred pleaded. "He's good for it. We know where to find him."

Alan folded his arms across his chest. I tried not to look at my watch.

"All right," he finally said.

"Great," said Fred. "Let's fill out the papers."

"We've got some coffee," Alan said, while his partner moved out of earshot to the rear of the small store, which had once been a gas station.

"How is he?" I asked softly.

Fred had had a heart attack the year before. It ranged, according to Alan, somewhere between medium and not too good. In the time Fred had been gone, Alan had been a different person. He had played Fred's good-guy role, holding the job open for him when he returned a month after his attack and bypass surgery.

"Doing good," said Alan. "I watch what he eats when he's here. His wife, Dotty, watches him at home. He takes his pills. Likes to stay busy. Business has been slow. When Fred retires, I'm selling out. The land is worth more than we bring in in four years. Fred will have a cushion and I can move back to Dayton."

Fred came hurrying back with the papers and the car keys. I signed and initialed in all the right places.

"Rides like a dream," Fred said, a hand on my shoulder. "A dream."

Car rides in my dreams were not something I thought of as selling points. My dreams were usually bumpy, lost, and dark with basements, which don't exist in Florida, and ghosts who wouldn't accept that they were ghosts.

I was thinking about my wife. There was a reason. I was about to deal with it.

2

TWENTY-TWO MINUTES LATER, I parked in an open space right in front of Sarasota News & Books on Main Street. I went in, picked up two coffees and two chocolate croissants, and walked the short block to Gulfstream Avenue.

Traffic whooshed both ways down Tamiami Trail in front of me, and beyond the traffic I could see the narrow Bayfront Park with little anchored pleasure and recreational fishing boats gently bobbing in the water.

Two homeless men made their home in the park across the street. One was an alcoholic, red-faced man with a battered cowboy hat and a guitar. He slept under a bench regardless of the weather and spent the hour or so every night that he wasn't too drunk playing and singing sad country-and-western songs on Palm Avenue or Main Street with his hat on the sidewalk accumulating coins and an occasional dollar bill until a police car pulled up and a cop leaned out. The cowboy didn't have to be told to amble on. He would nod to the policeman and move on. I had talked to the singing cowboy a few times because he had a look in his eyes I recognized as being very like my own.

We didn't talk about much, not who we were or where we came from. I told him I liked his playing. He told me he liked my baseball cap. I hadn't seen him around for a while.

The other homeless man in the park was black, in his thirties and almost always shirtless. He talked to himself a lot and I had talked to him once on the bench in front of the office where I was now heading. I had given him a cup of coffee. He had nodded something that might have been a thanks and had gone back to talking to himself. He, like I, was a man who preferred his own company.

I entered Ann Horowitz's office ten minutes late. Her inner door was open and I moved to it, holding out a coffee container and the white bag with the chocolate croissants.

She was seated in her leather chair next to her desk. The office was small. Three chairs, three bookcases filled with works on psychology and history. History was Ann Horowitz's passion.

She took the coffee and fished into the bag for a croissant, placing it on a napkin she laid out on the desk. I sat in the brown leather recliner across from her and took off the lid of my coffee.

"I thought you were going to bring almond," she said.

"They were out."

She looked at me as she held the croissant in her hand and said, "I'll endure the hardship."

Ann is a psychologist. She took me on as a challenge and charged me twenty dollars a session if I could afford it, ten if I could only manage that, nothing less.

Ann had come to Sarasota with her husband to retire a dozen years earlier, planning to write a book about forgotten Jewish figures in American history. She discovered that she would rather read and talk about them than write, and she also discovered that she missed working with people who challenged her.

She kept looking at me as she bit into her croissant. The ritual had begun. I was uncomfortable with it. Ann said my discomfort indicated that I was making progress.

"Discomfort will turn to return," she had told me during my last visit. "We started with reluctance, got you almost to hostility, and now you have attained discomfort. Progress."

I sipped some coffee, took a deep breath, and softly said, "Catherine."

Ann nodded, put down her croissant, and pulled the lid off of her coffee container.

"Which Catherine? Adele's baby?"

"My wife. Both maybe."

"Time for the question," she said.

I sighed and answered it before she could ask.

"I am not suicidal. I do not want to kill myself."

"You said that the way the police give the Miranda rights on *Law & Order*."

"Doesn't mean I don't mean it."

"You want to be dead?"

"Numb," I said. "I want to be numb."

"You still want to hold on to your depression?"

"Yes, I want to hold on to my depression."

"Would you be relieved or frightened if you knew you were about to die?

"Die how?" I asked.

"Hit by a car, shot by a bullet, know you have been fatally bitten by a coral snake."

"Relieved maybe. Maybe not. Hard to tell till it happens."

We had been here before and would be here again until the answers changed or she gave up. Ann is not the kind of person who gives up.

"No anger yet?" she asked, finishing the last of her croissant. I had broken off half of mine. The second half lay on a napkin on the little table next to the recliner. A book lay on the table. There was always a book for patients to look at in case Ann had an emergency phone call or an urgent trip to the rest room. The current book was a little one with short paragraphs by William Bennett.

"Lewis?"

"No anger," I said.

"You are not ready to hate the man who killed your wife?"

"Could have been a woman."

"Person," said Ann, accepting the remaining half of my chocolate croissant I handed to her.

"No anger. Nothing I can do with anger."

"But you can try to hide in your depression?"

"I try. It's hard work. You don't make it easier."

"That's why you come to me. Trying to feel nothing," she said, taking a small bite of the croissant to make it last. "Like a religion. Nirvana. Except without a god."

"Something like that," I said.

"Sleep?"

"I'm down to about fourteen hours a day," I said.

"Progress. Like an Atkins diet for depression," she said. "Lose a little more solitude and isolation each day. Adele, her baby, Flo, Ames, Sally."

"And Dave and you," I finished.

"All people you care about."

I turned my eyes away and shook my head.

"Things happen. People happen. I've been thinking about saving some money and buying a car."

"So you can run away again?"

"Yes."

"But you stay and come to me."

It wasn't a question.

"There's a lot to be said for it, but depression has its downside," I said.

"Why do you like *Mildred Pierce* so much?" she asked, now working on her coffee. "My husband and I watched it last night."

"You like it?"

"Yes. I have seen it before. What do you like about it?"

"I don't know. What do I like about it?"

"Maybe that bad things happen to Mildred, lots of bad things, but she keeps going. She never gives up."

"Her husband leaves her," I said. "One daughter dies. The other daughter betrays Mildred with her new husband, the husband who . . . She keeps going."

"But you do not."

"I do not, but maybe I have to."

"Abrupt change of subject," she said, wiping her hands with the paper napkin. "During the Civil War many people in the North still had slaves. There's a new book about it."

I nodded.

"On the other hand," she went on, tossing the crumpled napkin into her half-full wastebasket, "there were many Southerners, prominent Southerners, who fought and even died in the war, who did not believe in slavery and never had any slaves or freed the ones they had before the first shot was fired."

"I didn't know that," I said. "You going to tell me that I'm a slave to my depression, to my refusal to give up my wife's death? That I have to take off the shackles and start to live free?"

She smiled.

"No," she said. "I was simply making a reference to something that came to mind, but you've done a good job of finding something personal in it."

"Maybe I should be a shrink?"

"God, no. You think you're depressed now?"

"You're not depressed."

"I keep busy," she said. "I have my moments, but I am not chronically depressed. A little occasional depression is normal."

She shook her head and went on, "You are beginning to depress me," she said. "Most of us have suffered terrible losses."

"The Cubs have them every year," I said.

"Your baseball cap," she said, pointing at the cap still on my head. "It's a hopeful sign."

"My cap?"

"You wear it to mask your baldness," she said. "You have some vanity, some will to feel that others view you with approval."

"My head burns if I don't wear it," I said.

"A hat can have more than one function."

"You know what the ultraviolet index is?"

"You mean as a concept or the actual number today?"

"Today?"

"You are interested in the present?"

"I'm interested in my head not turning red and sore," I said.

"Wait, wait, wait," she said, holding up a finger. "I think I heard a touch of irritation in your voice, a very small one, smaller than the birth squeal of a pink baby laboratory mouse, but something. I see hope in that."

"The squeal of a pink baby mouse?"

"Vivid memory of a moment in a biology class in graduate school," she said. "You know what happened to the mouse? Of course you don't. One of my classmates took it home and fed it to his pet red corn snake."

"You know how to cheer a client up," I said.

"I do my best."

We went on for a while. We talked about Wilkens and Trasker, about my other client, about my relationship to Sally Porovsky and Adele's baby.

Stuart M. Kaminsky

"Time," she said.

I pulled one of the twenties Wilkens had given to me out of my pocket. She accepted it and looked at it.

"Lucky bill," she said. "There are four ones in the serial number. A liar's poker bill."

"Now you believe in omens?"

"Oh yes," she said, reaching for the phone. "The universe is connected down to the smallest segment of an atomic subparticle. Past, present, and future are part of a continuum."

"I love it when you talk dirty," I said, moving toward the door.

I heard Ann chuckle and say, as I opened the door, "Lewis Fonesca made a parting joke. I'm making a note of it. Bring me three jokes on Friday. That's an assignment. At least three jokes."

I closed the door. There was no one in the tiny waiting room.

The homeless black guy wasn't sitting on the bench. I had decided to break precedent and give him a dollar. It might open the door to him expecting more from me in the future, but since I didn't have a lot of faith in the future, a buck in the present wouldn't hurt.

But he wasn't there.

I found a phone and a phone book at Two Senoritas Mexican Restaurant a few doors down from Sarasota News & Books. William Trasker was listed.

I called. After five rings, a woman picked up and said, "Hello."

"Mrs. Trasker, my name is Lew Fonesca. Is your husband home?"

"No." She had a nice voice, a little cold but deep and confident.

"Could I stop by and talk to you?"

"You can but you may not," she said.

I was going to ask if she had been a grade-school teacher, but I said, "It's about your husband."

"Who are you?"

"A man looking for your husband," I said. "All I need is a few minutes of your time. I could talk to you on the phone but I'd rather—"

"I don't care what you'd 'rather' or who you are."

She hung up.

I didn't know Trasker's wife, but I did know when someone was frightened. She was frightened.

I got back to my car, pulled out carefully, and headed for Flo Zink's.

I took Tamiami Trail down to Siesta Drive, made a right, crossed Osprey, and then took a left onto Flo's driveway just before the bridge to Siesta Key.

The white minivan was in the driveway. Flo couldn't legally drive it. This was the third time her license had been taken away. Adele could drive. She wasn't sixteen yet, so she needed an adult supervisor with her. In Florida, even though she had no license, Flo qualified as copilot.

The door opened before I could knock or ring the bell.

"Baby's sleeping," Flo said.

Flo was wearing one of her country-and-western uniforms: her favorite denim skirt, blue-and-red checkerboard shirt. Her hair was white, cut short, and looking frizzy. Flo always reminded me of Thelma Ritter.

Patsy Cline, Roy Orbison, Garth Brooks, or Faith Hill were usually playing backup for conversation at the Zink house, but not today, not now. The baby was sleeping.

Flo was carrying a drink in her hand. It was in a wineglass. The liquid was amber. She caught me looking.

"Diet Coke," she said, handing me the glass. "Smell it."

I did.

"I thought you'd take my word," she said with disappointment.

"Can't afford to," I said as we moved out of the late morning heat and into the air-conditioned house.

"Can't afford to?"

"I'll get to that in a little while," I said.

"There's no alcohol in the house," she said, leading me toward the kitchen. "Not the drinking kind anyway, just some baby kind. Want a Diet Coke? Iced tea?"

"Diet Coke," I said.

She got me one from the refrigerator. I popped the tab and took a sip as I followed her through the living room and down the hallway to a half-open door. She motioned me in ahead of her and put her finger to her lips to let me know I had to be quiet.

The curtains were drawn but there was enough light coming through for me to see the face of the baby Adele had named for my wife.

Catherine was on her back, face turned toward me, eyes closed. She had a small crown of yellow hair, a round pink face. She looked vulnerable. I thought of the snake that had eaten Ann Horowitz's pink mouse and I shuddered. The baby sensed something, fidgeted, and turned her head away.

Flo took my arm and led me out of the room. When we were back in the living room, Flo pointed at a small white plastic box on the tree-stump coffee table.

"Intercom," she said, patting the box as if it were a pet dog. "She makes a peep, I hear her."

I worked on my Diet Coke.

"So," she said. "Take off your hat and sit a while."

Flo had the twang of New York in her voice and the grammar

of Oklahoma picked up from more than half a century of listening to western music.

I took off my cap, brushed what remained of my hair back with one hand, and said, "You're getting your driver's license back," I said.

"No shit," she said, sitting upright.

"None," I said. "If you get another DUI, you, me, and an influential local politician will wind up on the front page of the paper."

"It'd have to be a slow news day," she said.

"No. He's big enough to make the front page."

"I'm clean and sober, Lewis," she said. "On my dead husband Gus's grave, I swear. Don't need it anymore. I've got Adele. I've got the baby."

"Adele is . . . ?"

"Straight arrow," Flo said, gliding a flattened hand through the air. "Straight A's. No boys. No men."

Adele had been a child prostitute, sold by her father to a pimp. She had straightened herself out and then let herself get involved with a married man, the son of a famous man. The married son of a famous man was Catherine's father, who was serving life for a pair of murders.

"Getting my license back," Flo said with a grin, looking at her Diet Coke in a wineglass. "I was about to say 'fucking license,' but I'm working on my language. The baby. Adele's heard everything I can say and more, but Catherine is something else."

"Gus was on the County Commission," I said.

"Till he joined the ghost riders," she said, holding up her glass in a toast to her late husband.

"You know William Trasker?"

"Yep. Two terms on the council. Now he's on the County Commission. I know Willie Trasker."

"His wife?"

Stuart M. Kaminsky

"Yep again. Known Roberta Trasker for more than twenty years."

"Friends?"

"Have been. Sort of. Mostly when Gus was alive and he had business with Willie, but Roberta? Not for a while. Why?"

"I'd like you to call her and ask her to let me talk to her."

"Why don't you just call her yourself?"

"She won't see me."

"You tried?"

"I tried."

"What did she say?"

"Good-bye."

I explained why I wanted to talk to Roberta Trasker. Flo nodded her head as I spoke, finished her Diet Coke, and put the glass down.

"I'll call her now," she said, getting up and moving to the phone on the wall of the kitchen. A thin, rectangular white board about the size of a small computer screen hung next to the phone with a black marker Velcroed to the top. There was a list on the board but I couldn't make it out from where I sat.

"Roberta? It's Flo, Flo Zink. How the hell are you?"

Flo looked at me as she listened. Flo made a face.

"Is Billy okay? . . . Sure. How about coming over here sometime, the two of you, and see the baby . . . ? No, not 'sometime soon,' sometime real . . . Okay, but you'll call. Make that a promise . . . Good. One more thing. I've got a friend wants to talk to you, a good friend, name's Lew Fonesca. I owe him big time, Bobby, big time . . . How busy can you be? Give him a few minutes . . . Right. I'll send him right over. Remember, you're calling me next week to set up a time to come over. I don't hear from you and I call back with hell to pay. This is some special baby."

Flo hung up and turned toward me.

"Something's wrong," she said. "Could hear it in her voice."

"I heard it when I talked to her."

I told her what the situation was and she told me Roberta Trasker's address.

"She's waiting for you," Flo said. "But don't expect much, Lewis. Roberta Trasker can be a frozen cod and I get the feeling she doesn't like kids very much, not even her own."

Flo told me what she knew about Roberta Trasker. William Trasker did his best to make excuses for the absence of his wife at social and public functions over the years. She was ill or she was touring Europe or visiting her brother in Alaska, Montana, California, or Vermont. The Traskers had two grown sons and a daughter and four grandchildren. Flo had never seen them. One son and his family lived in Seattle. The other in Australia. They didn't even have an address for the daughter, or so they said when they were backed into a social corner. The rumor was that the daughter was deformed, retarded, behind bars, or living as the fourth wife of a Mormon in Utah.

Roberta and William Trasker were not close to their children.

"Roberta looks like a lady, drinks a little but not too much, can outcuss me if she wants to, and likes being the woman of mystery. Won't say much about her life before she moved here. Mystery woman. It's an act. I don't know who the actress is behind the character. Doubt if you'll find out. She doesn't take off the makeup."

"She get along with her husband?"

"Roberta? She worships the ground he bought her. They get along in public. Times I've seen them in private, back when Gus was alive, they looked as if they felt comfortable together. That's about it."

"What does she do with her time?"

"Spends it," said Flo. "And Bill's money, but he's got plenty to spend, more even than my Gus."

I put my cap back on, used the bathroom, washed my face

Stuart M. Kaminsky

and hands, and moved back to the living room, where Flo had risen.

"When do I get that license back?"

"I think it'll come in the mail," I said. "Maybe a day or two."

"Take care of yourself, Lew," she said at the open door.

"Take care of Adele and the baby," I said, opening the Nissan's door.

"With my life," she said. "Anything else I can do for you?"

I paused. "You know any jokes?"

3

I HAD TO GET as much done today as I could and it was already a little after noon. I'd have to devote at least the next day to my other client.

My other client was a very burly two hundred and twenty pounds with a pink round face. His name was Kenneth Severtson. He had been waiting in front of my office when I came back from lunch at the Crisp Dollar Bill on Friday. He was in his late thirties and knew how to dress.

"You're Fonesca?" he asked, clearly unimpressed by what he was looking at. He was in a neatly pressed, lightweight tan suit complete with a bold red designer tie. I was dressed in contemporary Fonesca, complete with my Cubs cap.

"I am," I said, opening the door and stepping in, with him behind me.

I flicked on the air conditioner, pulled up the shade to let some light in, and sat behind my desk. He looked around my office clearly as unimpressed with it as he was with me.

My office is a cube about the size of a small Dumpster. One small, scratched desk, a wooden chair—no wheels, no swivel—behind it, and two chairs—simple, wood, secondhand—in front of it.

Thumbtacked on the wall behind my desk was a *Touch of Evil* poster, a reproduction of the original with Charlton Heston and Orson Welles glaring at each other. The poster was beginning to curl. On the wall across from my desk was a painting about the size of an eight-by-eleven mailing envelope. Flo had given the painting to me as a Christmas gift. The artist worked at the Selby Gardens on the Bay. There was an orchid in my painting. The Selby specializes in orchids, but that didn't tell you what you needed to know about the painting.

"Looks like you," she had said when she handed it to me.

And it did. It was a dark, almost ebony jungle with black jagged mountains and dark clouds in the background. The only touch of color was a small yellow orchid on a gnarled tree in the foreground. The dark jungle, night sky, and the gothic mountain was definitely me, and the small touch of living color was about the right size.

I got to meet the artist, Stig Dalstrom, one afternoon at Patrick's restaurant on Main Street. He specializes in paintings like the one Flo had given me but Flo said he also did commissions.

Dalstrom was taller than me, a little broader, with glasses, a slightly receding hairline, dark blond hair, and an echo of his dark paintings in his eyes. He had a slight Swedish accent.

Our conversation had been brief and I wondered what haunted his past. I wondered how much one of his paintings or prints would cost. I told him I'd like to look up from behind my desk and see more of that haunting darkness and those little touches of light.

I was deep inside that tiny orchid when I heard a voice.

"Mr. Fonesca, are you all right?" the man across from me said, and I brought myself back from the jungle.

"You're . . .?" I asked.

"Severtson, Kenneth Severtson. She took the kids," he said to me to open the conversation.

"Nice to meet you," I answered.

"She had no right," Severtson said, leaning toward me and staring into my eyes without a blink.

I don't play "who blinks first." I didn't speak. He waited. It was my turn. I wasn't playing.

"You've got to find her."

He won.

"Who do I have to find?"

"My wife, Janice, and the children."

"I'm a process server," I said. "You want the police."

"There's no crime, not yet."

I was about to give him my standard line about needing a private detective.

"You find people," Severtson said.

"That's what a process server does," I agreed.

"Find my wife and children."

"Mr. Severtson, I don't do that kind of thing."

That was a lie. The truth was that whatever "that kind of thing" was I had probably done it when someone pushed the right tender buttons of my despair.

"Sally Porovsky said you might be able to help."

"How do you know Sally?"

He turned his head away and lowered his voice.

"There was an incident about a year ago," he said. "Janice and I had an argument. The neighbors called the police. The police called child protection. Sally Porovsky was the caseworker. She saw us a few times. So when Janice left three days ago, I called Sally. She told me to wait a few days and then come to see you if Janice and the kids didn't show up."

I held up a hand to stop him, reached over, picked up the phone, and dialed Sally's cell phone.

"Hello," she said, her voice cell-phone crackly.

"Kenneth Severtson's here," I said.

"He's in your office?"

"Yes."

"Can you help him?"

"Can you?"

"No," she said. "But my deep-down instinct is that if you don't help him, he'll try to help himself, and I think he has the kind of personality that could snap."

"Professionally put," I said.

"If I put it into social-work babble, it would say the same thing but you wouldn't understand it. I doubt if the people I write reports for understand them. I doubt if they even read the reports. Lewis, you are starting to depress me."

"I have that effect on people," I said.

I looked at Severtson, who strained to figure out what was going on. I didn't say anything.

"Lew, you still there?"

"Yes," I said.

"Well?"

"You want me working instead of spending the afternoon in bed with Joan Crawford."

"Something like that," she said.

"Dinner Sunday? My place," she said. "Seven?"

"I'll bring the pizza."

"Kids want Subway sandwiches. They like the ads on television."

"What kind of sandwiches?"

"Your choice. Seven?"

"Seven," I said.

"Call me later," she said. "I've got to run down to Englewood."

I hung up the phone.

"You like movies?" I asked him.

"Yes," he said cautiously.

"Old movies?"

"Sure, sometimes."

"Really old movies," I pushed. "From the Thirties and Forties?"

"Not particularly."

He was beginning to look at me as if he had come to the wrong place, which was fine with me. He didn't move so I pushed ahead.

"How old are your children?" I asked, looking at Severtson, taking off my hat, and putting it on the desk. "You have recent pictures of them and your wife?"

"Yes," he said, reaching into his inside jacket pocket. "Sally said I should bring them."

He handed me a brown envelope with a clasp. I opened it and looked at the three pictures. There were individual color photos of a boy and a girl. Both were smiling. Neither looked at all like their father. The third photograph told me who they looked like. The kids stood on each side of their mother, who wore jeans and a white shirt tied about her belly to reveal a very nice navel. Her hair was blond, just like both kids, and all three had the same smile.

"My daughter's name is Sydney, after my father. She's four. My son is Kenneth Jr. He's six. He says he has a loose tooth."

"Nice family," I said, returning the photographs to the envelope and placing it in front of me.

"Used to be," he said. "Then . . . . wherever Janice has the kids, Andrew Stark is probably with them."

"Friend of your wife?" I asked.

"More than a friend," Severtson said.

He looked as if he were about to cry.

"I see," I said.

"Stark is my partner," he said. "We own S & S Marine on Stickney Point Road. Upscale boats."

"I've seen it," I said.

"I caught them on the phone. Janice didn't deny it. She says it's my fault, that I've changed, that she needs attention not grunts."

"Have you?"

"What?"

"Changed," I said.

"Yeah," he said. "We've been married eleven years. I gained about four pounds a year. It's in my genes. So now Andy Stark is in my wife's jeans."

"You talk to him about it?"

"They were gone before I could," he said. "Janice left me a note saying she wants a divorce and that she'll get back to me as soon as she's settled somewhere. That's what she says she wants."

"What do you want?"

"My kids back," he said. "I'd probably even take Janice back if she'd come. She's going through some midlife thing or some woman's thing. I don't know. But she has no right to run away with Andy and take the kids. I want you to find them and bring them back."

"I can find them, maybe," I said. "It's hard to hide in the age of computers. But I can't force her to come back. If she doesn't want to come back, I can tell you where she is. It might be a good idea for you to let a lawyer know what's going on while I'm looking."

"I'll do that," he said.

"Did you bring the note she left?"

He went into an inside jacket pocket and came out with an envelope. He handed it to me. It had "Ken" written neatly on the front in blue ink.

I opened the envelope and unfolded the piece of unlined paper inside. The note was handwritten, neat, blue ink. It read: "Ken, the children and I are going. Please don't try to find us. I'll write to you when we are settled. I think a divorce would be for the best." It was signed "Janice."

"Show this to your lawyer and start thinking about whether you want custody of your kids," I said, returning the note and envelope to him. "That note is the start of a good case. And if she's in a hotel room with Stark and your son and daughter, and I see them spend the night together, I can testify if it comes to that."

I waited to see if this was sinking in.

"Ask my lawyer," he said.

"That's what I would do."

"I want my kids," he insisted. "I may want my wife, but if I can't have her, I want Kenny and Syd."

"I told you what I can do," I said.

He thought about that for about a minute.

"Okay," he said.

We worked out the payment and he gave me a five-hundred-dollar cash advance, all in fifties. I told him I'd check in with him and if it started to take a lot of time he could reassess the situation, especially if I had to go out of town or out of the state. He agreed.

"Find them," he said, placing a business card in front of me. "Please find them."

And he was gone. His office number was on the front of the card along with his home number. I pocketed the card as my phone rang. I picked it up and said, "Fonesca."

"Colleen Davenport," Warren Murphy's secretary said.

She worked for one of the partners at Tycinker, Oliver, and Schwartz, where I was on a retainer. In exchange for that retainer, I got paid a fixed sum each time I served papers and I got the reasonable use of the services of Harvey the Hacker, who had an office in the back of the law firm.

"Two jobs," she said. "One has to be done today. The other by Friday."

"I'll be right over," I said. "Can I talk to Harvey?"

Colleen said Harvey was out of town, which could mean that Harvey was out of town or Harvey had fallen off the wagon. I hung up and went to my backup, Dixie Cruise, no relation to the actor.

Dixie was slim, trim, with very black hair in a short style. She was no more than twenty-five, pretty face, and big round glasses. Dixie worked behind the counter at a coffee bar in Gulf Gate Plaza. About six months back, I had sought her out to answer a summons about a reported assault she had witnessed in the coffee bar and found that Dixie, who had as down-home an accent as any Billy Bob, was a computer whiz.

I called her at the coffee bar and she agreed to meet me when she got off of work at her apartment in a slightly run-down twelve-flat apartment building near the main post office. She had a small living room with a sofa bed, a large kitchen, and a bedroom devoted to her two computers, two large speakers, and all kinds of gray metal pieces with lights.

When I got to Dixie's apartment and she got in front of her computers, it took her ten minutes and cost me fifty bucks, which I would bill to Kenneth Severtson. Andrew Stark belonged to AAA. Three days earlier he had purchased two adult and two children's tickets to Disney World, Sea World, and Universal Theme Park. Dixie got a list of hotels in Orlando. Andrew Stark had Visa, MasterCard, Discover, and American Express cards. He had used the Visa to check into an Orlando hotel yesterday.

"Embassy Suites on International Drive," Dixie said, pointing at the screen as if her right hand were a handgun. "Checkout Thursday. Want to know what he ordered from room service?"

"Should I?"

Dixie shook her head and said, "A lot of burgers, fries, and Cokes, both diet and the new vanilla one,"

In the old days, prehacker, I would have gone to AAA, told a sad story, and hoped for the best. Then I would have tried airlines, travel agencies, and friends of Janice Severtson and Andrew Stark. Sarasota isn't huge but it might have taken me days, which means that without Dixie, Stark and Janice would have checked out before I found them.

I went to the law offices of Tycinker, Oliver, and Schwartz on Palm Avenue. Colleen Davenport gave me two sets of papers to serve: one was urgent, the other had a few days.

"How's Harvey?" I asked her.

She was young and inexperienced and trying to look a little older and filled with understanding of the world. She did a fair job.

"Truth?" she said softly as I stood next to her in her cubicle outside of Murphy's office. "He's had a relapse."

"Bad?"

"He's been at this place in Mississippi for two weeks," she said. "Firm is paying the bill. Harvey's too valuable to lose."

I went back to the Nissan with the papers. I put one aside for a Mickey Donophin and read the one for Georgia Heinz. There was an address on a street behind Gulf Gate Mall. I drove there. It was a small house, white, one bedroom, maybe two. No car in the driveway.

Paper in my pocket, I went up to the door and knocked. No answer. I found an almost hidden bell button. I pushed it. No sound.

"She's not home," a woman's voice came from my left.

The woman came from behind a tangelo tree, holding a green hose. Water was spraying weakly from the nozzle. A little rainbow ran through the spray.

"At work," the woman said.

She was about seventy, maybe more, dry, wearing a flowery gardening dress and a big green floppy hat that shaded her face.

"You happen to know where she works?" I asked.

"I happen to know. Yes I do. Who is asking? I'm not sending her no bill collectors. Poor thing got enough trouble."

"Trouble?"

"Lost her job at the bank, leg infection, even her old dog died. Then she had to see what happened."

"What happened?" I asked.

"Swear you're not a bill collector."

"I swear," I said. "I just want to give her something."

It didn't really matter what I told the woman. I could have said I was a hit man out to get Georgia Heinz. This was a lady determined to tell a story.

"Happened right out there," she said, pointing her hose at the street just behind my car. "Night, around ten maybe. Victor and I were watching a *Nero Wolfe* when we heard the scream. I said, 'Victor, somebody screamed.' And he acknowledged the fact. Victor has a hearing aid, you know."

"No, I didn't," I said.

"Of course you didn't," she said with faint exasperation. "You don't know Victor. I was just using a phrase. Victor's a retired detail man. Thirty years with Pfizer."

"Impressive," I said.

"Minneapolis," she said. "Minnesota, Wisconsin, Iowa, the Dakotas, all his."

"A scream. You were watching *Nero Wolfe*," I reminded her.

"Yes, right. Well, Victor and I came running out and there she was standing on the sidewalk and there was the boy on the street, and there was the pickup truck and there was this young man leaning out of the pickup truck window and he looked at her and he looked at us and he got back in that truck and drove away. I guess it's not a hit-and-run exactly because he did stop after he hit the boy."

"Leaving the scene of an accident," I said. "What happened to the boy?"

"Hurt bad. The Krelwitzes' son, goes to Manatee Community College. He'll live, though. I'm the one who got the license number of the pickup truck. Victor can't see worth diddly-squat, but I've got twenty-twenty, laser corrected, two thousand dollars but Medicare covered most of it."

"That's good," I said. "But you said you know where Georgia Heinz is."

"Of course I do," she said.

"Would you mind telling me? I have something to give her."

"Give it to me," she said, holding out her hand and aiming the hose in the general direction of the tangelo tree.

"I have to give it to Georgia Heinz," I said.

"I'm Georgia Heinz. You just knocked at Vivian Polter's door."

I checked the address on the summons. There had been no number on the door I had gone to, but the house on the other side of it had been one even number lower than the one I was looking for. The summons had been wrong.

I started across the lawn with Georgia Heinz keeping her eyes on me.

"What's this?" she asked.

"Court order," I said. "For you to testify about what you saw, the license number you took down. The lawyer I work for has a client who's been arrested for what happened. His pickup truck's license number doesn't match the one you gave."

"Than whose pickup truck was it?" she demanded, holding the summons in her hand.

"I don't know," I said, starting back toward my car.

"It was a trick all the time," she shouted. "You tricked me."

I was going to turn and reassure her that I hadn't tricked her when I felt the blast of water on my back. She had turned the hose on me.

I hurried out of range and got in my car. She was advancing across the lawn with her hose aimed in my direction. She had adjusted the stream on the nozzle so that the rainbow was gone and a long thin snake of water spat toward me.

I pulled away from the curb, being careful not to hit anybody who might be walking in the street.

My pants weren't too bad, but my shirt was drenched. I pulled into the Gulf Gate parking lot and went into Old Navy, where I bought a blue pullover shirt that went with my pants.

I had one more set of papers to serve. I'd worry about them later.

4

NOW, AS I PULLED into the driveway of the Traskers' house, I was thinking about the kids in the photograph Severtson had shown me.

The house was big, new, Spanish-looking, with turrets and narrow windows. It was on the water at Indian Beach Drive, not far from the Ringling Museum of Art and the Asolo Performing Arts Center. I've seen the outside of both, never felt the urge to go in the first and look at paintings in the second.

I rang the doorbell and waited. In about a minute, the door opened and I found myself facing Roberta Trasker.

Flo could have done a better job of describing her, but Flo was a woman and saw her through a woman's eyes. I was looking at her through my eyes, which might be even less reliable.

Roberta Trasker was probably well into her sixties and maybe she looked it, but she was the best-looking sixty-plus grandmother I had ever seen. She was model slender, wearing tight black jeans and a silky white short-sleeved blouse. Her face was unlined and beautiful. She reminded me a little of Linda Darnell, except Roberta Trasker had short, straight, gleaming white hair. Plastic surgery was possible but I couldn't detect it.

"Who're you?" she asked.

"Lew Fonesca," I said. "Flo Zink called a little while ago."

"What do you want?"

"To come in and talk," I said.

"About what?"

"Your husband," I said.

"I recognize your voice," she said. "You called a few hours ago."

"I did."

"I'm sorry, Mr. Fonseca . . ."

"Fonesca," I said. "Lots of people make that mistake."

"That must be annoying," she said, now playing with a simple silver band around a slender wrist.

"Depends on who makes the mistake."

"Did I annoy you?"

"Yes," I said. "Not because you got my name wrong but because you did it intentionally. But I'm used to that, too."

She looked at me with her head cocked to one side. I was being examined to see how much if any of her precious time I was worth.

"My husband is out of town on business," she said.

I could hear that hint of emotion in her voice, the same hint Flo and I had heard on the phone.

"Your husband is missing," I said. "He is also very ill, too ill, from what I hear, to be traveling on business or pleasure."

"You are wasting my time, Mr. Fonesca," she said, starting to close the door.

"I'm here to help find him," I said.

"And you are . . . ?"

"By trade? A process server. I'm good at finding people. I can find your husband and I can do it quietly."

"And you want money," she said.

"No," I answered. "I've got a client. I'm poor but honest."

"I can see that," she said. "The poor part."

I was wearing my freshly washed black jeans, Cubs cap, and a yellow short-sleeved shirt with a collar and a little toucan embossed on the pocket. My socks were white and clean. So were my sneakers.

"Take off your hat and come in," she said after a long pause.

I took off my cap and little smile lines showed in the corners of her mouth. I wasn't sure what amused her, my receding hairline or the total picture of a less than threatening, poorly dressed creature.

I stepped in and she shut the door. We were in a massive living room. The floors were cool, tavertine marble. The place was furnished like something out of *Architectural Digest*, something that a movie star might live in, if the movie star liked early Fred Astaire movies. Everything was either black or white. White sofa and chairs, white bookcases filled with expensive-looking glass animals, black lamps, black, sleek low table that ran almost the length of the wall across from the bookcases. A stack of unopened mail stood on the table. Over the table was the only real color in the room, a huge painting of a beautiful young woman in a satin white dress, sitting on a black sofa. The woman's legs were crossed and she leaned forward, her head resting on the fist of her right hand, her other hand dangling languidly at her side.

The room had been furnished to complement the painting. It was also a room that wouldn't welcome the intrusion of grandchildren with unwashed hands and shoes that tracked in sand from the beach.

"That's you," I said, looking at the painting.

"You're showing your brilliance already," she said, sitting in one of the white chairs.

"You're Claire Collins," I said.

"Now, I am impressed," she said.

Claire Collins had been a starlet in the late Fifties and early Sixties. She was in a handful of RKO movies, usually as a bad girl with a smoldering cigarette in the corner of her mouth suggesting close encounters of the third kind with the likes of Glenn Ford and Robert Mitchum.

"I've seen a lot of your pictures," I said.

"There weren't a lot," she said with a sigh. "There were twelve, none of them big, only three in color."

I looked at her.

"I think I can name them all," I said.

"Please, no. I'll take your word for it," she said, shaking her head.

"On television, videotape," I said. "*Black Night in December, Blackmailed Lady, Dark Corridors, When Angels Fall, The Last—*"

"Stop," she said. "I believe you."

I was afraid to sit on her white leather furniture so I kept standing.

"Mrs. Trasker . . . ," I began. "Do you know where your husband might be?"

"No," she said, "but he can't be far and I don't think . . ."

"He's a very sick man," I said.

She gave me shrug, which suggested indifference or that I was simply repeating something she already knew. I recognized the shrug as one she had given Dane Clark, in *Outpost*, one of the movies she made in color.

"Who told you that?"

"My client," I said. "My client is well-informed. My client wants your husband found."

"Why?"

"So he can be at the commission meeting on Friday," I said. "There's an important issue. His vote is needed."

I didn't like the way I had said that. It sounded hollow.

"I want him back too," she said. "I don't care about any vote. I want to be with my husband when he dies. I owe him that and a lot more."

"He's really that close to dying?" I asked.

"He is really that close," she said.

Her eyes were moist now. She looked like her character in *The Falcon in Singapore* in the scene where she was trying to convince Tom Conway that she was broken up by the death of her sister. It turned out that her character had killed the sister over a small man and a lot of money.

"Tell me about your husband," I said.

She stiffened a bit and looked at me as if what her husband was like was none of my business. But she saw something in my face, knew I would pay attention and be nonjudgmental. People seemed to feel safe talking to me.

"Bill? Now, he's a little bit bitter and a lot crotchety," she said. "Not with me. He knows better. When he was young, he didn't just walk over people, he trampled them into submission. And he had and still has a temper. All three of our children left us the moment they were of legal age. It wasn't just Bill. Bill runs far too hot and I run far too cold. It may add to the appeal I built my career, for what it was worth, on, but it didn't serve me particularly well with my family. Does everyone open up to you like this?"

"Almost," I said.

"I can't believe I'm . . . where was I?"

"Your family."

"I can't say I was particularly unhappy about my sons and daughter leaving," she said. "I was happy with Bill. He was happy stepping on people. Then we moved down here so he could find new fields of grass to trample."

"You admire your husband's ruthlessness," I said.

"As he admires what he calls my 'mystery.' "

"Midnight Pass," I said.

"Midnight Pass," she repeated, pursing her lips and looking at her portrait. "Since he found out he was dying, my husband's interest in trampling people has turned to nearly sweet compassion, at least for him. That makes him less attractive to me than what the disease has done to his body. If he lives long enough, he might even decide to publicly declare every shady deal he's ever made, though I doubt if he'd go so far as to try to provide restitution. There are just too many he's wronged and not enough money to go around and leave me comfortable."

"And you'll be comfortable?" I asked.

"Very," she said. "I like money. I like spending it and I love my husband."

"Any idea of what happened to him?"

"I don't know," she said, looking at me. "Maybe he didn't want me to see him die. My husband used to be a big, powerful man. As I said, tough, ruthless. He would probably prefer that I remember him that way."

"So you think . . . ?"

"He is dead or in some hotel room or with some friend."

"He didn't call you?"

"Nobody called me," she said, straightening her back as if she had just remembered that good posture was essential to a beautiful woman.

"Any suggestion about where I might start looking?"

"You can try the *people* at his office," she said. The word "people" came out with the suggestion that they were something less than what she considered real "people." "I've called repeatedly. His secretary, Mrs. Free, says she has no idea where William is or might be."

"Enemies?"

This time she did an Audrey Hepburn, narrow-shouldered, almost gamine shrug with a matching who-knows pursing of her lips.

"My husband is a politician and a contractor. Two occupations that make very few friends and very many enemies. You'd get a better sense of who his friends and enemies are from his *secretary*. If Bill is in a hotel or motel, she might even know that. I know he's not in any of the hospitals in Sarasota, Manatee, or any adjoining county."

That was all I had to ask for the moment. I liked looking at her, but I was getting a little tired of standing.

"Thanks," I said.

She got up.

"If you find him, you will let me know."

She was touching my arm now, her eyes searching mine. I had the feeling that performance and persona were merging for a second.

"I'll let you know," I said.

Outside the door in a blast of heat and humidity I put my cap back on. I knew where William Trasker's office was on Clark just east of Beneva on the south side of the street. I'd passed the two-story white brick building dozens of times, and a few of those times the big red-on-white sign that said "Trasker Construction" had managed to register.

I stopped at a phone booth outside of a 7-Eleven on Beneva and called Dixie at the coffee shop. The manager told me she had taken the day off.

"A cold, flu, *tuchisitis*, who knows," he said. "I'm up to my ass in latte orders and I'm getting a migraine from the smokers. Good-bye."

He hung up and I called Dixie at home. She answered after three rings. Her voice was hoarse when she said, "Hello."

"Me, Lew Fonesca."

"Hi, Lew," she said, the hoarseness gone. "I thought it was Creepy Cargroves, my boss."

"You're okay?"

"Got a good freelance hacking job for a local merchant whose name and business are confidential. You know what I'm saying?"

"I know. Can you do a quick check for me? See if you can find William Trasker's trail. He's missing."

"The County Commission guy?"

"That's the one."

"He's been in the shop a few times. Last time about a week ago. Looked awful. Likes his coffee straight and black with something sweet."

"He come in alone?"

"With something straight, black, and sweet," she said.

"Know her name?"

A massive truck whizzed by and I missed what Dixie said next.

"What was that?"

"Don't know her name, but she's always dressed for business."

"Hooker?"

"Not that kind of business. Business business. Suits, serious shoes, white blouses, pearls, costume ones. I've got an eye. How long's he been missing?"

"About four days," I said.

"I'll do the job for thirty bucks if I don't run into complications," she said.

"How long?"

"No more than half an hour, if I don't run into complications."

"I'll call back. Dixie, you know any good jokes?"

She told me one. I wrote it down in my notebook.

Twenty minutes later I was talking to a woman who was black, sweet, and dressed for business right down to the serious shoes and costume pearls.

Before I got to her, I had to get by the receptionist at Trasker Construction, who was well-groomed, late forties, early fifties, with a nice smile. She seemed like more than receptionist material when she deftly parried my lunging questions about Trasker. I figured her for a mom who was just rejoining the workforce and starting at the bottom.

She finally agreed to talk to Mr. Trasker's secretary, which she did while I listened to her side of the phone conversation. She handled it perfectly, saying a Mr. Fonesca wished to speak to her on a matter of some urgency regarding Mr. Trasker and that Mr. Fonesca would provide no further information. There was a pause during which I assumed Trasker's secretary asked if I looked like a badly dressed toon or acted like a lunatic. The receptionist cautiously said, "I don't think so," to cover herself.

Two minutes later I was sitting in a chair next to the desk of Mrs. Carla Free. Her cubicle in the gray-carpeted complex was directly outside of an office with a plate marked "William Trasker."

Mrs. Free was tall, probably a little younger than me, well-groomed and blue-suited, with a white blouse with a fluffy collar. She was pretty, wore glasses, and was black. Actually, she was a very light brown.

"I have to find Mr. Trasker," I said.

"We haven't seen him in several days," she said, sounding

like Bennington or Radcliffe, her hands folded on the desk in front of her, giving me her full attention.

"Does he often disappear for days?" I asked.

Mrs. Free did not answer but said, "Can I help you, Mr. Fonesca?"

There was no one within hearing distance. Her voice sounded all business and early dismissal for me. I decided to take a chance.

"Where do you live?" I asked.

She took off her glasses and looked at me at first in surprise and then in anger.

"Is this love at first sight, Mr. Fonesca?" she asked.

"You don't live in Newtown," I said.

"No, I live in Idora Estates. My husband is a doctor, a pediatrician. We have a daughter in Pine View and a son who just graduated from Pine View and is going to go to Grinnell. Now, I think you should leave."

"I have reason to believe that if Mr. Trasker goes to the City Commission meeting Friday night, he *will* vote against the Midnight Pass bill and that members of the commission will try to divert the money they would have spent on opening the Pass to helping with the renovation of Newtown," I said.

I waited.

"Who are you working for?" she asked quietly.

"Someone who wants to find William Trasker and help Newtown," I said.

"I was born here," she said so softly that I could hardly hear her. "In Newtown. So was my husband. My mother still lives there. She won't move."

"Where is Trasker?" I asked.

"Off the record, Mr. Fonesca," she said. "Mr. Trasker is not well."

"Off the record, Mrs. Free," I said, "Mr. Trasker is dying and I think you know it."

She nodded. She knew.

"You really think he'll vote against opening the Pass?" she asked.

"Good authority," I said. "A black man of the cloth."

"Fernando Wilkens," she said with a sigh that showed less respect than resignation.

"You're not a big fan of the reverend?"

"I'd rather say that he serves the community when that service benefits Fernando Wilkens," she said. "Fortunately, the two are generally compatible."

"You know him well?"

"I know him well enough."

She looked away. She understood. The sigh was long and said a lot, that she was considering risking her job, that she was about to give away things a secretary shouldn't give away.

"One condition," she said, folding her hands on the desk. "You are not to tell where you got this information."

"I will not tell," I said.

"For some reason, I believe you," she said. "God knows why. You've got that kind of face."

"Thanks."

"You've heard of Kevin Hoffmann," she said.

"I've heard," I said.

"He has a large estate on the mainland across from Bird Keys," she said. "Owns large pieces of land all along Little Sarasota Bay."

"So he'd make money if the Pass was opened."

"Now boats have to go five miles past the Pass site to the end of Casey Key and then come up Little Sarasota Bay another five-plus miles."

"I get it."

"Only part of it," she said. "If the Pass opens, a lot of Kevin Hoffmann's property, now a bog, could be turned into choice waterside home sites. Trasker Construction has done almost all of the work for Kevin Hoffmann. It's been said that Mr. Trasker is in Kevin Hoffmann's pocket. It's also been said that Hoffmann is in Mr. Trasker's pocket. They are certainly close business associates and have been for many years."

"It's been said," I repeated. "You think Hoffmann's done something to Trasker to keep him from voting against opening the Pass?"

"I wouldn't put it past him."

"You've put some thought into this," I said.

"Some," she admitted, adjusting her glasses. "You can check out Kevin Hoffmann's holdings in the tax office right downtown," she said. "Which would be more than the local media have done."

"Thanks," I said, getting up.

"No need," she said, rising and accompanying me down the hall. "We haven't had this conversation. I've told you nothing."

"Nothing," I agreed.

"Why doesn't Mrs. Trasker like you?" I asked.

"Five years ago when I came to work here," she said, "Mr. Trasker was looking less for a competent secretary than a possible sexual conquest. By the time he realized that he would not be permitted to even touch me, he had also realized that I was probably invaluable to the business. Mrs. Trasker is a smart woman. I'm sure she knew what had been on her husband's mind. I'm also reasonably sure that she knew he had failed, but Mrs. Trasker is a vain woman not likely to be kindly disposed toward any woman her husband found attractive."

When we stood in front of the receptionist's desk, she shook my hand and said, "I'm sorry I couldn't help you, Mr. Fonesca, but I will give Mr. Trasker your name and number as soon as he returns."

It was almost four, but I drove up Swift and made good pre–rush hour time. Rush hour in Sarasota was still not a big problem, compared to Chicago or even Dubuque, but it slowed me down.

I got to the parking lot in front of Building C in a complex of identical three-story buildings marked A, B, C, and D off of Fruitville and Tutle. It was just before four-thirty.

Building C housed some of the offices of Children's Services of Sarasota. Buildings A, B, and D had a few empty office spaces but most were filled by dentists, urologists, investment advisers, a jeweler, an estate appraiser, a four-doctor cardiology practice, and three allergists.

John Gutcheon was at the downstairs reception desk, literally twiddling his thumbs. John was thin, blond, about thirty, and very openly gay. His sharp tongue was his sole protection from invaders of his life choice. His world was divided into those who accepted him and those who did not accept him.

I was on John's good list, so I got fewer verbal barbs than a lot of Children's Service parents, who usually sullenly and always suspiciously brought in the children they had been charged with abusing. He looked up at me and shook his head.

"That cap has got to go," he said. "You are not a hat person and only real baseball players and gay men with a certain *elan* can get away with it. You look like an emaciated garbageman or, to be more socially correct, an anorexic sanitary engineer."

"Good afternoon, John," I said. "She's expecting me."

"Good afternoon," he answered. "I'm glad you prepared her. Are you saving someone today or are you going to try to pry Sally away from her caseload for dinner? She could use the respite."

"Both."

"Good. I'll sign you in."

"Thanks."

"It's been drearily quiet here today," he said, looking out the window at the cars in the parking lot. "I'm giving serious thought to moving."

"Key West?" I asked.

John rolled his eyes up to the ceiling.

"No," he said. "Care to try for a second stereotype?"

"San Francisco," I tried.

"You are a George Sanders–level cad, Fonesca," he said. "Providence, Rhode Island, the city of my birth, the birth of my life which still puzzles my parents."

"Providence," I repeated.

"My parents are very understanding people," he explained. "Very liberal. They walked out on *Guess Who's Coming to Dinner?* when they first saw it. Couldn't accept that a beautiful man like Sidney Poitier, who played a world-famous, wealthy, and brilliant surgeon, would be in love with that dolt of a white girl."

"I get the point. You know any good jokes, John?"

"Hundreds," he said, opening his arms to indicate the vastness of his comic memory.

"Tell me one."

He did. I wrote it down in my notebook.

"Flee," he said with a wave of his right hand when I finished writing. "Your lady awaits."

He pulled the clipboarded sign-in sheet on his desk and began to carefully enter my name.

I took the elevator up to the second floor unannounced and went through the glass doors.

In most businesses, with the clock edging toward five, the employees would be in the act of preparing for their daily evacuation. Not here. The open room the size of a baseball infield was vibrating with voices from almost every one of the small cubicles that served as office space for the caseworkers.

Most of the workers I passed were women, but there were a few men. Some of the workers were on the phone. One woman looked at me in a dazed state and ran a pencil through her thick curly hair as she talked on the phone. She closed her eyes and tilted her head back.

"Then when will you and your wife be at home?" she asked.

Never, I thought. Never.

Sally's cubicle was big enough for her to sit facing her desk with one person seated to her left.

The person sitting was a thin black woman in a sagging tan dress. She was worn out, clutching a little black purse against her small breasts. She looked up at me with tired eyes as Sally spoke to a boy of about thirteen standing to the right of the desk. The boy looked like the woman with the purse. His eyes were half-closed. His arms were crossed and he was leaning back against the thick glass that separated Sally from the caseworker across from her, Julio Vegas. Vegas, on the phone and alone, gave me a nod of recognition.

"Darrell," Sally was saying evenly, "do you understand what I'm telling you?"

Darrell nodded.

"What am I saying?"

"I get in trouble again, maybe a judge takes me away from my mother."

"More than maybe, Darrell, almost certain. And you heard your mother say that if you didn't straighten out, she didn't want to see you till you went somewhere else and came back a responsible man."

"Yes," Darrell said.

"You think you can straighten out?"

"Yes," said Darrell without enthusiasm.

"Really?" Sally said, sitting back.

"Maybe," the boy said, avoiding his mother's eyes.

"Mrs. Caton?" Sally asked, turning her eyes to the thin woman. "You willing to try once more?"

"I got a choice?"

"Considering his police record and breaking into the car last night, I can start the paperwork now, put Darrell in juvenile detention, or we put him into Juvenile Justice and see how fast we can get in front of a judge if you say you can't handle him anymore."

It was a lose-lose situation. I recognized it. Sally had told me about it a few dozen times. Kid goes back to his mother, and there is no way outside a miracle that he is going to straighten out. Kid goes into the system, and the odds were good that if a foster home could be found, he wouldn't straighten out and the foster home might even be worse for him than living with his mother. There was at least a shot if a good foster home could be found, but generally it was lose-lose.

Mrs. Caton looked at her son, at Sally, and at me. Sally watched the woman's eyes and turned to me. She held up a finger to indicate that she would be finished in a minute. Normally, Sally's minutes were half an hour long. She turned back to Mrs. Caton.

"Guess we can try again," the woman said with a sigh and a shake of her head.

"Darrell?" Sally said, turning her head to the boy.

"I'll habilitate," he said.

"Good word choice," Sally said. "Now make a good life choice."

"Let's go home, Darrell," Mrs. Caton said, shaking her head to show that this was no more than she expected.

Darrell, who stood about three inches taller than his mother, moved past me. Darrell whispered to me, "What'd you do to your kid?"

Since I had no kid, I had no answer. He didn't expect one. I didn't put high hopes on Darrell's habilitation.

When they were gone, Sally swiveled her chair toward me, took off her glasses, and rubbed the bridge of her nose. Sally is dark, pretty, maybe a little overweight, and definitely a lot over-worked.

"That boy is thirteen," she said. "His mother is twenty-eight. Do the math, Lew. I was bluffing. There's no space in juvenile and no basis for any action. She's stuck with him till he commits a felony, she kicks him out of their one-bedroom apartment, or he decides to live on the streets or with the crack dealer he picks up a few dollars from as a lookout."

"Darrell is lost?" I said, sitting in the chair where Mrs. Caton had been.

"No," she said, brushing back her dark hair with both hands. "Percentages are against him. I'm not. I'll do an unannounced drop-in in a few nights, maybe take them out for coffee or an ice cream for which I will not be reimbursed."

Sally was a widow. Her husband had died five years ago and she was raising her son and daughter in a two-bedroom apartment about five minutes away on Beneva. She worked sixty-hour weeks for thirty-seven and a half hours of pay and once in while she sent someone to me for the kind of help I can give. Someone like Kenneth Severtson.

"Use your phone?" I asked.

She handed it to me and I called Dixie.

"It's Lew," I said when she answered with her I've-got-a-bad-cold voice. "Anything on Trasker?"

"Not a trace after last Thursday," she said in normal Dixie. "Thursday night he paid for gas on an Amex card. That's it. No hotels, motels, escort services, bank withdrawals, bagels, café lattes, or bank deposits. Nothing. Whatever he's spent since last Thursday has been with cash."

"Thanks."

"Did find something," she said before I could hang up. "He's got a record. Goes back thirty-two years. Spent two years in a

California prison for nearly killing a man who he said was diddling his movie-star wife."

"Claire Collins," I said.

"That's the one. William Trasker was Walter Trasnovorich when it happened. Legally changed his name when he got out in 1972."

"Who was the man he almost killed?"

"Actor," said Dixie. "Movie name, Don Heller. Real name, Franklin Morris. Want to know Roberta Trasker's name before it was Claire Collins? Roberta Goulding, but I think there's a name even earlier. There's a big blank in her life from the age of zero to about seventeen. I'll keep working on it."

"Trasker have any family?" I asked. "Brothers, sisters?"

"I can find out," she said.

I thought for a second. I could call Roberta Trasker for an answer, but I don't like telephones. I don't like the dead space I'm expected to fill on them and Roberta Trasker might give me a lot of dead space.

"See what you can find," I said. "I'm going out of town tomorrow. You can leave a message on my answering machine if you find anything. And there's someone else I'd like you to check on: Kevin Hoffmann, the real-estate developer."

"Got it. I'll have to bill you some more," Dixie said apologetically. "I'm a working girl with two cats."

I hadn't seen any cats in her apartment but I believed her.

"Okay," I said, and hung up to look at Sally, who was looking back at me with slightly raised eyebrows that held a question.

"Long story," I said. "You have time for the China Palace buffet?"

Sally looked at her watch.

"No," she said. "I've got to put in at least another hour filling out reports and then get home to the kids."

"I'll bring you some carryout. Cashew chicken and hot-and-sour soup?"

The China Palace was three minutes away on Fruitville.

"And a bunch of egg rolls for the kids," she said, reaching down for her purse under the desk.

"On me," I said. "I've got a paying client, remember?"

"Kenneth Severtson."

"I'm going to Orlando tonight," I said. "His wife and children are there with—"

"Andrew Stark," she finished. "You have a plan?"

"No," I said. "Find her, watch, maybe talk to her. Maybe I just tell Severtson where they are. He tells his lawyer. Think that's a good idea?"

"Probably not," she said. "I don't think Kenneth Severtson's likely to handle the situation very well. It's better if you talk to her. If she won't come back, Severtson can get a lawyer. They're his children, too."

"But that would take time," I said.

"And money," she added. "And she could be out of Florida before the paperwork could get done so someone like you could serve it."

"What do you have on the family?"

She reached over to a stack of files leaning against the glass at the back of her desk, fished through them, and came up with the one I wanted. I knew she couldn't let me read it, but that didn't stop Sally from answering some questions.

"Your own words," I said.

"My own words," she said, pursing her lips. "Kenneth Severtson is not the Cosby dad, but he's not Homer Simpson either. He's got a temper. He's tough to get through to. They have credit-card payment problems, even talked about bankruptcy. His business is good, but they spend like its Microsoft. He took it out on his wife. The police were called in. He needed help. He doesn't trust therapy and resented our intervention. Janice isn't a mouse, but she isn't a dragon. Good mothers can do dumb things when it comes to their kids. I had her down as a loyal wife who was willing to put up with a lot to keep her marriage and family together."

"Things have changed," I said.

"Andrew Stark," she said. "Stark isn't an old friend of the family. Went into partnership with Kenneth Severtson a few years ago. Definitely a shady background. He's done some very soft time for consumer fraud, and he has not been particularly polite in dealing with women who are, unaccountably, attracted to him."

"You met him?"

"No, just made a few calls to friends in the sheriff's office."

"So?" I asked.

"She'll probably stay with Stark until he gets tired of her. Or maybe it's true love. Truth is, Lewis, I don't care about the future of Andrew Stark and only dimly about Janice Severtson. It's the kids. Do what you can, Lew."

I nodded.

Sally looked over at Julio Vegas, who was in animated conversation on the phone in Spanish.

"I'll be back with Chinese in a shopping bag," I said, getting up.

"I'd kiss you if we weren't in the equivalent of South Gate Mall," she said with a tired smile as she touched my hand. "Be careful."

"At the China Palace?"

"In Disneyville."

5

HAD ALREADY PACKED my blue carry-on for a couple of nights and had my Chicago Cubs baseball cap in the front seat of the Nissan Sentra. I look like a big-eared dolt in the cap, but it protects my ever-growing forehead from burning under the Florida sun and even though it was close to seven at night, the sun was still huge and hot in the sky behind me as I headed east on Fruitville for I-75.

I had delivered the bag of Chinese food to Sally and got twelve egg rolls, three of which sat in a brown sack on the seat next to me. Another one was in my hand. I had also bought four egg rolls for John Gutcheon.

I drove past Target and the malls on my left and right and headed north on I-75. Traffic wasn't bad for three reasons. Rush hour was over. It was summer and the snowbirds had left, reducing the population of Sarasota and the entire state of Florida significantly. People who worked were already home and people who didn't were in their air-conditioned homes or at the beach on the cool white sand ignoring the ultraviolet index.

I was on my way to Orlando armed with three photographs and wearing a Cubs cap. I listened to a talk-show guy who badgered his callers, made crude jokes, and kept saying he was just using common sense while he got the history of Israel, Iraq, France, and the United States almost completely wrong. I chewed on egg rolls and kept to a few miles over the speed limit.

There was construction on I-4 from the Tampa interchange to Orlando. I-4 is four lanes, two lanes in each direction, and it always seems there are as many trucks as cars. Still, it only took me a little over two hours to get to International Drive, a street of glitz, restaurants, hotels, a water slide, plenty of places that sell T-shirts and souvenirs, and a Ripley's Believe It or Not house built at an odd angle, as if it had just been dropped from outer space.

The hotel wasn't full, but all they had for me was a room at almost two hundred a night. I didn't have a credit card, but I had taken all my cash with me. I paid a day in advance and got a receipt I could show Kenneth Severtson. The young woman behind the desk did a great job of ignoring the fact that my luggage was a single blue carry-on.

When I got to my room, I threw my cap on the table, took the John Lutz novel I was reading out of the carry-on, and went down to the atrium lobby, where I used the house phone to connect me to Andrew Stark's room. No answer. I asked for his room number. The young woman on the phone said they weren't permitted to give out room numbers.

I went down to the lobby. There were plenty of wrought-iron seats at tables and tastefully upholstered chairs scattered around the area. I found a chair in the atrium facing the door to the hotel and sat with my paperback open in my lap.

Little kids ran screaming in their swimsuits heading for the pool. Families went by speaking German, French, and something I couldn't place.

Stark, Janice Severtson, and the kids came in a little after nine-thirty. Stark was carrying the little girl, Sydney, who was sleeping. Kenneth Jr. was walking slowly with a less-than-happy look on his face. His mother was definitely a beauty, but there was something less than ecstasy in her face. She was carrying a colorful shopping bag with a picture of Shrek on the side.

Stark was a good-looking if slightly beefy-looking man with wavy salt-and-pepper hair. He was at least twenty years older than Janice Severtson.

There wasn't too much I could do to be inconspicuous. I don't have the kind of face people remember in any case. It's a blessing in my work and in my private life.

I managed to get on the elevator with the four of them and smiled.

"Floor?" I asked pleasantly.

"Seven," Janice Severtson said, closing her eyes.

I hit the "seven" and "eight" buttons.

When we passed the third floor, she opened her eyes and looked at me.

"I know you," she said.

Stark turned to face me. He was wearing black jeans and a black shirt with buttons and sleeves that came down to his elbows. He was also wearing muscles and a scowl. His face was sun-browned. His brown eyes were firmly focused on me.

"I don't . . . ," I began.

"Sarasota YMCA," she said. "Downtown. You work out there."

So much for my keenly developed internal storehouse of names and faces. How could I not remember someone who looked like Janice Severtson? How could she remember me?

"I do," I said with a grin. "Every morning before I go to work. I'm the men's wear department manager at Old Navy in Gulf Gate. Brought my wife and kids here, for our annual week of torture."

"I know what you mean," she said.

"Who's that?" the little boy asked, looking up at me.

"A friend of your mother's," said Stark with more than a touch of suspicion.

"You a friend of my daddy's, too?" the boy asked.

"No," I said, holding out my hand to Stark. "Pleased to meet you."

"He's not my daddy," the boy said.

"He's your grandfather?"

Stark's jaw was tight now. I ignored him and looked down at the little boy, who was shaking his head no.

"He's Andy," the boy said.

"I think we've bothered the man enough," said Janice Severtson.

The elevator stopped at seven and they shuffled wearily out.

"Nice to meet you," I called as the doors closed.

When the doors opened on the eighth floor a few seconds later, I got out quickly and moved to a spot on the atrium landing not far from my room where I could see them moving slowly toward their room.

After they went in, I stayed at the railing for another hour, pretending my novel was a sketchbook when anyone went by, keeping an eye on the door to the room I was watching on the seventh floor. I even drew a crude stick figure and a tree on the inside cover of the novel at one point. My watch hit eleven, and I went to my room and set the alarm clock for five in the morning. I shaved, showered, shampooed, brushed my teeth, and watched a Harold Lloyd silent comedy on Turner Classic Movies. Harold wound up running around an abandoned ship being chased by a murderer and a monkey in a sailor suit. The movie was short. I went to sleep. Everything was going just fine.

By seven in the morning, I was eating the free Continental buffet breakfast at a two-person table. When I finished, I slowly drank cup after cup of coffee with *USA Today* in front of me. A little before nine, Andrew Stark, Janice Severtson, and the kids came down. The kids were bouncing and arguing. The adults were just arguing. I couldn't hear them, but it looked as if the brief honeymoon was in trouble.

I followed them out after they breakfasted. The rest of the day was moppet heaven for the kids and nightmare alley for me. They went on and saw everything at the Disney-MGM Studios theme park while I watched from a discreet distance. I don't know what I was watching for. Possibly signs of intimacy in front of the children. A stolen passionate kiss and a little groping while the kids were in the Muppet Vision show, or maybe I was hoping for a chance to catch Janice Severtson alone.

We watched the *Beauty and the Beast* show, the *Hunchback* show, the *Honey I Shrunk the Kids* show, the Indiana Jones Epic Stunt Spectacular, and had lunch at Disney's Toy Story Pizza Planet Arcade. By the time we hit Voyage of the Little Mermaid, I was strongly considering calling Kenneth Severtson and telling him that I was on my way back to Sarasota.

They went on The Great Movie Ride and ended the day with The Making of *Tarzan*. I wished Stark would carry me or better yet, that Janice Severtson would carry me.

They stopped for dinner at a seafood restaurant. I didn't eat. The chance of being spotted was too great and I didn't put much faith in talking my way out of an accidental encounter with, "Well, we meet again. Small world after all."

I wasn't hungry.

When they went back to their suite, I followed and stood outside the door, trying to listen through the curtained window

                                                   Stuart M. Kaminsky

without giving the impression to anyone that I was a peeping tom. There was an alcove with doors to more rooms and a stair-well ten feet away. If I heard anyone open the door inside the room, I could get to the alcove and up the stairs before I was spotted.

The rooms were set back from the railing, so I couldn't be seen from the atrium floor. I made sure no one was watching me from a floor above and put my ear to the window. I couldn't make out words inside the room but the voices were hard and angry.

I went back to my room. I hadn't been able to get Janice Severtson alone. Stark had stuck too close to her. I would call Severtson in the morning, give him his wife's room number, advise him to pass it on immediately to his lawyer, and head back home. I'd alert Sally before I called Severtson in case she wanted to contact him and try to talk him into being reasonable when he heard from me. I couldn't spend any more time in Orlando. I had a missing commissioner and two days to find him.

I took a hot shower, got into my boxer shorts, and turned on the television. I was going to look for a movie, but the channel guide told me there was a Cubs game on WGN.

It was the fifth inning. Kerry Wood was pitching. The Cubs were up, three to nothing. The announcer said Moises Alou had hit a home run with two men on to give the Cubs the lead.

I tried to lose myself in the game. I almost succeeded. The Cubs were ahead, five to nothing, going into the ninth. They were playing at home. The Pirates were batting. Wood was going for a complete game shutout.

I tried not to think about the little girl in Stark's arms, of the little boy who had asked me questions about his mother and father, about Adele and the baby, Sally and her children, Darrell Caton, who had looked at me with contempt in Sally's office.

The Cubs helped. They almost blew the game. Wood got

wild, gave up two walks and a double. Score was five to two. Reliever came in. I didn't recognize his name. He had just come up from Triple A. He walked the first man. The next batter hit into a double play, but the runner on second scored after a bad throw to the plate by the first baseman, Mueller. Five to three. The next man up got on with a broken-bat single to right. The tying run was on base.

Two outs. The batter hit one deep and high. It kept traveling toward the vines in right field. Sammy backed up to the wall, eyes on the ball. He timed the little leap and pulled the ball down for the final out.

In baseball, sometimes things went right.

In baseball, there was always a clear end, a final score.

I turned the lights out and got in bed. I was asleep in seconds.

Someone was knocking at my door. I sat up dizzy and looked at the clock with the glowing red numbers. It was a little after three in the morning. The knock came again. I got off the bed and went out of the bedroom to the door.

"Who is it?" I asked.

"Janice Severtson."

I opened the door and flipped on the lights. The children were both in pajamas and robes, crying. Janice Severtson needed a comb and a good dry cleaner. Her white robe was splotched with blood.

"Can we come in?" she asked. "Please."

I stepped back and the weeping trio came in. I closed the door and turned to watch them sit on the small sofa. Janice Severtson was trying to comfort them, kissing the tops of their heads, hugging her children.

"How did you find me?" I asked. "And why?"

"I called the desk after I recognized you earlier," she said. "I said I didn't remember your name but that we knew each other from Sarasota. I described you. They found someone who remembered checking you in."

"I hope the description was kind," I said, putting my jeans on over the orange boxer shorts I had been sleeping in.

She didn't answer that one. I pulled my shirt on over my head.

"I called some friends I can trust in Sarasota," she went on, looking at the dark television screen and hugging her sobbing children. "Found someone who knew you. My husband sent you, didn't he?"

"Yes," I said.

"Can I trust you?" she asked, continuing to soothe her children. "I have no one else to turn to."

"You can trust me. But I'm not sure why you should believe you can."

"No choice," she said with a shrug. "I want you to take Sydney and Kenny back to their father."

Both children said, "no," but Janice wasn't listening.

"At three in the morning?" I asked.

She sat the children on the little sofa against the wall and told them she would be back in a second. Kenneth Jr. turned his head into his mother's shoulder. The little girl looked down and bit her lip. Then Janice motioned for me to follow her into the bedroom, where she closed the door.

"I just killed Andrew Stark," she said. "I've got to go back to the room and call the police. Take my children home. Please. My husband is a good father. I don't want them involved."

"Let's go to your room and have a look before we call the police."

I slipped my bare feet into my unlaced sneakers and opened the door.

Janice Severtson hugged both her children and told them she would be gone for just a minute. They weren't crying anymore. They looked as if they were nearly asleep.

"Can we watch television?" Kenny asked.

"Sure," I said, handing him the remote.

He clicked it on. A voice in Spanish rattled excitedly about a soccer match going between guys in green uniforms and guys in yellow ones.

"They play soccer in Mexico in the middle of the night?" he asked.

"It's a tape," I said.

He nodded knowingly, eyes blinking as he changed the station and watched a crocodile slither into a pond of water.

"Be right back," Janice Severtson said, following me through the door after I checked my pocket to be sure I had my room card.

Even at three in the morning, the atrium wasn't empty. Five men were seated eight stories down talking softly. A crew of cleaning people was sweeping and scrubbing. Janice Severtson looked down across the open space at the closed door of her room a floor below.

"What happened?" I asked quietly.

She wiped her eyes with her sleeve, took a deep breath.

"He tried to rape me," she said. "He hit me, pulled my hair. He'd gotten up during the night. He was drunk. There was a knife on the table. His knife along with his wallet and keys. I told him to stop. He didn't. I told him he'd wake the children, that they would see us. I begged him. He grabbed my wrist and laughed. We were standing there, just . . . I twisted my arm and pulled free and then I brought the knife down. He looked surprised. The children slept through it all. Thank God, the children slept through it. Andrew, he lay there with the knife in his chest. I didn't know what . . . You know the rest. I'll go back and call the police. You take care of my children, please."

"You're sure he's dead?" I asked.

"Yes. I covered his body with the blanket so the children wouldn't see him when I woke them up."

"I'll go take a look. You go back to your kids and give me your room card."

"Why?" she asked.

"Because I'm asking you," I said. "I won't take long. If the phone rings, it'll be me. Answer it."

She brushed her hair back with her long fingers and pulled the room card out. I took it and let her back into my room. The television was on. Kenny had switched to an old *Dick Van Dyke* rerun, the one where Rob goes off to a cabin to write a novel. The episode, as I recalled, was funny. Sydney was asleep and Kenneth Jr. wasn't laughing.

I went down the fire stairs and made my way to the room on the seventh floor. I opened the door and wiped the door handle clean with my shirt. Then I kicked the door closed. The lights were on. There was a vague body shape under the blanket on the open hide-away bed.

I moved alongside the bed and pulled the blanket back. Andrew Stark lay there, bloody, eyes closed. His T-shirt had a picture of a grinning cartoon turkey on the front. The turkey was covered in blood. A knife was plunged deep into his chest. Stark was naked from the shirt down.

I didn't touch anything else. I looked around the room and into the bedroom. There was a teddy bear and stuffed elephant lying back on a pink blanket. I went back into the room where Stark was lying, checked my watch, and started for the door.

The moan wasn't loud, but it was clear and it came from the supposedly dead Andrew Stark. I went back to the body and knelt. Stark' s eyes opened and moved in the general direction of my face. I didn't bother to tell him not to move.

I could have just called 911, but a few minutes probably

wouldn't make much difference. At least that's what I told myself.

"You'll be all right," I assured him as I examined his wound.

He looked around the room as if he had no idea of where he was. He smelled of alcohol. There was plenty of blood.

"You'll live," I lied. "I'm going to try to stop some of this bleeding. Then I'll call an ambulance."

His right hand came up suddenly and gripped my wrist. For a dying man, he was damned strong. I tried to pull loose as he croaked, "Why?"

"You want to live?"

"Why?" he asked.

Since it was the same question I've asked myself a few thousand times since my wife was killed, I had no good answer for him, but I had the feeling that his "why" didn't mean the same thing mine did.

His eyes began to roll. A very bad sign.

He whispered something I couldn't hear, pain in his face . . . Then he closed his eyes and I leaned over to be sure he was still breathing. He was.

I picked up the phone, not worrying about fingerprints any longer, and dialed my own room. Janice answered before the second ring.

"Yes?" she said with a quivering voice.

"It's me, Fonesca. Get down to your room fast. Leave the kids there."

"What . . . ?"

"He's still alive."

She didn't answer and I had no time to talk to her now.

"Fast," I said.

I hung up, checked my watch, sat on the bed, and said, "Stark, you still with me?"

His groan suggested that he was. I checked my watch.

Almost a minute passed. If she didn't show up fast, I'd have to call 911.

The knock was soft, but it was a knock. I let her in. She was a ghostly pale, beautiful vision of white and blood red. I closed the door and she walked over to Stark, who hadn't moved.

"Andy?" she asked.

He groaned in response.

She turned to me and, voice and hands shaking, said, "I didn't kill him."

"You've got to call 911," I said. "You've got to call now. Just tell them a man has tried to kill himself. Tell them where we are. Don't answer any more questions."

She shook her head no. I picked up the phone and handed it to her. I hit 9 for an outside line and then 911.

I could hear a voice on the other end because the phone wasn't close to her ear, but I couldn't make out the words.

She said exactly what I had told her to say and hung up.

"Good," I said. "I think we've got at least five minutes, maybe more. I'm going to be back in my room with the kids. You understand?"

She nodded again, looking at the half-naked, bloody man on the bed. He made a series of short gasping sounds, managed to reach the handle of the knife with his right hand, and tried to pull it out before I could stop him. Then he stopped struggling and his hands flopped to his sides.

I checked for a pulse in his neck. There wasn't any.

"You want to tell me what really happened here, or you want me to guess?" I asked. "Faster if you tell me."

"He didn't tell you?" she said, clasping her hands together to keep them from shaking.

"He didn't say anything other than 'Why?'" I said, determined to be out of there in three minutes. "You said he hit you. There's not a mark on you. You said he tried to attack you and you fought him, but the kids didn't wake up. And your robe is bloody and I don't see a tear in it or a button missing. You stabbed him while you were wearing the robe. You stabbed him while he was lying in the bed. You stabbed him when he was asleep. You got up, put on your robe, and stabbed him."

"You don't understand," she said, crying, her hands, white-knuckled, clasped in mock prayer.

"Maybe I do. Which kid?"

"Which . . . ?"

"You woke up and saw something. Which of your children was he going to molest?"

"Sydney," she said wearily. "The bathroom light was on and the door open a little, a night-light. He was sitting on Sydney's side of the bed, his hand between her legs. She was asleep. Andy had been drinking while I was asleep. I could smell it across the room. He started to touch her. Before I could get up, he came back to bed. A few minutes later when he started to snore I got up and put on my robe. I took the knife and . . . the rest of what I told you was true."

"Does Sydney know what Stark was trying to do to her?"

"No, I don't think they even looked at the bed when we left the room," she said. "They weren't even really awake."

I checked my watch. Florida police had been under fire for months over not responding to 911 calls quickly enough. Time was running out.

"You came out of the bathroom," I said to Janice Severtson. "You could tell he was drunk, mumbling. Words you couldn't understand. Saw him stab himself. You called 911 and remembered that you had seen me, an old friend of your husband's, in the hotel. You called me, brought the children to my room, and came back here to wait for the ambulance and police. You understand?"

"I . . . ," she said, looking at Stark.

Stuart M. Kaminsky

"He's been talking about killing himself for running away with you, his partner and best friend's wife. He's been talking about regretting things he did in the past. He's been drinking and he got depressed when he drank. You've got that?"

"I . . ."

"Mrs. Severtson," I said, "if you want to keep your kids out of this, you better remember. You tell the truth about what happened and why, and you lose your kids. Television news will get it and make it all very ugly. Your picture, the children's picture all over the place, maybe network. Good-bye kids. Good-bye husband. Probably jail time. So, can you remember what to say?"

"He killed himself," she said. "But why can't I just say he attacked me and I defended myself?"

"That's what you told me, and it took me about two minutes to figure out you were lying," I said.

Stark's hand and fingerprints were on the knife handle. Even if a smart cop thought something was more than a little suspicious, he probably wouldn't pursue it. Stark had a record. Stark, Janice, and her children weren't rednecks in a cheap motel room. Class still has its privileges.

"I'm going," I said. "They'll be here any second. You'll be all right."

It wasn't a question but she answered more strongly than I expected.

"I'll be all right."

I moved toward the door.

"Wait," she said.

I turned toward her. She went into the bedroom and came back almost immediately. She handed me the teddy bear, the stuffed elephant, and the pink blanket. I went out and moved fast without running toward the stairwell. Below, out of sight, I could hear the sound of voices in the lobby. I ran up the one flight and came out close to the wall where I couldn't be seen by anyone eight flights below. I made my way to my room, opened the door, and found Sydney asleep on the sofa next to her brother, who was nodding off as he watched the end of the *Dick Van Dyke* episode. In her sleep, Sydney took the elephant and the pink blanket and clutched them to her chest.

Kenny looked at me. I handed him the teddy bear.

"What happened?" he asked, eyes blinking heavily. "Where's my mom?"

"Mr. Stark had an accident," I said.

"I don't like him anymore," the boy said. "Sydney doesn't like him anymore either. He smiles, buys us stuff, but he's a fake. We told Mom. She wouldn't listen."

"She's listening now," I said. "What did you see tonight before your mom brought you to my room?"

Kenneth didn't hesitate.

"Andy was sleeping on the bed," the boy said. "All covered up."

"You want to get some sleep, Kenneth?"

"Yes," he said.

"Get into the bed in the other room," I said.

"Sydney might get up and be scared."

"I'll put her next to you."

That seemed acceptable to him. I picked up the girl, who clung to her blanket and elephant. She smelled clean. She smelled like a little girl. I followed Kenny into the bedroom, where he watched me put his sister down on the bed. Then he climbed into the bed, put his head on the pillow, and fell asleep almost instantly with one hand touching his sister's arm.

It was just a question of how long it would take some cop to knock at the door to my room. My story would be simple, always best to keep it simple. Friend of Janice's husband, taking a few days off to enjoy the Orlando glitz, ran into them in the

Stuart M. Kaminsky

elevator. Then she brought me the kids. I didn't know Stark. I didn't know what he was doing there. Janice would have to swallow the humiliation and tell them the truth on that one. The cops would probably just go through the motions. No need to do anything else.

I was halfway through a Diet Dr Pepper and an ancient rerun of a *Bob Newhart Show* when the knock came.

The two uniformed cops looked as if they had been awakened from a deep sleep. They were both young. The older of the two, who was about thirty, asked the questions. The other one took the notes.

They stayed long enough to get statements from Janice Severtson and me. They didn't wake the kids. Janice told them she had seen Stark stab himself but the kids hadn't even seen the body. She told them she had brought them up to me when Stark stabbed himself. She said she had quickly run back down and found him on the bed. She got the blood on herself, she told them, when she tried to help him.

She was a good liar. So am I. She agreed to stay in Orlando the next day to come in, answer a detective's questions, and sign a statement. They said the kids should stay in Orlando in case a detective wanted to talk to them. Then the cops said I could do whatever I wanted.

I asked Janice if she was going to be all right, took her to my room after the police let her gather some clothes, gave her my door card, packed in about a minute, put on my cap, and moved to the door.

"You might want to shower," I said, "and get some sleep on the sofa."

She nodded.

"Thank you," she said. "I don't think they believed me."

"They believed me," I said. "Shower, sleep."

"Yes," she answered, drained, automatic.

"You be all right?"

"Yes."

I left, stopping at the desk, where the night manager heard my story, looked serious and sympathetic, and said he would be happy to give me a room for the rest of the night.

I checked my watch. It was almost five-thirty in the morning. The sun would be up in less than an hour.

"I don't feel like seeing Mickey Mouse anymore," I said.

"I had enough the first week I was here with my niece," he said. "How much bouncy and jolly can an adult take?"

"A lot less than a kid," I said.

I drove for a while on I-4, got off at a Lakeland exit, had an Egg McMuffin and coffee, and headed for Sarasota.

6

TRAFFIC WAS WEEKDAY-MORNING heavy on both I-4 and I-75. I was back in the DQ parking lot and climbing the concrete stairs to my office and home a little after nine-thirty.

I called Kenneth Severtson's number. No answer. I was relieved. I didn't want to talk to him. I didn't want questions.

"Your wife and kids will probably be back tomorrow," I told his machine. "They're fine. Be nice. Stark's dead. Killed himself. A long story. Your wife will tell you."

There was one message on my answering machine. It was one of the secretaries in the law offices of Tycinker, Oliver, and Schwartz.

"Mr. Fonesca"—her voice came through flat and dry—"Mr. Tycinker asked me to remind you that he needs those papers served on Mickey Donophin before Saturday. If we do not hear from you, he will assume you are unable to do this and will contact the Freewell Agency."

I called Tycinker, Oliver, and Schwartz. There was no one there, but there was an answering machine.

"This is Lewis Fonesca," I told it. "Tell Mr. Tycinker I'll have the papers in Mickey Donophin's hands within twenty-four hours."

I hung up, got my soap, a towel, toothbrush and toothpaste, and my electric razor and moved toward the rest room I shared with the other tenants and Digger, an otherwise homeless old man, who was standing in front of the mirror over the sink when I went through the door.

"Ah," he said, looking at me in the mirror. "The little Italian."

The rest room was almost always clean, which came as a stunning surprise to most visitors. A smiling, retarded man named Marvin Uliaks, for whom I had recently done a job, kept clean the rest room and most of the stores and storefront businesses on the three-block stretch of the seven short blocks of 301 between Main and the Tamiami intersection. He accepted whatever the business owners wanted to give him and smiled even when he was given only a quarter.

"How do I look?" Digger said, turning to me.

He looked like a disheveled mess of a human being who had put on a wrinkled gold tie that had nothing to do with his wrinkled blue-and-red striped shirt and sagging dark trousers.

"Dapper," I said as he gave me room to get to the sink.

"Got a job interview," he said over my shoulder, checking his tie in the mirror.

There was no hint of alcohol on his breath. There never was. Digger didn't drink. He couldn't afford to. He had told me when we first encountered each other by the urinal a few months ago that he neither drank nor took drugs.

"It's my mind," he had said. "Doesn't function right. I lose days, weeks, get headaches, fall a lot."

"Where's the job interview?"

He moved out of the way so I could brush my teeth.

"Jorge and Yolanda's," he said, checking his own teeth over my shoulder and rubbing them with his finger.

I held up my tube of Colgate, and he held out a finger for me to drop some toothpaste on it.

"Obliged," he said as I stepped out of the way after rinsing my mouth so he could work on his teeth.

Jorge and Yolanda's was a second-floor ballroom-dance studio right across the street. I could see it from my office window.

Satisfied with his teeth, Digger rinsed with a handful of tap water and stepped back. I turned on my razor.

"Want to know what I'll be doing?" he asked.

To the hum of my razor, I looked at him in the mirror and said, "Yes."

"Dancing," he said.

"Dancing?"

I stopped shaving.

"They have dances for their clients and prospective clients every Friday night," he said. "They need extra men because they have more women than men. What're you looking at me like that for? I'm a terrific dancer. Anything, you name it, waltz, tango, fox-trot, rumba, swing. You name it. I get fifteen bucks and all the appetizers I can eat every Friday night providing I don't make a hog of myself."

Digger used to be a pharmacist. He sometimes slept in a closet of one of the twenty-four-hour Walgreen's. There was a seemingly infinite number of Walgreen's and Eckerd drugstores in Sarasota, an even greater number of banks, and a supply of cardiologists, oncologists, and orthopedic surgeons that probably rivaled Manhattan's.

I knew little about Digger's past, didn't want to know more.

"Sounds great," I said, returning to my shaving. "Good luck."

He looked at himself in the mirror again.

"Haven't got a chance, have I?"

"Not a chance in the world," I said, finishing my shave and checking my face for places I might have missed.

"What the hell. I said I was coming in, answered an ad in the paper. Said I was coming in. What the hell? It's just across the street. What have I got to lose? You know?"

He started to loosen his tie.

"Got this tie at the Goodwill for a quarter," he said. "Real silk, just this little stain where you can't even really notice, but what the hell."

"What time's your appointment?" I asked, washing my face.

"Just said I should drop by some time after ten, but what the hell."

"You've got time to shave, use a comb, get a pair of pants that fit, a white shirt, and a pair of socks and shoes at the Women's Exchange."

The Women's Exchange consignment and resale shop was a few blocks down Oak Street.

"That'd cost," he said, looking at me with eyes showing a lot of red and little white.

"How much?"

I dried my face.

"Ten, fifteen bucks," he said.

I fished out a twenty and held it out. Digger took it.

"I gotta pay this back?" he asked.

"Get yourself something at the DQ if there's anything left," I said.

"Don't worry," Digger said, some of his confidence returning. "This isn't a precedent."

"I know," I said. "Good luck."

"Thanks. I tell you something? Now that the twenty is in my pocket?"

I nodded.

"You never smile."

I nodded again.

"Some things are funny," he said.

"Some things."

"I mean, I'm not talking about a big smile like one of those yellow stickers. Just something besides doom and gloom."

I imagined Lillian Gish in *Broken Blossoms*, pushing up the corners of her mouth into a pathetic smile when her brute father ordered her to smile.

"I'm working on it," I said, towel folded around my soap and shaving gear. "Know any jokes?"

"Couple maybe, if I can remember them," he said. "Never could remember jokes. Wait, I've got one."

He told it. I took out my notebook and wrote it down. The list for Ann Horowitz was growing. I already had the start of a second-rate stand-up act.

Digger looked as if he had something more to say but couldn't come up with it.

"Wish me luck," he said, going out the rest-room door ahead of me.

"Luck," I said, and headed back to my office.

There were three new messages on my answering machine. I didn't play them back. I knew I had a dying politician to find and not much time to do it and some papers to serve for the law firm of Tycinker, Oliver, and Schwartz, but there were other things more important at the moment, like spending the day on my cot sleeping when I could, watching a video of *Panic in the Streets* or *A Stolen Life*. I was trying to cut back on my dosage of *Mildred Pierce*.

I took off my pants and shirt, draped them on the wooden chair, and lay down after removing my shoes.

I didn't have to sleep. Dreams came while I was awake. The dying Stark would be added to my sleeping nightmares. My waking dreams always came back to moments with my wife, little moments. A laugh shared across the table at the Bok Choy Restaurant, our buttery fingers meeting in a box of popcorn while we watched a movie I couldn't remember. Her holding my face in her cool hands and looking into my eyes after we had an argument until I grinned and conceded her victory. Picking out the car in which she was killed.

There was an endless supply of pain. I savored every image, my depression fed on it. It wasn't simply self-pity. There was some of that, but it was that deep sense of void, loss that I wanted to hold onto and lose at the same time.

I fell asleep before I could insert a videotape. I dreamed of nothing and was awakened by the ringing of the telephone. It was still light outside. I checked my watch. It was almost seven at night. The sun was going down. I went into the office and picked up the phone a ring before the machine kicked in to take the message.

"Fonesca," I said.

"What happened?"

It was Kenneth Severtson asking a reasonable question.

"I left a message on your machine."

I looked at the battered metal box I had picked up in a pawnshop on Main Street.

"So?" he asked anxiously.

I told him the story and ended with "They should be home soon. Your wife had to answer a few questions for the police."

Long, long pause.

"He killed himself in front of Kenny and Sydney? She was in bed with him in front of Kenny and Sydney?"

Stuart M. Kaminsky

"They were in another room. They're young," I said. "I don't think the sex part sunk in."

I didn't believe that and I wasn't sure he would either, but it was a lie he could pretend to hang onto if he really wanted it.

"I'm thinking about a divorce and asking for custody of the children," he said.

"Talk to Sally."

"I don't know. I want things the way they were," he said, thinking out loud.

"I know, but it won't happen. You take her back, you take the pain. There are things harder to take. Talk to Sally."

"If there's ever anything I can do," he said.

I thought of asking him if he knew any jokes, but decided to say, "Thanks, you owe me some money. You can send it to me or drop it off."

"How much?"

"Three hundred," I said. "I've got to go."

I played the messages, erased Severtson's and two from Dixie to call her. I dialed Dixie at home.

"It's me, Lew," I said before she could cough or say hello in her fake hoarse voice.

"Roberta Goulding had a brother and a sister," she said. "Brother, seven years younger, Charles. Sister, six years younger, now Mrs. Antony Diedrich living with her husband in Fort Worth. He's got a Toyota and a Buick dealership. Don't know where the brother is."

"Thanks, Dixie," I said.

"That's not why I called mainly," she said. "Kevin Hoffmann, member of the board of just about everything in Sarasota, major contributor to the Ringling Museum, Asolo Theater, Sarasota Ballet, Sarasota Opera, Pine View School and Booker School Scholarship funds, Committee to Open Midnight Pass. Goes on and on."

"He's bought lots of friends."

"One might conclude," said Dixie. "Makes lots of money, like *lots*."

"Like?"

"Taxes on income over the past six years show over a million and half a year, some years over two million," she said.

"Thanks," I said.

"You haven't heard the best," she said. "He's going to have a birthday Sunday."

"I'm happy for him," I said.

"You might want to give him a present," she said, and told me why.

When I hung up with Dixie, I called Roberta Trasker. She answered after three rings.

"It's Lew Fonesca," I said.

"You found William?"

"You know Kevin Hoffmann?"

The pause was long. I opened the phone book and searched the pages for Hoffmann's number while I waited. He wasn't listed.

"Yes," she said. "Socially. He and his wife, Sharon, and William had business with him. Sharon left him about five or six years ago."

"You said 'William had' business with Hoffmann."

"I'm sorry," she said. "I suppose I'm . . ."

"I understand. Mind if I call Hoffmann and ask him if he has some idea where your husband is?"

"No," she said. "I gather you haven't gotten very far in finding William."

"One small step closer," I said. "I'll call you when I have more. You have his number, Hoffmann's?"

When I hung up I looked over at the Dalstrom painting on the wall, the deep dark jungle and darker mountains, the single touch of color in the flower.

Then I dialed the number Roberta Trasker had given me. A man answered.

"Mr. Hoffmann?"

"Who's calling?"

"Lew Fonesca," I said. "Mrs. Trasker give me this number."

"What do you want to speak to Mr. Hoffmann about?"

"William Trasker," I said.

"What about Mr. Trasker?"

"He's missing," I said. "I want to ask Mr. Hoffmann a few questions that might help me find him."

"You're making this inquiry on behalf of Mrs. Trasker?"

"Yes."

"You're with the police?"

"I'm not against them," I said.

I was tired. I wanted to go to a back booth at the Crisp Dollar Bill across the street, listen to the bartender's tapes, eat a steak sandwich, drink an Amstel, get back in bed, and watch a videotape, something old, something black-and-white, something with William Powell.

"May I have a noncryptic answer?" the man said.

"I'm not a police officer."

"One moment."

The phone was placed down gently, and I looked at the painting on my wall while I waited. The jungle was inviting and I wanted to smell the orchid. I didn't know if the orchid in the painting had a smell.

"Mr. Hoffmann is busy. If you leave a number, he'll get back to you tomorrow."

"Tell him I have a birthday present for him," I said. "It can't wait."

The phone went down again and this time a different man's voice, a higher voice, said, "This is Kevin Hoffmann. And you are?"

"Lew Fonesca."

"You told Stanley that you have a birthday present for me." He sounded amused.

"Yes."

"And you are looking for Bill Trasker?"

"Yes."

"And you are representing . . . ?"

"Someone who wants to find Trasker."

"Come on over," he said.

He gave me the address.

"I'll be there in forty minutes."

I called the *Herald-Tribune* office and got a young reporter named John Rubin who maybe owed me a favor.

"Midnight Pass," I said.

"I'm on a deadline," Rubin said. "Call me back tomorrow, early afternoon."

"Two minutes," I said.

"Something in it for me?"

"Might be," I said.

"Something big?"

"A woman I know, " I said, thinking of Ann Horowitz, "says all size is relative. A hit-and-run on Webber might not be worth more than a paragraph on page ten unless the victim or the driver was someone with power, pelf, or notoriety."

"Pelf?" Rubin said with a laugh. "You're a funny guy, Fonesca."

"I don't try to be but I'm working on it, my shrink's orders," I said. "Midnight Pass."

"That's your big story?" he asked. "Midnight Pass? I'm working on a double murder, guy goes nuts, stabs his wife with a screwdriver, batters her boyfriend with a foot stool, shoots himself with a speargun."

"A speargun?"

Stuart M. Kaminsky

"Yeah, and if you think that's easy, try it some time."

"There are better ways to kill yourself."

"Much better, but they don't make good stories. Any case, they're dead, he'll live. Midnight Pass, huh?"

"There's a vote on Friday on whether to start reopening it," I said.

"The vote will be to open it," Rubin said. "If I count my votes right."

"Maybe you're counting them wrong," I said.

"You know something," he said, sounding interested.

"You tell me something," I said.

"Okay," said Rubin. "Pass started closing up when Casey Key drifted closer to Siesta Key. In 1983 two property owners got permission from the county to fill in the Pass and reopen it a little bit south. They filled Midnight Pass and tried to open it a little south. It didn't want to reopen. Two very small armies lined up across from each other, sometimes literally. One cried, Open the Pass for traffic and nature. The other cried, It was too expensive to open it and keep it open and nature was doing just fine without it."

"And?"

"Both sides tried to line up environmentalist backing, but that hasn't led to much. One pack of environmentalists didn't like the fact that man and not nature had closed the Pass. That pack didn't like the fact that the closing created a dark-watered and not always fragrant-smelling Little Sarasota Bay the Gulf waters couldn't flush out."

"And that is bad," I said.

"Some say it was good, that nature was about to close the Pass anyway and will close it again if it is opened. New ecosystem for marine life, a rare Florida ecosystem they think makes it worth keeping the Pass closed. Then came the studies ordered by the county commissioners. Bottom line and a quarter of a million dollars later, the county was told it could reopen the Pass for five and a half million dollars and keep it open for another two hundred sixty thousand dollars a year."

"The U.S. Army Corps of Engineers?" I prodded.

"Right, the U.S. Army Corps of Engineers reviewed the study and weren't all that happy with it. Now, before the commissioners can apply for state and federal money to open the Pass, there would have to be another study, a big one, estimated cost, one million plus."

"And the commission is voting tomorrow on whether to have another study," I said.

"And if they vote to have it, they're pretty well locked in to going ahead with opening the Pass if the study says they should. And I think that's just what the study will say if it's approved. That answer your question?"

"Yes," I said. "And who makes money on this?"

"Besides the company being paid for another study? Landowners. People with land in Little Sarasota Bay if the Pass opens. People with land on the Gulf Coast if it stays closed. But money's not the only issue. A lot of people with plenty of time and money look for religions to invest their time, heart, and money in. Midnight Pass is nearly a religion for a lot of people in South County."

"Thanks," I said.

"Welcome. So what do I look for?" he asked.

"Be at the commission meeting," I said. "Stay till it's over. Then you might want to interview one or two of the commissioners after the vote on the Pass is taken."

"And the commissioners will talk to me about it? I mean talk and say something with shark teeth?"

"At least one will be quotable, possibly more."

"You're sure?"

"Since I have no reputation, I can't stake mine on it. It won't cost you anything but a few hours sleep."

"I'll be there," Rubin said. "I gotta get back to my suicidal speargunner. You still smiling, Fonesca?"

"Always," I said, and we hung up.

I put on my blue slacks, my only white shirt, and my only tie, blue-and-red striped. I put on blue socks and my ancient black Rockport shoes.

I was going to a party.

Hoffmann's fortress was on the mainland opposite Bird Keys. The sun was just going down when I got there. I had stopped at Walgreen's on Bahia Vista and Tamiami Trail to pick up Hoffmann's present.

I parked next to the ten-foot-high brick wall. I could hear the surf somewhere in the distance behind the wall. The black steel gate was locked. I pressed the button in the wall to the right of the gate and waited. The gate opened a few seconds later. I walked up to the house on the inclined, cobble-paved driveway. The house, big, Spanish-looking, was on a small ridge, a few feet of added protection from rising bay water when a hurricane or gale storm hit.

The door was open. The man standing in it was a little over six feet tall, lean and well-muscled, a little younger than me. He was wearing dark slacks and a short-sleeved green polo shirt. He was also wearing glasses.

"Fonesca?" he asked.

"Stanley?" I responded, recognizing his voice.

He stepped back to let me in, closed the door, and led me into a gigantic living room with a long bar to the right and an open French door to the left, facing the water. A man stood with his back to me, looking out at the water. He was about my height but broad across the shoulders. His white hair flecked with black was cut short and glistened as if he had just gotten out of a shower or pool.

He turned. Kevin Hoffmann's face was unlined, handsome. I had seen his picture in the *Herald-Tribune*. He looked even better in person. He was wearing white slacks and a short-sleeved New York Yankees shirt. On his feet were white deck shoes. No socks. I was overdressed.

Hoffmann looked at me with an Arnold Schwarzenegger grin. Stanley stood off to my right, adjusted his glasses, and stood at ease, military at ease.

"You like baseball," Hoffmann said, looking at my Cubs cap.

"I like the Cubs," I said.

"Right," he said. "You're from Chicago. Process server now. Used to work for the state attorney's office in Cook County. Lost your wife in an accident. Sorry about that. I lost my wife about the same time."

I wondered how much more he had learned about me in the time since I had called. I knew he wanted me to wonder.

"Come with me," Hoffmann said, motioning with his right hand.

I followed. Stanley didn't. We moved into a dark room beyond the tasteful Southern plush furniture in the living room. He flicked a switch and motioned for me to step in.

The room was an office with an antique desk and chair in the middle with a phone on it. No computer. There was a window on one wall, facing the water across a wide stretch of grass and sand. There was a small dock but no boat that I could see. The walls of the room were covered ceiling to floor with glassed-in cabinets. Inside the cabinets were hundreds of baseballs, and in one corner were four racks of baseball bats.

Over my shoulder I sensed Stanley standing in the doorway.

"All autographed," Hoffmann said, bouncing athletically on his heels and looking around. "All fully authenticated. I've got Babe Ruth, Ty Cobb, Ted Williams, DiMaggio, Hank Aaron, Clemente, Sandy Koufax, even a Carl Hubbell. Cubs corner is on the lower shelf over there. Banks, Dawson, Pafko, Sandburg, Sosa, Hank Sauer, Frankie Baumholtz, thirty Cubs. Almost two hundred Yankees. Take a look."

I moved forward, holding the small box I had brought, and looked at the baseballs Hoffmann was pointing to. I was impressed.

"And the bats," he said, picking one out of the rack. "Brooks Robinson. And I've got a Willie Mays, Roberto Clemente, Orlando Cepeda, a Mark McGwire, and a Pie Traynor."

Hoffmann took a cut through the air with Brooks Robinson's bat. It swished about three feet in front of my face.

"I still play," Hoffmann said. "Senior softball league out on Seventeenth Street. Had a doubleheader this morning. A few of the players were in the majors, a lot played college ball or minor league. Of course we use aluminum bats. I keep mine in the back of my car.

"Want to handle one of these?" he asked, shouldering the big bat.

"Some other time," I said. "Let's talk about William Trasker."

I looked back at Stanley in the doorway.

"Let's," Hoffmann said. "A great man. Lots of people don't like him, but I admire him. He lets people know what he wants and he lets them know he plans to take it. We've had business dealings together for years. I've learned a lot from Bill Trasker."

"You know where he might be?"

"I know where he is," said Hoffmann with a smile. "Like something to drink?"

"No, thanks," I said.

Hoffmann looked around the room.

"I don't just collect these things," Hoffmann said. "I told you I play. Two leagues. All year around. One of the great things about Florida. One of many reasons I moved here when I was younger."

"Twenty years ago," I said.

He nodded, holding the bat in front of him and examining Brooks Robinson's autograph.

"Something like that. You play baseball, softball, Fonesca?"

"Used to, a little. Babe Ruth League. Good field. No hit. I got to the point where I just waited for walks and hoped the pitcher didn't hit me with a fastball. Gave up the game after one season."

"I'm a first baseman," he said. "I make a good target on the field and at the plate and I didn't give up when I was a kid. What position did you play?"

"Outfield. Babe Ruth League. I wouldn't make a good target at first base."

"Don't underestimate yourself," he said, pointing the bat at me as if it were a rifle. "You'd make an adequate target."

"Trasker," I said.

He shook his head and carefully placed the bat back in the rack.

"Upstairs, in bed. My dear friend is gravely ill. Can't be moved. Doctor's orders. Bill is in the terminal stages of cancer. He's comfortable, well, as comfortable as modern medicine can make a dying man with cancer. He is watched over twenty-four hours a day."

"Shouldn't he be in a hospital?"

"Can't be moved. If you like, you can talk to Dr. Obermeyer. That is if Mrs. Trasker says it is all right."

He moved behind the desk and sat in the leather swivel chair.

"I love this room," he said, looking around.

"Mrs. Trasker doesn't know her husband's here," I said.

"Of course she does," Hoffmann said. "Stanley called her when we brought poor Bill here, didn't you, Stanley?"

We both looked at Stanley, who adjusted his glasses and said, "I forgot."

Hoffmann looked at me with another shake of his head.

"Stanley is normally the most reliable of my employees," he said confidentially but not so confidentially that Stanley couldn't hear. "Stanley is bright and he has the virtue of complete loyalty. But he has many duties and sometimes little things and, yes, even big ones slip past him."

"That speaks well of Stanley," I said. "Then I can see Mr. Trasker?"

"I'll call Mrs. Trasker right away, but I'm afraid Dr. Obermeyer means it when he says no visitors," Hoffmann said, closing his eyes and nodding sadly.

"Mrs. Trasker's going to want to see him," I said. "She's going to ask him if he wants to go to a hospital, maybe make the decision herself if he's not up to it. Bring in another doctor or two to examine her husband."

"Mr. Trasker has stated quite clearly that he wishes to remain here," Hoffmann said, smiling up at me.

"Mrs. Trasker might want to ask him herself with a policeman or two at her side," I said.

"She is welcome to proceed with any legal action she wishes," he said. "I've sworn to my old friend that I will follow his wishes, and that I will do until the law orders me to do otherwise."

"Which means warrants, lawyers, Dr. Obermeyer."

"At the very least," Hoffmann said amiably. "And that will take several days, perhaps a week."

"At least till after Friday's County Commission meeting?" I said.

Hoffmann looked as if this were something he hadn't considered.

"I suppose that's true," he said. "But even if it weren't, Bill is definitely in no condition to attend any meetings."

"You're a true friend," I said.

Hoffmann made a fist with his right hand, put it up to his

chest, and said, "I try to be. I want nothing more than to follow the wishes of my friend and mentor and let him exit this world, if he wishes, in the bed upstairs. He's getting the best medical attention money can buy. I only wish that money could buy him more time and a return of his health."

"I'm deeply moved," I said.

"I can see that. But you plan to pursue this?"

"Yep."

"I'm willing to go to great lengths to protect William Trasker," he said, looking at the rack of bats.

"I'm moved even more deeply," I said.

Hoffmann scratched his cheek.

"You are being threatened, Mr. Fonesca," Hoffmann said. "I'll be blunt. If I asked him to, Stanley could make you disappear. Is that right, Stanley?"

"That's right," Stanley said.

I think I smiled, a small smile.

"Are you suicidal, Mr. Fonesca?" Hoffmann said, puzzled.

"Someone asked me that yesterday. I'm not sure about the answer. It's one of my problems," I said. "But I'm working on it and I'm not going to take my own life. I've got a good shrink."

Hoffmann looked genuinely interested.

"You mean what you're saying, don't you?" he said.

"I mean it."

"Ah, a good Italian Catholic," Hoffmann said. "You won't take your own life but if someone else kills you . . ."

"I'm not a Catholic," I said. "None of my family is."

"What are they?"

"Episcopalians."

"Then we are at an impasse," Hoffmann said. "I think our visit is over. You can follow Stanley to the gate."

He stood up.

"I've got a present for you," I said, holding out the gift-wrapped box of chocolates I'd picked up at Walgreen's.

He took it.

"I think you are more than a little bit crazy," Hoffmann said.

I had shaken him, but not enough. So far I was just a determined little man who couldn't be intimidated.

"Why are you giving me a present?"

"Yesterday would have been your birthday," I said. "If you had lived."

7

KEVIN HOFFMANN SAID nothing. He tapped his fingers on the wrapped box of chocolates, and I said, "Don't you want to know what's in it?"

"I'm not dead," Hoffmann said.

"Then you must not be Kevin Hoffmann," I said. "That confuses me. You're using Kevin Hoffmann's name and Social Security number. But the Kevin Hoffmann born with that number died in Modesto, California, twenty years ago yesterday at the age of fifteen, according to a county death certificate which I can have faxed or mailed to me. If you are Kevin Hoffmann, you're thirty-five years old and much too young for senior softball. You're breaking somebody's rules."

He considered me with eyes holding no fondness for humankind. But I'll give him this: he didn't try to lie.

"I've committed a minor misdemeanor," he said evenly. "I've

paid my taxes every year and legally took the name of Kevin Hoffmann two decades ago."

"I don't want to know who you were before that," I said. "I don't want to know what you were running from. I want to get Roberta Trasker, come back here with her and a doctor, and see her husband."

"Now you're threatening me," he said as if he were enjoying our talk, which might in fact have been the case.

Hoffmann reached over and pushed the phone on the desk toward me.

"You know her number?" he asked.

I started to reach for my notebook but he lifted the receiver and hit seven buttons. He handed the phone to me.

"Yes," Roberta Trasker said.

"Lew Fonesca. Your husband is at Kevin Hoffmann's house. Hoffmann says your husband wants to stay here. According to a Dr. Obermeyer he shouldn't be moved. I think it would be a good idea for you to get over here with a doctor or two of your own."

"Bill is at Kevin's house?" she repeated.

"Can you come with a doctor?"

"His, our internist is Gerald Kauffman," she said. "I'm sure he'll meet me there if he's in town and I tell him it's an emergency. His oncologist is, well, he has several, all in the same practice on Proctor."

Hoffmann watched as I spoke and then reached for the phone. I handed it to him.

"Roberta," he said. "Stanley was supposed to have called you about this. I wondered why you hadn't called back or come over. I'm sorry. If you like, I'll have Stanley come right over and pick you up."

Hoffmann was smiling at me as he listened to Roberta Trasker. I heard his side of the conversation.

"You don't have to, Roberta . . . Yes, that's exactly what I'll do . . . You know I will . . . Yes . . . Of course . . . Yes, you know you can believe me . . . I'll keep you informed and let you know when Dr. Obermeyer says you can see William. Believe me, he is resting quite comfortably."

He held the phone out for me. I took it.

"I believe him," she said, her voice quivering, about to crack.

"You believe him?"

"Yes," she said, having trouble getting the single word out. "Bill should stay there. He's being well cared for."

"I think your doctor—"

She hung up. I handed Hoffmann the phone. He hung it up and started to open the box of candy. I watched him.

"Some people can be threatened," I said.

"Most. A Whitman sampler," he said, holding the box open and reaching over with it to offer me first choice. "In your position, I would have brought Ghirardelli or at the least Frango mints. When's your birthday?"

"September twenty-ninth," I said, taking what looked like a chocolate-covered cherry.

"If you're around in September, I'll have a large box of assorted Ghirardelli chocolates delivered to you."

"Aren't you going to write the date?" I asked.

"I'll remember," he said, "if you are around."

He put the top back on and handed the box to me.

"Give it to someone who likes carbohydrates and cheap chocolate," he said.

I took the box.

"Good night, Mr. Fonesca, and don't even consider returning here. You won't be welcome."

Stanley led me out through the house and down to the gate.

"Got a last name, Stanley?" I asked.

"LaPrince," he said.

Stuart M. Kaminsky

He put his hand in his pocket and the gate opened.

"Any suggestions about what I should do next?" I asked.

He thought for a beat and said, "Who brought the flaming imperial anger? Who has brought the army with drums and with kettle drums? Barbarous kings. A gracious spring, turned to blood-ravenous autumn."

"Shakespeare?"

"Ezra Pound, " he said.

I got into the Nissan as the gate closed. Darkness had come. Darkness and wet heat. I started the engine and turned on the air conditioner. Stanley stood behind the closed gate, watching me as I drove away.

Roberta Trasker wasn't my client. My client was the Reverend Fernando Wilkens. I went back to my office and called the number Wilkens had given me. It was a little after ten. I got his deep bass voice on the answering machine: "You have reached the home of Reverend Wilkens. Please leave a message. May the Lord grant you peace."

After the tone I asked Wilkens to call me in the morning. Then I went across the street to the Crisp Dollar Bill, the box of chocolates under my arm.

There were seven people at the bar and people at two of the booths. Teresa Brewer was just finishing "Till I Waltz Again With You." By the time I got to the back booth, Chet Baker was playing "You Don't Know What Love Is" on the coronet and singing. He sounded as if he knew what he was singing about.

The bartender and owner Billy Hopsman's taste in music had no bounds. He was a lean creature with hair a little too long, nose a little too large, taste in music a lot too broad. Regulars were used to stepping into cool air, comforting darkness, and anything from Maria Callas to Pat Boone or "The Pizzicato Polka."

Billy called to me, asking what I wanted. I ordered a glass of the coldest beer he had and a steak sandwich with a side of potato salad.

"Coleslaw," he called back. "Out of potato salad."

I told him that was fine. I knew fries came with the sandwich. Maybe I'd talk to Ann about my diet again, ask her if she thought I was subtly and slowly eating myself to death on unhealthy food. If I were, so were millions of others. An epidemic. Maybe eating anything but fish and green vegetables should be declared a health hazard. Maybe I was babbling nonsense to myself.

I got the beer first. It was cold. I didn't ask what kind it was. I gave Billy the box of chocolates and told him to pass it around.

"Birthday present," I said.

"Your birthday?"

"No. I gave it to someone. He didn't want it. I think he's on some kind of diet and didn't want to be tempted."

"He should have taken it," Billy said. "Just to be polite."

"I think you're right."

"Well," said Billy, picking out what looked like a peanut cluster. "His loss is your gain."

"That's the way I look at it. What do you know about Midnight Pass?" I asked Billy when he brought my steak sandwich with a pile of fries and a bowl of coleslaw.

"Jack shit," he said. "You know who that is singing now?"

Chet Baker had finished. I heard a woman's deep voice with strings behind her.

"Sarah Vaughn," I said.

"Right, 'Make Yourself Comfortable,'" he said, and strode back toward the bar where he offered the box of candy to a guy with a biker's body, beard, and fisherman's hat.

The biker, his mouth full of chocolate candy, said, "Hey, Billy, you settle this for us. Ace says that's Ella Fitzgerald. I say it's Peggy Lee."

I didn't hear Billy's answer.

I worked at my sandwich. It was overdone but hot. Just the way I like it. The onions were undergrilled but hot. Just the way I like them. The coleslaw was too sweet, just the way I like it. A feel-good meal as a reward for a job badly done.

"Saw your car in the lot, the one you're renting," came the voice across the table.

Digger was sitting there in a white shirt, a wide red tie, and a blue jacket at least one size too large. His face was pink and clean-shaven. He didn't look happy.

"Didn't get the job?"

"I got it. You should have seen me. It all came back. Kept my back straight, led like George Raft, didn't miss a beat, smiled like a waiter at a fancy restaurant. Even tested me on the bolero. I think maybe I was a professional dancer or something when I was younger. Can't remember, but you should have seen me, Fonesca. I almost had them clapping their hands."

"Then why don't you look happy?" I said with a mouthful of steak sandwich.

"You don't look happy either. But you never do. When you see that guy in the mirror, don't you ever tell him something to pep him up?"

"So, you didn't take the job."

"I took it," Digger said. "By God, I took it and I'll be there on Friday and I will dance with old ladies and I will smile and I will drink unspiked punch and eat little sandwiches and collect my fifteen dollars for just showing up, an additional five if I do a good job. I've taken the first small step back to respectability and I don't think I like it much."

"Give it a chance," I said.

"I will. But I don't know if my brain can take it. You gonna eat all those fries?"

"Half of them."

He reached over and took three at a time. I asked what he wanted to drink.

"A beer, like you."

"I thought you didn't drink?"

"A beer ain't drinking," Digger said, reaching for more fries.

I ordered him a beer and handed Billy a five-dollar bill when he brought it over.

"I've got three bucks left of the money you gave me this morning," Digger said. "Mind if I spend it on a place to flop tonight?"

"No."

"One more favor. Can I hang my jacket, shirt, tie, and the rest in your place? Want them clean for Friday."

"Sure."

"This morning as I recall you asked me for a joke. I think I told you one. You want to hear another?"

"No," I said. "I've had enough fun for one day."

The next day was even more fun. The phone woke me at six in the morning. I ignored it but couldn't get back to sleep. I looked at the ceiling, mouth dry, trying to focus on nothing. That usually worked. It didn't this time.

The phone rang again at six-twenty and at ten to seven. I got up. I was wearing a pair of faded black boxer shorts with a pattern of white airplanes. I knew I needed a shave. I always need a shave. Maybe I'd grow a beard. I remembered my grandfather Tony when he had a beard. He kept it trim, made him look wise, but he told me once that it was harder to keep it looking good than it was to shave.

"Fonesca, are you there?" Kenneth Severtson's voice came frantically. "For God's sake, pick up the phone if you're there."

I picked up the phone.

"I'm here," I said.

"They're holding Janice," he said. "Just got a call from her. The kids are in some kind of place they keep children."

"Where are you?"

"In my car, on the way to Orlando. What the hell happened?"

Paranoia is the patron saint of the guilty. I didn't think anyone had the time or inclination to bug my phone but I wanted to take zero chances.

"Did you get the message I left you yesterday?"

"Yes," he said impatiently. "Stark killed himself. Well, the Orlando police say they're not sure. They've been badgering Janice. What the hell did she do?"

"Looks like she got herself involved with a violent alcoholic," I said. "Your partner."

"So now it's my fault? Is that what you're saying? You're saying it's my fault. The hell with it. I'm not forgiving her, not for what she's done to my kids. I talked to my lawyer. I'm getting Ken and Sydney and bringing them back home and Janice can . . . I don't know."

"Stark killed himself," I said.

"In front of my children?"

"No."

"Janice was there?"

"Yes."

I heard the sound of a horn and Kenneth Severtson cursed bluely and loud.

"That son of a bitch," he said.

I didn't know if he meant Stark or the other driver.

"Get her a lawyer," I said. "You know any in Orlando?"

"Why should I . . . No . . . Yes, a group that does tax law."

"Call them. Ask them for a criminal lawyer. See if someone can meet you. Has your wife been charged with anything?"

"I don't know," he said. "I don't care."

"You care," I said.

"Okay, okay. I'll call the lawyer," he said. "What are you going to do?"

"Make a call, get back to Orlando, talk to the police."

"And tell them what?"

"My story," I said.

He gave me his cell-phone number. I wrote it on the pink Post-it pad on my desk and told him I'd call him back.

I called the Reverend Wilkens. This time I got an older-sounding woman. I told her I had to speak to Wilkens and who I was. He was on a few seconds later.

"Mr. Fonesca, you've found William?"

"I have and I haven't. He's at Kevin Hoffmann's house, too sick to be moved according to Hoffmann and a doctor named Obermeyer. You know this Obermeyer?"

"No," he said. "Do you believe Hoffmann? What does Trasker's wife say about all this?"

"She says she believes Hoffmann."

"Do you believe Hoffmann?"

"I don't believe Hoffmann and I don't believe her," I said. "I've got to get to Orlando. I should be back by late in the afternoon. I'll talk to her. I don't know if she'll cooperate."

"My questions are simple," Wilkens said. "Why is William Trasker in that house? Why isn't he at home or in the hospital if he is ill? Is he too ill to come to the Friday-night meeting if he is, indeed, that ill? It does not have the odor of honest concern on the part of Mr. Hoffmann. Hoffmann wants Midnight Pass open."

"I know. He told me," I said. "He also not very tactfully told me that he'd break my head with a genuine Babe Ruth bat or have a man named Stanley shoot me if I didn't stop bothering him."

"Is it essential that you go to Orlando? We are running out of time."

"It is essential," I said. "I'll call you when I have more."

Three hours later I was back in Orlando and with a few questions found the detective who was handling Stark's death. His name was Tenns, Sergeant Jacob Tenns. He came out to meet me in the waiting room at the station, where people sat with their heads in their hands, their briefcases on their laps, their eyes open and looking at nothing or their eyes shut and looking at too much.

Tenns was a throwback. Lean, dark slacks, suspenders, white shirt, and a tie. His glasses were perched on the end of his narrow nose. His hair was dark, combed straight back. He wore broad suspenders. He was trying out for a part in *Inherit the Wind*.

"You Fonesca?" he said approaching me.

"Yes."

"You made a statement the other day about Andrew Stark's death," he said.

"Yes," I said.

"Officer who took your statement was given a reprimand," Tenns said. "You should have been held as a material witness till a detective talked to you. Follow me."

I did, through a wooden door, down a narrow corridor to a small room with a table surrounded by six chairs. There was a humming refrigerator on one side of the room and two vending machines on the other: one gave out Cokes and Sprite if you inserted seventy-five cents or a dollar bill, the other gave out candy if you put in a dollar or correct change. Along the wall facing us as we entered was a counter and sink with closed cupboards over it. A half-full Mr. Coffee pot sat in one corner of the counter with Styrofoam cups nestling inside each other.

"Coffee?" asked Tenns.

"Yes," I said, sitting.

"Anything in it?"

"Sugar, milk," I said.

He nodded, got me a cup of coffee and one for himself. He sat down and looked at me.

"Her story's a crock of shit," he said calmly.

"Janice Severtson's?"

"No, Madonna's autobiography," he answered. "Mrs. Severtson says she went to you for help because she knew you from Sarasota."

"That's right. We both work out at the Y."

"You do any other kind of working out with Janice Severtson?" he asked.

"What?"

"She was here with a man who wasn't her husband," Tenns said. "Coincidentally, you, a *friend*, happened to be here, too."

"You're saying maybe Janice Severtson and I . . . ?"

"Stranger things have happened," Tenns said, working on his coffee.

I tried mine. It wasn't bad. Wasn't good either.

"I had a case two years back," Tenns said. "Little dwarf, half-black, half–who knows what the hell else, ugly as a possum. He and this full-size stripper were lovers, killed her husband. Little guy had to stand on a chair behind the husband to hit him with a bat."

"What was her name?" I asked.

"Stripper? Elaine Boulenbar. Why?"

"Conversation," I said. "I'm not a dwarf. I'm not rich. I'm not good-looking."

"She could have hired you," he said. "I checked. You're a process server."

"I thought that was considered honest work," I said.

"It means you deal sometimes with some bad people," Tenns said. "Sometimes it rubs off a little."

"You deal with bad people more than I do," I said.

"Which is why I'm going down this street."

"Why would she hire me to kill a man she ran away with?"

"Don't know. Conversation. Did she hire you?"

"No, I was here because her husband asked me to find her. I found her. She spotted me, remembered me from Sarasota. What I told the officer was the truth. I went back to Sarasota and told her husband. He's here someplace trying to get his kids."

"I know," said Tenns, turning his cup in circles. "He's in another room. We're bringing the kids. You don't have a private investigator's license, Fonesca."

"I don't want one. Severtson came to me, asked me to help him find his wife and children. I said I would."

"He pay you?"

"Yes. Where's Mrs. Severtson?"

"Medical examiner says Stark stabbed himself downward, not straight in," Tenns said, demonstrating the thrust with his right hand. "Odd. Awkward."

"I didn't know the man," I said.

"Nothing else you want to tell me?"

"No."

"I talked to the kids," he said. "Girl was asleep. Boy can't remember anything."

"We're not talking about murder here," I said.

"Doesn't look like we've got a case there, does it?" he said. "But she did run away with the kids, did shack up with a man with a record, probably screwed him in front of the kids. Husband wants to take the kids and leave her here. And . . ."

"And?"

"Why did Stark want to kill himself?" Tenns asked.

"Drunk, depressed, suddenly saddled with responsibility, guilty about running away with his partner's wife. Maybe the ME can do some exploratory and find out he was dying of something."

"Maybe," Tenns said. "I checked. Stark was single. Wife divorced him twenty years ago and moved to San Diego. Business he was in with Severtson is booming. No confirmation so far that he was alcoholic. Some evidence from people the Sarasota police checked with that he wasn't. Some evidence from the same people that Stark wasn't the kind to feel guilty about running away with his partner's wife. People he worked with say Janice Severtson wasn't the first wife to spend a weekend with Andrew Stark. But with two kids along, it looks like Stark was in for a lot more than a weekend."

"And what does Mrs. Severtson say?"

"Dialogue right out of one of the soaps my wife watches when she isn't selling costume jewelry," he said with a sigh. "Janice Severtson says she thought she loved Stark, but then again maybe she was just running away with him to get away from her husband."

"You've been busy."

"Very," he said. "I'm faxing a report to the Sarasota sheriff's office. I'm sending the Severtsons home. I'm telling them not to think about moving out of the state. I'm signing off on this as a probable suicide but I'm keeping the file open. My board's full. I've got a bruised thigh. I couldn't sleep last night and there's a drooling drug dealer with an attitude in another room waiting to tell me lies. I'll get back to Stark's death when I get a chance, and I *will* get a chance."

Tenns got up, scrunched his empty coffee cup, and threw it in the wastebasket near the Coke machine.

"I checked a little deeper on you, Fonesca," he said, turning and looking at me over the tops of his glasses. "Lost your wife, went a little nuts, quit your job with the state attorney's office, wound up in Sarasota."

I sat. There was still some coffee in my cup. I was getting hungry.

"So anyway, your story checks out with hers. I'm letting her go."

"I'd like to see her," I said.

"Go back to the waiting room. She'll be there in a few minutes."

"Sergeant, know any jokes?"

"Cop jokes," he said. "Why?"

A few minutes after I was in the waiting room, looking at wanted posters, Janice Severtson came through a metal door. Her hair had been brushed but not well. Her makeup had been applied but not well. Her clothes had been put on but not neatly.

She spotted me and I got up as she moved quickly in front of me.

"They told me Kenneth took Sydney and Kenny," she said. "Where are they?"

"Probably on the way back to Sarasota. You hungry?"

"I don't know," she said, running her fingers through her hair.

"Let's get something to eat," I said.

"I've got to get back to Sarasota," she said. "Talk to Kenneth. Oh, those poor babies. What've I done to those poor babies?"

Everyone in the waiting room was listening to us. Most were looking. Some probably had tales a lot worse than Janice Severtson's. I guided her out the door, down the steps, and to my car, which had about two minutes left on the meter.

We stopped at a nearby Shoney's. She had a salad and a reasonably well-controlled cry. I had a chicken sandwich and a strong desire to be alone.

"You want me to talk to your husband?" I asked while we ate.

"Yes."

"I will," I said, reaching for a sagging fry.

I found a phone near the cash register and called Kenneth Severtson's cell phone.

"You have the kids?"

"Yes, I'm on I-75 just passing exit 42. We're going home. What about Janice?"

"You know the First Watch on Main Street?"

"Yes."

"Can you be there at ten Saturday morning, without the kids?"

"I can get a sitter, but . . . Yes."

"I want your wife with you."

I thought I heard the voice of a small boy over the phone but the words weren't clear. I hung up and went back to Janice. She had finished her salad and was shredding a napkin.

"I talked to him. I think you can go home, at least for now."

I drove her back to her car where it was still parked at the hotel. I waited for her to get out of my car, but she just sat.

"I killed a man," she said.

"Yes."

"It doesn't feel real."

"I know."

"My God, can you really just kill people and get away with it?" she said.

"Happens every day," I said.

I told her to be at the First Watch Saturday. I watched her get into her car, start it, and pull out of the hotel lot. She held up a good-bye hand to me. I returned the gesture and headed for the highway.

When I got back to my office, it was a little before one. I thought about calling Dixie for more help but decided I wanted to do this one the old-fashioned way. If that didn't work, there was always Dixie.

It took two phone calls and two lies and I had my answer, not as complete and detailed as Dixie would have given me but enough for me to do what I was going to do.

I can be fooled, but I'm not a fool.

I called Ames McKinney at the Texas Bar and Grill. I told him to bring a gun, something not conspicuous.

8

I SAT AT MY DESK, thinking, listening to the window air conditioner, and looking at the small painting of the dark jungle and
small orchid. I knew that over my shoulder Charlton Heston and
Orson Welles were looking down at me.

"Do what must be done," Heston's Vargas character said
with conviction.

"Take care of your ass," said Welles's Hank. "No one else
will, partner."

I got up and changed into my best work clothes: an old,
only slightly frayed pair of blue slacks, well-ironed; a colorful
pink-and-white short-sleeved shirt, my best; and the most
expensive item I owned, my black patent leather shoes with
dark socks.

It took Ames McKinney less than ten minutes to get to me.
I was back in the chair behind my desk when I heard his motor

scooter come into the DQ lot and park below. I didn't hear him climb the metal stairs to the second floor or hear his footsteps approach my door. Ames McKinney was polite, born seventy-three years ago, a child of polite, God-fearing Methodists in Texas near the Oklahoma panhandle. Ames knocked. I told him to come in. Ames had once been close to rich and had lost it all. He had trailed the partner who had cheated him to Sarasota, where the partner had changed his name and grown even richer, a steel pillar of philanthropy and high society.

I found Ames's partner, and the two of them, in spite of my attempts to reason or threaten them out of it, had an old-fashioned shoot-out on the beach in the park at the far south end of Lido Key. Ames was the better shot. The former partner took a bullet in the heart. Ames served eight months for having an unregistered weapon and engaging in a duel, a law that still existed in Florida. Ames's age and the evidence of what his former partner had done and my eyewitness testimony about the gunfight had kept the sentence reasonably short.

Now Ames lived in Sarasota, in a room with a bed in the back of the Texas Bar and Grill on Second Street. Ames's job was to keep the place from being broken into at night and see to it that the owner Ed Fairing's gun collection was maintained. Ames got the room, food, and a very small salary. It didn't cost Ames much to live, but even shopping at Goodwill, the motor scooter needed gas, and once in a while a man needs a new toothbrush.

Ames came in, standing tall and lean in jeans and a long-sleeved shirt. The jeans were worn white in patches but clean and the shirt was a solid khaki that looked more than a little too warm for the weather. On his head was the battered cowboy hat he had putt-putted into town with three years ago. Once Ames must have been close to six-six. I figured age had brought him down a few inches. Age seemed to be the only thing that could bring Ames McKinney down.

"Have a seat," I said.

Ames sat.

"How've you been?" I asked. "How's Ed?"

Ed was Ed Fairing, owner of the Texas Bar and Grill and collector of antique guns that didn't work, which were on display in the Grill, and the more modern kind, which were kept in a wall-sized cabinet in Ed's office. Ed's face was the color and texture of high-quality tan leather. His hair was clear, pure white and likely recently cut by himself or one of the four-dollar old-time places still trying to compete with First Choice and the other new chains and mens' salons. Ed looked as if he had served shots of whiskey to Wyatt Earp and smiled when he poured a sarsaparilla for the rare teetotaler who wandered in. Ed, in fact, was from New Jersey and gave up a nine-to-five job in Manhattan to follow his dream of owning a saloon.

"Fine," said Ames.

"Got something you can help me with," I said.

"I'm here," he reminded me.

"I'm looking for William Trasker, the county commissioner. You've heard of him?"

"Heard," said Ames, taking off his hat and putting it on his lap the way his mother had taught him back when Hoover was president.

I filled him in on Trasker, Hoffmann, Hoffmann's man Stanley, Reverend Wilkens, and Roberta Trasker.

"I make it clear?" I asked.

He nodded.

"Gun?"

He patted his brass belt buckle. It was about four inches across, had an embossed little gun on it and the letters "FA" over the word "Freedom Arms."

Ames reached down with his right hand, clicked something

on the buckle, and the embossed gun popped off the belt and into his hand.

"Five shots, .22 caliber, single-action. Stainless steel," he said, holding up the weapon. "Uses black powder or Pyrodex. Accurate, deadly at close range."

"Where did you get that?"

"Freedom Arms, Freedom, Wyoming. No federal forms or record keeping. Ed just charged it on his credit card and it came three days later."

My plan was simple. Go to Roberta Trasker, try to find out why she had backed away from getting her husband away from Kevin Hoffmann, and get her to go with us to Hoffmann's to get William Trasker out of there and, if necessary, to the hospital.

With Ames riding silent shotgun, I drove to the Spanish-style house with the turrets on Indian Beach Drive. A blue-black Mercedes was parked in the driveway. I pulled up next to it and we got out.

There was a smell of rain in the air and the clouds were starting to come darkly together.

I pushed the bell button next to the door, with Ames behind me. There was no answer. I kept pushing. I tried the door. It wasn't locked. I opened it enough to peek in and call out.

"Mrs. Trasker?"

There was no answer. I thought for a few seconds and went in, calling out, "Mrs. Trasker? It's me, Lew Fonesca. Your door was open. I need to talk to you about your—"

She was lying on the white tile floor, splats of blood on her neck and chest. One arm was straight out, the other at her side. She had her head turned. She looked very dead. She looked very beautiful.

I heard Ames behind me clicking his little .22 off of his belt.

I knelt at her side to be sure of what I was already sure of. She was dead. She was also pale and cold.

"I know her from someplace," Ames said.

"Claire Collins," I said, nodding at the picture on the wall. "She was in the movies."

I was still on my knees. I wanted to tell her that I'd never forget her in that one scene with Glenn Ford. I wanted to ask her who had killed her and I wanted her to answer me. I stood up.

"What now?" Ames asked.

"We call the police," I said.

I found a phone in an office at the back of the house. I didn't think I should touch the one in the living room in case the killer had used it. The office smelled faintly of cigars, and it seemed to be the only room not a shrine to the memory of a Busby Berkeley 1930s musical. The furniture was all old wood and cracking brown leather.

I called the only cop I knew. He was in.

"Viviase," he answered when they put me through.

"Fonesca," I said.

"What now?" he said with a sigh. "Try not to tell me you found a body."

"I can try, but I'll fail. Roberta Trasker."

"Wife of William Trasker?" he asked.

"Yes," I said.

"You're going to tell me she's been murdered."

"Yes," I said. "She lives on—"

"Big Spanish house on Indian Beach Drive," he said. "Been there. Don't touch anything. Just sit somewhere far away from her body and wait."

He hung up.

"Might be a good idea for you not to be here when the police come," I said to Ames, who stood, cowboy hat in hand, looking down at the dead woman the way Henry Fonda had in almost any John Ford movie he had been in.

"I'll stick around if it's all the same."

"It's not," I said. "You've got a record. You killed a man. You're carrying a weapon. You're not supposed to. You'd be right at the top of the suspect list if they found you here."

"Suit yourself," he said.

"You can catch a SCAT bus on the Trail," I said.

"I'll walk it," he said.

"Sorry," I said.

"We both are," he answered, turning his eyes from the dead woman to the picture on the wall. "Handsome woman."

"I'll call you later," I said.

"You know who did this?" Ames asked.

"Probably," I said.

When Ames was out the front door, I did a quick search of the house. I found a gun in one of Trasker's desk drawers. It looked as if it had never been fired. I found letters, papers, and shelves full of books, most of them best-sellers going back twenty years. I couldn't bring myself to go through Roberta Trasker's clothes.

"What are you doing, Fonesca?" Viviase asked me as I stood with my back to the bedroom door.

"Wondering," I said, not turning.

"About?"

"People," I said, turning to face him. "Why so many of them want to turn the world into—"

"Shit," Viviase finished. Viviase was a little over six feet tall, a little over two hundred and twenty pounds, a little past fifty, short dark hair and a big nose. It said, "Detective Ed Viviase" on the door to his office, but his real name was Etienne. He had a wife, kids, and a reasonable sense of humor. He probably knew a cop joke I could use. I wasn't going to ask him.

"Come on," he said, turning his back on me and walking into the hall. I could hear voices in the living room, knew that cops were taking pictures, being sure she was dead, trying not to contaminate the crime scene too much. I followed Viviase away from the living room and into William Trasker's office. He sat in the leather chair at the desk. I sat in an upright chair of black wood, tan leather, and arms.

"So, what happened?" he asked.

"I found the body," I said. "She was shot. She was dead. I called you."

"What were you doing here?" he asked.

"William Trasker is missing," I said. "I was trying to find him."

"William Trasker is not missing," Viviase said. "He's at Kevin Hoffmann's house. And you know it."

He scratched the top of his head and looked up at me with his hands folded in his lap.

"I was getting to that," I said.

"Hoffmann beat you to it," said Viviase. "His lawyer called us, complained about you threatening him."

"And he told you Trasker was in Hoffmann's house."

"Yes. Said he was too sick to move. Gave the name of the doctor on the case, said Trasker's wife, who now lies dead in the other room, knew all about it and approved. So, I have an important question."

"Yes."

"Why were you looking for William Trasker? And don't tell me it's privileged information. You're not a private investigator. You're a process server who gets himself involved in other peoples' business."

"Sometimes," I admitted.

"Sometimes? You've come up with five dead people in the last three years."

"I don't want to get involved in other peoples' business," I said. "It just . . ."

"Happens," he said. "I know. So, my question?"

"Why was I looking for Trasker? For a friend."

"And your friend possesses a name?"

"Fernando Wilkens," I said. "He wants Trasker found so he can vote on the Midnight Pass proposal on Friday."

Viviase was shaking his head. To himself as much as to me, he said, "This hits the blotter, these names are going to jump out and be all over television and the papers."

"Any cash, jewelry missing?" he asked hopefully. "And don't tell me you wouldn't know. You've gone over the place."

"As far as I can tell, there's nothing missing. Her purse is open on the table near the kitchen. I think you'll find two hundred and six dollars in it. Jewelry box in the bedroom is full. I think it's all real."

"So, who killed her?"

"My vote? Hoffmann, to keep Roberta Trasker from changing her mind and getting her husband away from the Hoffmann house."

"Trasker's going to vote against opening the Pass?" Viviase asked, showing some interest.

"That's what I've heard. Can we get Trasker out of there?"

"If he wants to," Viviase said. "He can get up and go anywhere. He can dance naked under the moon on Holmes Beach, get drunk and make a fool of himself. He can watch a movie at the Hollywood Twenty."

"Why don't you ask him?" I said.

"I've got no cause to go into Hoffmann's house," he said slowly, as if speaking to an idiot. "If I just showed up, Kevin

Hoffmann would turn me away and start pulling chains to make my life far less idyllic."

"Don't you think someone should tell Trasker that his wife is dead?"

He was listening.

"He may be well enough to give you some ideas about who might want his wife dead."

"And he might let us know that he wants out of Hoffmann's house. What the hell? Let's do it."

He got up and so did I.

"You want me to go with you to Hoffmann's? Why?"

"Would you believe I like your company?"

"No."

"How about I want you there so Hoffmann can identify the man he says threatened him?"

"No."

"Okay, last try. You made Hoffmann nervous enough that he called his lawyer and had him put pressure on us. I'd like to see how nervous you can make Hoffmann."

"Fine," I said, following Viviase down the hallway. "But there's something you should know."

"What?"

"Kevin Hoffmann's date of birth."

9

AFTER I TOLD Viviase about Kevin Hoffmann's name change and Social Security card switch, we drove our own cars to Kevin Hoffmann's estate. I parked behind Viviase and followed him to the gate, where he pushed the glowing button on the wall.

"Yes," a voice came from somewhere.

It was Hoffmann's man, Stanley.

"Detective Viviase. I'd like to talk to Mr. Hoffmann."

"Hold on."

Viviase stood looking at me, bouncing on his heels. He was not a patient man.

"Come in," Stanley said, his voice coming out of the afternoon overcast.

The gate opened and we walked up the cobblestone walk to the open door, where Kevin Hoffmann stood in white shorts, white sneakers, and a white tennis shirt with a little black New York Yankees emblem on the pocket. A dark new Lexus was parked in the driveway.

"Viviase," the detective said, introducing himself. "You know Fonesca."

"We've met," Hoffmann said.

"You complained about Mr. Fonesca bothering you the other day," Viviase said.

Hoffmann backed into the house and motioned us forward. We entered and he closed the door behind us.

"Bygones," Hoffmann said. "If that's why you've come, there's no need. I forgive him."

"Thank you," I said.

"Did Mr. Fonesca tell you about my baseball collection?"

"I haven't had a chance," I said.

"Well," said Hoffmann. "I'll be happy to show it to you. Who's your favorite baseball player of all time?"

"Ralph Kiner," Viviase said.

"I've got a ball signed by him," said Hoffmann. "Met him twice. Nice man."

"Some other time," Viviase said. "I'd like to see William Trasker."

"I don't think that's possible right now," Hoffmann said. "But it just happens Dr. Obermeyer is here right now, with Bill. Would you like to see him?"

"I'd like to see Trasker," Viviase said.

"Well, we'll have to talk to Dr. Obermeyer about that. This way," said Hoffmann, moving to the stairs and taking them two at a time.

Viviase and I came up at a decidedly slower pace. Hoffmann went past the open door of a bedroom and through the open door of a second bedroom. A man, Trasker, lay in the bed in blue pajamas, a paisley quilt pulled up to his chest. He was clean-shaven. His eyes were closed. He was thin, pale, sunken cheeks, mouth slightly open, skin almost white.

Beside the bed stood a man who was also wearing tennis shorts. His were blue and his shirt was an even lighter blue. There was no emblem on his pocket, just an understanding smile on his face. He was slightly overweight, probably slightly over sixty, and only slightly balding with a professional-looking gray thatch.

"Dr. Obermeyer," Hoffmann said, softly introducing the man near the bed.

Obermeyer shook our hands.

"Can Mr. Trasker be moved to a hospital?" Viviase asked.

"I wouldn't advise it," said Obermeyer in a very professional baritone.

"We might want a second opinion," said Viviase. "I'd like to talk to him."

"Mr. Trasker is sedated," the doctor said. "I've also given him a rather high dose of pain medication. I don't think he'd be very coherent if we did manage to wake him up."

Hoffmann was leaning against the wall near the door, his arms folded in front of him. His eyes met mine and he smiled.

"Mr. Trasker asked that he remain here," Obermeyer said gently but firmly.

"Unless his wife tells me otherwise," Hoffmann said. "Whatever Roberta wants is fine with me, but she's already said she thinks it's a good idea."

"Let's go in the hall," Viviase said.

We all moved to the hall and I closed the door on the sleeping commissioner.

"When did you last see or talk to Mrs. Trasker?" Viviase asked.

"Roberta?" said Hoffmann. "This morning. I told her to come over and see Bill after Dr. Obermeyer said it was all right."

"She's dead," Viviase said.

"Roberta?"

Hoffmann sounded genuinely surprised, but surprise was only part of it. There seemed to be a real touch of shock or even grief. The man was either innocent or a good actor. I bet on the good actor.

"What happened?" he asked as Obermeyer put his hand on Hoffmann's shoulder to steady him.

"Shot," said Viviase.

"Robbery?"

"No," the detective said. "Nothing taken. Where've you been today?"

"Me? Softball game in Venice early in the morning. Then tennis tournament at the racquet club. Jim and I are partners."

"Jim?"

"Dr. Obermeyer," Hoffmann explained. "We're partners."

"In tennis," I said.

"Yes, tennis," Hoffmann said, turning unfriendly eyes to me. "We started at eleven and finished just half an hour ago. We haven't even had time for a shower."

"Who was watching Trasker?"

"My assistant, Stanley. She's really dead?"

"Yes," Viviase said. "I've got a question for you and then I'd like to talk to Stanley. He's here?"

"Probably in his room, the next bedroom," Hoffmann said, nodding his head down the hall.

"We can talk to him in a few seconds," said Viviase. "First, my question. How old are you?"

Hoffmann closed his eyes and shook his head.

"Why doesn't that question surprise me?" he asked. "Fonesca here told you about my Social Security number."

"Yes."

"I've paid all my taxes," Hoffmann said.

"What's your real name?"

"I'm not wanted for anything," Hoffmann said.

"How about a direct answer? The question is simple."

Hoffmann thought for a moment and shook his head no.

"I'll talk to my lawyer first," he said.

"I think getting a lawyer is a good idea," said Viviase.

"You think I killed her? Why would I kill . . . I wouldn't hurt her, but I will guarantee that if you don't find the person who did it, I will, and I have the distinct intuition that the murderer will . . . I didn't kill her."

The man was good. If we were in a movie, I'd give serious consideration to nominating him for a Best Supporting Actor Oscar.

"Let's talk to Stanley," Viviase said.

"I'll stay here," Obermeyer said, looking down at his patient.

Hoffmann stepped past us and knocked at the closed door of the room next to the one where William Trasker lay sleeping.

"Come in," Stanley called.

In we went.

The room was less a bedroom than a library with a bed tucked in one corner. Every wall had a bookcase from floor to ceiling. Every bookcase was full. There was a small space in one bookshelf for a computer and oversized screen. On the screen was a view from a video camera showing the front gate of the house. There was also a window, dark curtains closed.

Stanley sat in a worn armchair near the window, an old wooden floor lamp next to him glowing down at the book on his lap. The room was cool. Stanley wore dark slacks and a yellow cotton shirt with a lightweight dark sport jacket.

"Stanley," Hoffmann said. "This is Detective . . ."

"Viviase," Viviase completed.

"And you know Mr. Fonesca," Hoffmann continued.

Stanley didn't nod. I didn't say anything.

"Mrs. Trasker has been murdered," Hoffmann said with a steely steadiness that was clearly supposed to send a message to Stanley, but I wasn't sure what that message might be. I had an idea, but I wasn't sure.

"I'm sorry to hear that," Stanley said, putting a leather strip in his book and placing the book on the table next to him.

Stanley was looking at Hoffmann. He took off his glasses, held them up to the light to be sure they were clean, and put them back on again.

"Where've you been all day?" asked Viviase.

"In and around the house, keeping an eye on things, taking care of Mr. Trasker," he said.

"Never left him alone for long?" Viviase said.

"Checked in on him every ten or twelve minutes except for the forty-five minutes in the weight room to work out, use the treadmill, weights, steps."

"And when you weren't working out or in and around the house?" Viviase continued.

"I was reading."

He held up the thin paperback book he had placed on the table to show us what he had been reading. I could see the cover clearly. It was *A Coney Island of the Mind* by Lawrence Ferlinghetti.

"You were reading this today?" Viviase asked.

Stanley looked at Hoffmann and said, " 'Cast up, the heart flops over gasping "Love." A foolish fish which tries to draw its breath from flesh of air. And no one there to hear its death among the sad bushes where the world rushes by in a blather of asphalt and delay.' "

"Ferlinghetti?" I asked.

"Yes," said Stanley, turning his gaze from Hoffmann to me. "There's one in here about depression."

"And don't forget 'Junkman's Obbligato,' " Viviase said.

Stanley blinked at the detective with respect.

"I read a lot of that crap when I was a kid," said Viviase. "I grew up. You read a lot?"

Viviase looked around the room.

"I don't like television, and I'm not all too fond of people," Stanley said with a small twitch of a smile aimed at the detective first and then at me. He ignored Hoffmann.

"You have a last name?" asked Viviase.

"LaPrince, Stanley LaPrince. Cajun."

"You own a gun, Stanley LaPrince?" Viviase asked.

"Three," he said, opening his jacket to show one in a holster. "A shotgun and a rifle in the rack in the den downstairs. All registered."

"And that's all?"

"That's all."

"Mind if I look at your gun?"

Stanley removed the weapon from his holster and handed it to the detective. Viviase smelled the barrel and shook his head slightly at me to indicate that it was not the weapon that murdered Roberta Trasker.

Stanley accepted his gun back and returned it to the holster.

"You walk around with a gun all the time?"

"I'm Mr. Hoffmann's assistant. That includes protecting him."

"From who?"

"Enemies," said Hoffmann, his eyes on Stanley. "Thieves. Someone tried to break in the house four years ago. You can check your records. Stanley caught them before they could get to the house. I think he may have shot one of them when they got away."

"What were they trying to steal?"

Stuart M. Kaminsky

"What do thieves try to steal?" Hoffmann said with some exasperation. "Money, jewelry, electronic equipment, maybe my baseball collection, and the house is filled with antiques."

It was Viviase's turn to nod.

"Enemies, Mr. Hoffmann?"

"Detective, I am a philanthropic son of a bitch," he said. "The philanthropic part of me gets me awards. The walls of my den are covered with them. Sarasota's charities love me. I'm invited to everything. I speak with passion and conviction about the plight of the homeless, the parentless, the children suffering from diseases both known and obscure, women who've been abused and Habitat for Humanity."

"You're a saint," I said.

"No," said Hoffmann. "I'm really the son of a bitch who undercuts business on deals and uses his connections among what passes for high society to obtain what I want. I like money. I like power. But I love baseball."

Viviase was clearly unimpressed. He turned back to Stanley.

"You have a record?"

"Four years, Folsom," said Stanley.

"What did you do?"

"I read."

"What did you do that got you those four years?" Viviase asked. "Overdue library books?"

"I almost killed a man," Stanley said evenly. "We had a political disagreement in a friend's house."

"Political disagreement?"

"Over drugs," said Stanley. "Neither one of us wanted them legalized, but for different reasons. Mine were libertarian. His were personal and economic."

"I don't care for your sense of humor, Mr. LaPrince," Viviase said.

"I don't think I have one," Stanley said.

"How did an ex-con get a license to carry firearms?" the detective asked.

Stanley looked at Hoffmann. Viviase turned to Hoffmann, who said, "With the support of some friends in the government and my persuasiveness, special dispensation was given after evidence was presented to show that Stanley was totally rehabilitated."

"Mind if I have a doctor look at Trasker?" asked Viviase.

"Yes," said Hoffmann. "I do. Bill Trasker and I have complete faith in Dr. Obermeyer."

"Any other questions for me?" Stanley asked, picking up his book.

"Later," said Viviase, letting Hoffmann lead us out of the room.

I was last. I glanced back at Stanley. When our eyes met, I felt cold. I was sure that was exactly what he was trying for.

"Anything else you'd like me to do?" Hoffmann asked.

"Get that lawyer we talked about," said Viviase.

"I'll do that. Normally, I'd offer you a drink or something I've baked. I was a chef for a few years, *cordon bleu*. Pastries are my specialty."

We were walking down the stairs.

"I'm watching my weight," Viviase said.

"And I am watching my back," Hoffmann answered. "That's why Stanley is in the house."

"You have that many enemies?" asked Viviase.

"I have that many people who either consider themselves my enemies or want something I have and are willing to do foolish things to get it."

There wasn't much else to say to him, so Viviase and I went through the front door and headed down the driveway. Hoffmann stood in the doorway watching us.

"You believe that crap about his being a chef?" asked Viviase.

"No. You really think Ferlinghetti is crap?"

"No," said Viviase. "I just don't like smug, pretentious sociopaths like Stanley LaPrince."

"They don't like each other," I said.

"Hoffmann and Stanley? You're right," Viviase said.

"Think you can get Trasker out of there?" I asked.

We went through the iron gate and it swung closed behind us.

"I'll check with legal, but I don't think so. I doubt if we can even get a doctor in there for a second opinion."

"So there's nothing you can do?"

I walked him to his car.

"I can check on Stanley LaPrince's story, find out Kevin Hoffmann's real name. I'm sure there's a federal law against using someone else's name and Social Security number even if you don't profit from it."

"Identity theft," I said.

Viviase opened his car door.

"Something, but we're a long way from getting Trasker out of there, definitely not by tomorrow for a commission meeting. Even if we did get him out, he's not in any condition to vote. Hell, he's not in any condition to drink a chocolate shake."

"I guess not," I said.

Before he closed the door, Viviase looked at me and said, "Fonesca, I don't really care if he votes or doesn't vote tomorrow. I'm looking for Roberta Trasker's murderer and between you, me, and Derek Jeter, I think the killer is in that house."

Viviase drove away.

I stood for a few seconds looking back at the house through the gate. The front door was closed now. I got in my car and waited. I waited over half an hour before Obermeyer came through the front door, got into his Lexus, and hummed down the driveway toward the gate, which opened for him.

He turned right. I followed him.

He drove north on Midnight Pass Road and made a right turn at Stickney Point. He pulled into the mall on his right just before Tamiami Trail, parked, and headed for a bar. I got out of my car after he went through the door and followed him.

There was no music coming from inside when I opened the door. There was a hockey game on the television over the bar. The sound wasn't on. The place wasn't full but it wasn't doing badly.

I spotted Obermeyer. He was seated by himself in a booth toward the back near the rest-room sign. I found a seat on the other side of the room where I could watch him with no chance of his seeing me.

A waitress brought me a beer and a plate of nachos with salsa. I looked up at the television screen and watched two men on skates go after each other with wooden sticks. One of the men had a very bloody nose.

I had a beer and a half and two plates of nachos while Obermeyer had four drinks of something something dark and brown with no ice in the next forty minutes while he watched the hockey game. He watched, but I had the feeling he wasn't seeing it. When he put the fourth drink down and looked as if he were trying to decide to go for number five, get up and drive home, or asked for a designated driver, I decided it was time. I took my almost flat second beer and moved over to sit across from Obermeyer, who looked up at me. I could see he was trying to place me.

"You were at Kevin's," he said.

"Yes."

"I just stopped for a drink," he said, as if there might be any other reason for being in a bar even if you did like nachos.

"Me too," I said, holding up my glass to show him. "Trasker's really sick," I said somberly.

"Very sick," Obermeyer agreed. "A very sick man. He's lucky to have friend like Kevin."

"Who needs enemies?" I said.

"What?"

"With a friend like Kevin Hoffmann, who needs enemies?" I explained.

"Oh," said Obermeyer, finishing his drink. "You're wrong."

Obermeyer held his liquor well, but I wondered what his blood-alcohol level was. Something was bothering him. The man had needed a drink. The man had needed four drinks and he looked toward the bar as if he might be considering number five.

"Trasker is dying," I said.

"Everybody is dying," Obermeyer said with a knowing doctor's smile. "It's the one fact my profession has to accept as a certainty. All we can do, if we don't screw up, is forestall the inevitable."

"Some of us take more time dying than others," I said. "Trasker . . ."

"Days, weeks, maybe even a month or more, but if I were one who bet on morbidity, I'd say he's closer than a few days to the end."

"He in pain?" I asked.

"Nothing we can't control."

"You mean shots?"

"We've got painkillers that could make you ignore a cannon-ball hole right through your stomach."

"That doesn't happen very often, though, does it? I mean a cannonball hole through someone's stomach."

He grinned and waved at the bartender, deciding another drink would be a very good idea.

"We're in Sarasota, Florida," Obermeyer said. "I've seen people who've lost their arms to sharks, had sunstroke that sent their temperature to one hundred and eight and survived, children hit by cars driven by ancient drivers who should have been declared legally blind."

"So Trasker is sedated."

"He is, to put it clinically, so far out of it that he can look back at the earth and see with clarity the floating eyeball of a corn snake."

"Colorfully put," I said.

"Thanks," Obermeyer said, looking up to hurry his drink. "Stanley recite any poetry for you?"

"Yes," I said.

"Smug little prick," said the doctor as his drink was delivered.

"So if Trasker wasn't sedated, his pain could be handled with something, morphine maybe?"

"Maybe," said Obermeyer.

He took a large sip.

"Normally, I don't drink like this," he said. "Normally, I drink a hell of a lot more when I've got something to drink about. But medical science is a wonderful thing. I've got a variety of options that keep me functional."

A group of people at the bar groaned. I looked back over my shoulder. The television was flashing the score. The Tampa Bay Lightning were losing to Boston, four to one.

"So, if you took Trasker off of sedation and gave him a shot or two, maybe one of your options, he could walk around, talk?"

"I wouldn't recommend it," he said.

"But . . ." I began as he lifted his glass again and held up his free hand to stop me.

"I'm drunk," he said. "I'm not a fool. Ask me now. Ask me in the morning. Ask me on the witness stand and I say I'm treating William Trasker properly. And given his condition, it would be the truth."

"Kevin Hoffmann's got a lot of money," I said.

"One hell of a lot of money," Obermeyer agreed, holding his

glass and looking at the contents he swirled in a small circle. "And he gives it generously."

"Any causes you're particularly interested in?"

"A campaign to build a center for state-of-the-art treatment of heart disease near the airport," he said. "A state-of-the-art center which I will have the honor of heading and for which I am already a leading candidate as first patient."

I dropped a five-dollar bill on the table to cover my two drinks and tip and stood up.

"You understand?" Obermeyer asked, as if he really needed understanding for whatever he was doing for Hoffmann.

"I understand," I said.

"I'll tell you a secret, Mr. . . ."

"Fonesca."

"Mr. Fonesca. I'm really a good doctor, but that's not what I was going to tell you. I'm a little overweight. I drink too much, have a slight cardiac problem, and I've got an arthritic knee but I could come close to shutting Kevin Hoffmann out every time we get on the court. He has no backhand. His forehand has no power and my nearsighted eight-year-old niece could return his serve. I have to cover for him in doubles to keep us in most matches and I have to do it without letting him know. Now that, Mr. Fonseca—"

"Fonesca."

"Fonesca, sorry, that is hard work. Kevin Hoffmann is not the athlete he thinks he is and maybe, some day, when I think I have nothing left to lose, I'll wipe his ass on the tennis court so badly that he'll realize I've been kissing that ass for years and he . . . Enough."

I left him and went back out to the parking lot.

Stanley, hands folded in front of him, stood in front of my rented Nissan, watching me.

"You read?" Stanley asked as I stopped in front of him.

There was traffic in the parking lot and the lights were bright.

"I'm basically literate," I said. "But I prefer old movies."

"Never could get into movies," Stanley said, adjusting his glasses. "Books? You can lose yourself in a poem, in a book, go to another space, time, world, a place better or worse than the one we're in, but definitely far from it."

"Kevin Hoffmann a reader?"

"A patron of the arts," Stanley said. "Theater, opera, symphony, ballet."

"And baseball."

"And baseball," Stanley agreed. "Dr. Obermeyer drinks a little."

"Dr. Obermeyer drinks a lot," I said.

"And when he drinks he talks."

"He talks," I agreed.

"Mr. Hoffmann would prefer that you not talk to Dr. Obermeyer."

"I can appreciate that."

"Mr. Hoffmann will be upset if you talk to Dr. Obermeyer again."

"Upset?"

" 'Who wills to know what weal awaits him, must first learn the ill that God for him hath wrought.' Benvenuto Cellini wrote that in his autobiography."

"And it means?"

"Simply put," Stanley said, "if you talk to the doctor again, you'll discover something bad waiting for you."

There really wasn't much more to say.

Stanley walked toward the bar. I had the feeling Dr. Obermeyer was about to have a new drinking partner. I wondered what Stanley's drink of choice might be. I guessed Diet Sprite.

10

IT WAS THURSDAY NIGHT, a little before nine. The rain had started again. It wasn't much of a rain but it was enough to hide the moon and stars and give me a feeling of protective isolation from people.

Traffic going north on Tamiami Trail was light, but there was the usual cast of coastal Florida characters on the road. I passed the infirmed and ancient, weak of sight, hearing, and judgment, hunching forward to squint into the darkness, driving twenty miles under the speed limit, trying not to admit to themselves that they were afraid of driving. These senior drivers were a potential menace, but I understood their loneliness, their unwillingness to give up driving and lose even more of their contact with the world.

Then there were the grinning kids in late-model cars or pickup trucks. They took chances, cut people off, and were unaware that death was a reality. You might challenge death fifty, a hundred, two hundred times, but the one time you lost, the game was over. They didn't consider losing. The game was everything.

There were families on their way back from somewhere or someone, one or two children sleeping in the backseat, mother and father in the front listening to the radio, just wanting to make it home and to bed for a few hours.

And then there was me.

I stopped at the video store a block from the DQ. They specialized in Spanish-language movies, but had a good collection of American movies from the Thirties, Forties, and Fifties, most of them second-generation copies.

Eduardo, overweight, sagging eyes, too-small button-down shirt, sat behind the counter at the back of the small store. He nodded when I walked in. Eduardo had been an almost promising middleweight in the late Seventies. Time had been no more kind to him than it had to me.

I didn't think I would find what I was looking for, but I did. I almost missed it. It was one I hadn't seen before called *Forbidden Destiny*. I recognized the title, knew who was in it. I found it in the bin of overused tapes for sale in a plain white box with the title printed in ink on the spine. I gave Eduardo three dollars.

"Rain," Eduardo said, looking out the window. "Bad for business. I think I'll just close up early and get a beer at the Crisp Dollar Bill. You want to come?"

"Tired," I said. "Busy day."

Eduardo understood tired. I don't think he knew much about busy days. He nodded.

When I got to my office just before ten, I found a message on the machine from Sally. "Lew, call when you get this if it's before ten."

I called.

"Hello," said Susan, Sally's daughter. Susan was eleven and was convinced that every time the phone rang it was for her.

"It's me, Lew," I said.

"I'll get her," Susan said, and put down the phone.

I could hear the television playing. The voice sounded like George Clooney in serious mode.

"It's Mr. Sunshine, Mom," Susan called.

"Dork," said Michael, who was going to be fifteen some time soon. "He can probably hear you."

"Lew?"

"Mr. Sunshine himself," I said.

"I have to talk to you about the Severtsons. I need to fill out a report and I want to quote you in it."

"Ken Severtson wants custody of the kids," I guessed. "And he wants a divorce."

"Neither," she said. "I talked to them a few hours ago. They're going to stay together."

"For the kids," I said.

"It's always for the kids," she said. "Even when it's the worst thing that can happen to the kids. Well, almost the worst thing."

The light in my office came from a line of fluorescent overheads, two of which were out, one of which was flickering and pinging. I could see the painting, the Dalstrom painting of the black forest and the single colorful flower.

"You think the kids should be taken away from the Severtsons?" I asked.

"It doesn't much matter what I think. There's not a judge in the state who would take kids away from parents who aren't criminal offenders, don't take drugs, and don't beat the kids. But a detective in Orlando faxed a report to the sheriff's office here, and the sheriff's office sent me a copy."

"Which says?"

"Mother and children present at a suspicious death. Mother in bed with a man who wasn't her husband. Family bears watching. We add that to the complaint about them from before and . . . I don't know."

"What?"

"Report on Stark," she said. "Lost his wife. Had some trouble with the law when he was young, but he's been a regular churchgoer for years. Upstanding businessman. Volunteer at the food bank."

"And child molester?" I added.

"Nothing in his past and no proof but Janice Severtson's word," said Sally. "Neither child remembers ever being touched by Stark."

"It would have happened. It was about to happen."

"But it didn't," Sally said. "Can you do me a favor and write out your version of what you know happened, what she told you, how Kenny and Sydney behaved? I'll attach it to my report and list you as a semiretired former member of the Office of State Attorney of Cook County, Illinois."

"When do you need it?"

"Soon," she said. "Tomorrow? The kids want to go to the movies Saturday. How about coming over here for dinner and you join us?"

Sally couldn't help it. It was her mission. Saving children and reclusive process servers. She knew I didn't like going to the movies. I preferred my cot, something old in black-and-white, and being alone. She had made progress with me. I had gone out to restaurants alone with Sally five times, and seven or eight times with her and kids. The kids liked The Bangkok. Susan liked getting a sugar high on Thai iced tea.

The rain started to come down harder. I could hear it beating on the concrete outside my door.

"Dinner is fine," I said. "I'll let you know about the movie."

"I was just joking when I called you Mr. Sunshine," Susan suddenly came on.

"I know," I said. "You know any real jokes?"

"Sure. Blond jokes. Lots of them. Why?"

"I'm collecting them for a friend I have to see in the morning."

Susan told me a joke. I jotted it down in my notebook and thanked her and then Sally came back on.

"Tomorrow," she said. "Afternoon. I have to be in court in the morning. Another crack child is going to be given back to his mother who just got out of rehab."

"And you'll fight it."

"And lose," Sally said. "And then I'll have the case back in a month or two or five and we'll start the same cycle again. Listen to me. I'm starting to sound like you."

"Did you hear the joke Susan just told me?" I asked.

"No."

"Ask her to tell it to you. I think it will make you smile."

"Did it make you smile, Lew?"

"No," I admitted. "I'll see you tomorrow afternoon sometime."

When we hung up, I turned off the office light, went into my cubbyhole room, hit the light switch, and got undressed. I put on a fresh pair of underwear, turned on the VCR and the television, and popped *Forbidden Destiny* into the slot.

I watched George Nader and Ernest Borgnine plan a bank robbery before Claire Collins appeared, her hair swept back, a knowing smile on her face, a dark sweater and skirt, her mouth pouting, her eyes darting.

When it was over, I turned off the television with the remote and lay in the dark listening to the rain.

Tomorrow was a busy day. I hated busy days.

• • •

The rain had stopped by morning but the sky was still dark and the DQ parking lot wet with puddles where the concrete was indented. Cars kicked up splashes and small waves on 301. My watch told me it was eight o'clock.

The phone rang. I got to it before the answering machine kicked in.

"Fonesca," I said.

"You know where the Seventeenth Street softball fields are?" Kevin Hoffmann asked, full of energy.

"I can find them," I said.

"Go east down Seventeenth past Beneva," he said. "You'll see the sign on the right. Drive past the big enclosed field where people run their dogs, and park in the lot. You'll see the fields. I'll be at the first diamond on your right."

"When?"

"If the rain doesn't come back, we'll start our first game in about half an hour."

"I've got a ten o'clock appointment," I said.

"It won't take long," he said.

"I can come to your house later," I said.

"I think it'll be better if you stay away from my house," he said.

"And from William Trasker?"

"Healthier," he said.

"For who?"

"Everyone involved. Get to the game as soon as you can."

I hung up, checked my watch again. I had time.

I put on clean underwear and my jeans, picked up my clean towel and green plastic bag with my soap, razor, toothbrush and toothpaste, and went out on the landing. The air was heavy and wet and I didn't want to deal with it.

The rest room was empty. Digger had moved up in the world, at least for now. The mirror could have been cleaner, but it

Stuart M. Kaminsky

was clean enough to show me the thin, hairy-chested bald man with sad, brown eyes.

"Good morning," I said to myself.

The guy in the mirror didn't think so. Besides, he needed a shave. Washed, clean-shaven, and toothbrushed, I left the rest room with the towel around my neck and my green plastic bag under my arm.

I had left the door unlocked.

Digger sat in the chair across my desk. He looked relatively clean and very nervous.

"The door was open," he said.

I nodded.

"I came in," he said. "Can we talk?"

"I'm going down to Gwen's for breakfast," I said, moving toward the back room. "I'll buy you breakfast."

"That'd be nice," he said. "Very nice."

I put on a shirt, white socks, and sneakers, and motioned for Digger to follow me. When we were on the landing, I locked the door.

"I'm scared," Digger said as we went down the stairs. "I gotta dance tonight. I don't think I can do it."

"You can do it," Knute Fonesca said evenly.

"No, it's too late. Life waltzed right by me while I was two-stepping in the desert of despair for all these years," Digger said.

"Colorful talk for a frightened dance instructor. Talk like that to the old ladies and you'll have your salary doubled in a month."

We crossed the DQ parking lot and turned right, staying as far away as possible from the curb where cars were spraying rainwater as they passed. We passed the workout club, antique shop, and a storefront for rent before we got to the diner.

Gwen's Diner is a holdover from a few years before the day Elvis supposedly came in and bought two cheeseburgers and a

Coke sometime in the Fifties. A poster of Elvis, guitar in hand, mouth open, arm reaching up in midsong, hung on the wall with a little index card Scotch-taped to it with Elvis's autograph.

If you sat in the right place at the counter, you could see both Elvis and any collisions that might take place where 301 met the curve at Tamiami Trail.

People who had been coming here regularly for a decade or two called the place Gwen's II. No one remembers the original Gwen's, if there ever was one. The place was owned and run now by a woman named Sheila and her two daughters, one of whom, Jesse, was eighteen and about to graduate a year late at Sarasota High School a block away. She was a year late because she had taken time out to have her second baby. The other daughter, Jean, had graduated a year ago. They were all natural blonds and all able to deflect a sharp or heavy innuendo with the skill of a seasoned and well-armed gladiator.

Digger and I took a booth in the no-smoking section. The no-smoking section was four booths against one wall with smokers surrounding it.

Gwen's was busy, and the three women were scurrying around but making it look easy, taking care of the counter-sitters and going from a table of roofers, to a single car salesman reading his newspaper, to three women who looked as if they were just going to or coming from the fitness center Digger and I had passed on our way here.

"Coffee?" asked Sheila, looking down at us.

All three women wore whatever they felt like wearing, which was generally tight jeans, when they weren't pregnant, and various brightly colored T-shirts.

"Yes. Waffles and an egg over easy with bacon for me," I said.

"Fueling up for the day, Fonesca?" she asked with a smile. "And you?"

She looked at Digger with a businesslike smile.

"The same," he said, looking at me to be sure it was all right.

I nodded to Sheila, who scribbled on her pad.

"How are the kids?" I asked.

"You mean my girls or their little ones?" she asked.

"Everyone."

"Dancing through life," Sheila said, turned, and moved toward the kitchen.

"That's it. That's it. It's the dancing," Digger said, leaning toward me across the table. "I don't trust my knees. I stopped dancing through life ten years ago and started to walk slow and for maybe the last two, three years I've been, to tell you the truth, crawling."

Sheila came back with two mugs of coffee.

"Big Cheese Omelet up," a woman's voice came from the kitchen out of sight from where we sat.

Help arrived in the form of Tim from Steubenville, who moved from the counter and sat next to me, facing Digger. Tim lived in an assisted-living home a short walk away at the end of Brother Geenen Way. He spent as much time as he could at Gwen's, reading the newspaper and telling those who'd listen that drugs, which he had never used, should be legalized, that there should be no income tax, that gays should do whatever they wanted including getting married, that anyone who wanted a gun and wasn't insane should have one. Since there was very little left of Tim, who was eighty-nine years old, the regulars at Gwen's tolerated him, a few even agreeing with him from time to time, which he appreciated, or argued with him, which he appreciated even more.

Tim had brought his coffee and newspaper with him. He looked at Digger.

"Seen you around," Tim said.

Digger nodded.

"You're looking better than I seen you before."

Digger nodded again.

"Off the bottle?" Tim asked.

"I don't drink," a melancholy Digger said. "No drinking. No drugs. Haven't smoked in twenty years or more."

"Nothing to give up," said Tim, nodding in sympathy.

Sheila looked over at me from the table of the three women and made a nod, which I took to mean that she would ease Tim back to the counter if I wanted him gone. I shook my head once to let her know Tim's presence was all right with me. I preferred Tim talking to Digger than my talking to either one of them.

I tuned them out, hearing only voices, not words, until Sheila came with our platters and a flip-top pitcher of syrup.

"I never thought of it that way," Digger was saying when I came back to earth.

"Well, what the hell you have to lose?" said Tim. "What the hell?"

Having accomplished his mission, Tim folded his newspaper, picked up his mug of coffee, and went back to his place at the counter, where he immediately engaged a burly trucker in animated conversation.

Digger dug into his food and finished long before I did, a determined look on his face. I was about halfway through when Digger said, "You mind if I get going? I've got stuff to do to get ready for work tonight."

"Sure," I said.

"Thanks for your help," Digger said, getting up.

"Sure," I said again, wondering for only a beat what Tim had said to him that had brought Digger back to the first small step of self-confidence.

I left a tip on the table and paid Jesse at the cash register with Elvis in midgyration a few feet to my right.

Less than fifteen minutes later I pulled onto the driveway at

Seventeenth Street Park. I passed a big open field on my left, where about a dozen people and the same number of dogs were running and barking. The parking lot a little farther down on the left was almost full, but there were spaces open if I was willing to step into shallow puddles left by the rain.

I could see ball games going on beyond the mesh fence, and I went through an open gate and down a concrete path. Voices were traveling in the heavy air. The sound of an aluminum bat hitting a ball clanked clearly, followed by shouts of encouragement.

Hoffmann was waiting for me at the first field on my right. He was wearing jeans, a New York Yankees cap, softball shoes, and an orange T-shirt with "Double Tiger Productions" printed on the front. The men on the bench behind more meshed metal were wearing the same Double Tiger shirts.

"Glad you could make it," Hoffmann said cheerfully. "I'm up this inning if we get a man on base."

The men out in the field were wearing blue shirts. I couldn't make out what was written on them. Both the men in the field and the ones on the bench ranged in age from not young to decidedly old.

"They know you're only thirty-five?" I asked.

Hoffmann laughed. It wasn't bad, but it wasn't authentic either.

"Watch this next batter," he said.

A heavyset man came off the bench, two bats in his large hands. He wore shorts, and both knees were reinforced with white elastic bands. He moved slowly, swinging the bats, handed one of the bats to a wiry man who had to be seventy, adjusted his glasses, and moved to the plate.

"That's Alan Roberts," Hoffmann said. "The Boomer. No knees. Has to hit it deep off the fence to make it to first. Then he gets a pinch runner."

I watched. The pitcher was a lean man with a dirty white

cap. He put his feet on the rubber, stepped off, and delivered the ball. The ball arced. Roberts swung and missed.

"Harder to hit a slow-pitch softball than a fast pitch," he said. "Fast pitch, the ball comes straight at you. You swing even, make contact, and that's it. Slow pitch, you have to hit up into the ball, time your swing perfectly, and supply your own power. It's an art."

There was supportive chatter on the field, encouraging the pitcher, whose name seemed to be Winston. There was also supportive chatter from the bench for Boomer, who took a couple of practice swings and cocked his bat back. Winston delivered. The arc was low. The ball was about to cross the plate chest-high when the batter swung. The ball sailed up and out about twenty feet in the air and rocketed toward the fence and over it. The bench cheered.

"That's more than two hundred feet," Hoffmann said happily as Boomer shuffled around the bases. "A lot of these guys played college ball, minor leagues, even a few made it to the majors. The hitting stays with you. The fielding, too. The body goes. Legs, back, arms."

Boomer crossed the plate and accepted high fives from the bench and Hoffmann, who moved over to meet him and then came back to me.

"I'll get up this inning," Hoffmann said. "I'll make this quick and straight, Fonesca. See that gym bag at the end of the bench, the red one with the white handles?"

"I see it."

"I can get an envelope out of that right now," he said. "Inside of the envelope is five thousand dollars. Cash. I'll get it for you now. You take it and disappear till after the commission meeting."

I didn't answer. Another player, this one tiny and at least seventy, was at the plate.

"That's Cal," Hoffmann said. "He's from Chicago, too. Big Cubs fan. You should meet him."

Hoffmann wasn't looking at me but he understood my silence.

"There are two envelopes in that bag," he said. "Each with five thousand dollars. They could be in your pocket in ten seconds."

I still didn't answer.

"Okay," said Hoffmann, looking at me now. "What if that ten thousand dollars is a payment to you for your services. I have a job for you in . . . what's your favorite city?"

"Sarasota," I said.

"New Orleans," Hoffmann said, ignoring my answer. "You'll like New Orleans. Go there till Saturday or Sunday and find someone for me."

"Who?"

"The fill-in piano player at Preservation Hall," he said. "The mime in front of the church in that square near the place where everyone goes for those puffy things covered in sugar. Find me the best antique dealer in the French Quarter."

"Why?"

"Why? To get you the hell out of town, Fonesca. Can you use ten thousand dollars?"

"Yes, but I don't need it."

He sighed deeply and looked down at the ground. We were standing in wet red dirt. It would take me time to get my shoes clean.

"I've got a client," I said. "I've got two clients."

"Remember my man Stanley?" Hoffmann asked.

"Vividly," I said.

"He has no temper at all. He reads a lot, works out a lot, practices with a wide range of firearms, and has been diagnosed by competent analysts both in prison and out as being violent and sociopathic."

"Must get invited to a lot of parties," I said as Cal from Chicago sent a blooper into short right field and moved surprisingly quickly to first base.

"He does what I tell him to do," Hoffmann said, applauding Cal's hit. "Sometimes he does things he thinks I want without telling me. Sometimes he . . ." Hoffmann's voice trailed off. "Sometimes he makes terrible mistakes."

I had the feeling that I was seeing the real Kevin Hoffmann for the first time. His face lost its tightness, his eyes closed, his head went down. I knew that look. It was grief. Real grief. But for who? William Trasker? Mrs. Trasker? And why had mention of Stanley triggered it?

"He's very loyal," Hoffmann said, lifting his head and opening his eyes, his smile returning, his false front restored. "You don't want to deal with Stanley."

"I don't want any more literary lessons from him," I said.

"You don't want any kind of lessons from him," Hoffmann said.

A bite of bitterness? Did I detect the hint of it in his voice? Whatever it was, it was gone when he said, "Take the envelopes, drive to New Orleans, come back Saturday or Sunday."

"I don't think so," I said. "I've got a dinner date for Saturday."

"So, money doesn't interest you?" Hoffmann said.

"Not very much."

"Threats don't bother you?"

"Not a lot."

Hoffmann gave me a hard look.

"You need a good psychiatrist, Fonesca," he said.

"I've got a psychologist," I said. "I have an appointment with her in about twenty minutes."

"Kevin," someone called from the bench. "You're up."

Hoffmann reached for a bat leaning against the fence.

"You *do* know you've been threatened?" Hoffmann said. "I mean you have enough contact with reality to know that much?"

"Offered a bribe first and then threatened," I said.

"I'm up," he said, and bat in hand, jogged to the plate.

I watched him hit a ball foul, miss a pitch, and then hit another ball foul. Rules of the game. Foul ball with two strikes and you were out. Hoffmann threw his bat on the ground and looked at me with less than love in his heart for his fellow man.

I checked my watch. I had fifteen minutes.

I drove west on Seventeenth to Orange, went south, turned right on Main, and found a parking spot on Palm Avenue next to an art gallery. I stopped for two coffees and two biscotti from Sarasota News & Books, and I was in Ann Horowitz's office a minute early.

While she finished her early-morning appointment, I worked on my coffee and read an article on what quasars are in an old *Smithsonian* magazine. She was only ten minutes late, but she always made it up by giving me an extra ten minutes at the end of our session, which in turn meant the next client, patient, or lunatic would be equally late or later.

The man who came out of Ann's closed office door wore a suit. He was short, fat, and moving quickly out the door, avoiding my eyes.

"Come in, Lewis," she called from inside her office.

I went in and closed the door behind me. I had finished my biscotto in the waiting room while reading the four-year-old *Smithsonian*. I placed the white paper bag with the coffee and her biscotto on her desk.

"Chocolate?"

"Almond," I said.

She nodded her approval as I sat in the recliner across from her.

"You're wearing new earrings," I said.

"My husband made them from stones we found on the beach," she said, touching one of the earrings. "Crafted for hundreds of thousands of years by the sea. The ocean can be a great artist."

I drank some coffee and she nibbled on her biscotto and took out her coffee.

"The operative word is 'can,'" she said, smelling the coffee. "The ocean also produces a near eternity of shapeless, colorless rocks and shells. Nature is not selective. It creates the neutral, the beautiful, and the ugly. It is up to humans to search for the beautiful."

"You've cheered me already," I said.

"I can see that. Jokes," she said, taking a sip of coffee. "You have jokes for me?"

"Someone just threatened to kill me," I said.

"New symptom?" she asked. "Paranoia?"

"No," I said and explained.

"All the more reason you should have jokes," she said.

I took out my notebook and flipped to the pages where I had written the jokes people had told me over the past three days.

"I don't tell jokes well," I said.

"Why does that not surprise me?" she said. "You tell. I'll listen."

"I want to die in my sleep like my grandfather did," I read. "Not screaming and yelling like the other people in the car he was driving."

"You find that funny?" Ann asked.

"You didn't even smile," I said.

"I've heard it before. You think it's funny?"

"I . . . no."

"Tell me another one."

"I went home last night and discovered that someone had replaced everything I own with exact duplicates."

"And what do you think about that one?"

"I like it."

"But is it funny? Never mind. Tell me another."

"A new patient got an emergency visit with a therapist," I read. "The patient said, 'Doctor, I'm depressed. I lost my wife. My children hate me. I hate myself. Sometimes I have suicidal thoughts.' 'Well,' said the therapist, 'the world's greatest comedian, Santoro, is in town tonight for one performance. Get a ticket to see him.' 'But, Doctor,' the patient said, 'I am Santoro.' You've heard that one, too?"

"Yes," Ann said, working on her coffee. "You find it funny?"

"Sad," I said.

"Have you noticed people tell you sad jokes?"

"I seem to have a gift. You want more jokes?"

She nodded her head to indicate that I should go on.

"Mrs. Quan Wong had a baby. The nurse brought the baby in for the Wongs to see and said, 'The baby is fine,' the nurse said. 'But there's something wrong. This can't be your baby.' 'Why not?' asked Mr. Wong. 'Because,' said the nurse, 'two Wongs don't make a white.' "

"You like that one?" Ann said, wiping crumbs from her fingers.

"No," I said.

"I don't think I do either. You have more?"

"Four more," I said.

"Do you think any of them are funny?"

"No," I said.

"It doesn't matter. Do you know why I told you to collect jokes?"

"To cheer me up," I said.

She shook her head no vigorously, and said, "It was to get you to make contact with people, to ask them for something that might help you, to let you know that people are willing to respond to a request for a little help. The important question isn't whether the jokes are funny, but whether the people who told them to you smiled when they told you. Did they smile?"

"I think so," I said. "I don't know about the ones I got over the phone."

"Next assignment," she said. "Memorize these jokes and the other ones you have and tell them to someone you care about."

"I can't tell jokes," I said.

"Of course you can. You just did. You simply tell them badly. Memorize them and tell them to someone."

"You want me to do a stand-up comedy act?"

"If you want to put it that way," she said. "Before we get together again you present your act to someone."

"Who?"

"To Catherine," she said. "Not the baby. Your wife. Imagine her responses. Come back and tell me if she finds your jokes funny, if she smiles, makes faces, groans."

"I can't," I said.

"You can do it," she said soothingly. "You can do it."

"I'll try."

"Don't try, succeed. You know who was a great teller of jokes and stories? General Patton. Loved to tell jokes and funny stories. I think he was depressed, too. I've been told he sometimes had his jeep driver completely naked when he drove him around after a battle. He'd pretend not to notice and people were too embarrassed to look at the driver or say anything. Patton thought it was hilarious."

"That reassures me," I said. "But I don't think the world's ready to see me walking around naked."

"Sarcasm," she said. "A small step toward recovery. A step to one side of comedy. Let's try something. You've told me all the wonderful things about your wife, her beauty, wit, kindness, idiosyncrasies. Tell me things you didn't like about her."

"There are none," I said.

"She was a human being, not a goddess. It is not disloyal to remember her as a human being. Besides, it is easier to tell jokes to a human being than a goddess."

I looked down at my cup of coffee, cocoa brown with two packets of artificial sweetener. I drank.

"Start small," Ann prompted.

"She left cabinet doors open," I said. "I always had to close them. I told her about it at first and then I just gave up and did it."

"You liked doing it, closing the cabinet doors?"

"I didn't mind. Sometimes it bothered me but usually . . ."

"You smiled and did it," said Ann.

"Yes," I said.

"I'm not sure I'd count that as a fault, but it's a start."

"She told me what to do when I drove, told me if I was going too fast or too slow, or not passing other drivers when I should or passing them when I shouldn't."

"That bothered you."

"Yes."

"Because you're a good driver?"

"Yes."

"Progress. More."

"She was always telling me to stand up straight, sit up straight. We'd be out somewhere and she'd come up behind me and press her hand into my lower back to remind me to straighten up."

"She press you hard? Did it hurt?"

"No, it wasn't that she was wrong. I guess I didn't like the criticism."

"Keep going."

"She was almost always late when we had somewhere to go. She'd tell me she would be ready in five minutes and it was always fifteen or even twenty and we'd have to drive like hell to get where we were going on time."

"And she would be telling you how to drive during all this?"

"Yes," I said.

"Do you want to cry?" Ann asked.

"Yes," I said.

"Because you feel disloyal to her memory?"

"Because I miss her faults," I said.

"So cry?"

"I can't."

"I'm pushing too hard," Ann said. "You want a Diet Coke? I'm still thirsty. I've got some in the refrigerator."

"Sure," I said.

While she left the office to get the Cokes, I tried to imagine Catherine reacting to the joke about the Wongs. I tried to see her face. She would groan and then she would smile supportively. Or maybe she wouldn't.

Ann came back with the two Diet Cokes, sat down, and said, "So, in the time we have left, do I tell you what I've learned about recently discovered innovations in surgery that were employed by the South during the Civil War or why Serbians are so good at preparing Middle Eastern food, or do you tell me what you've been doing for the past three days?"

I opted for the last three days. I had already told her about Hoffmann and Stanley and Roberta Trasker, so I told her about Digger and the boy named Darrell Caton and his mother in Sally's office. I told her about Dr. Obermeyer. I told her about Ames's little gun. And I told her about the Severtsons.

"And this is all true?" she asked with great interest. "You're not creating any of it?"

"I don't know how to create it," I said. "And why would I make it up?"

"To please your therapist," she said. "People do it all the time. I suggest something and the patient, wanting to please me, agrees even if they don't believe it. Don't try to please me. It gets in the way."

"I didn't make any of this up," I said.

"For a man who is trying to hide from the world, you seem to have been drawn very deeply into it."

"Not by choice," I said.

"You could have said no. No, I won't look for the woman and her two children. No, I won't try to find the county commissioner. So, why did you say yes?"

"I don't know. You want me to think about it?"

"Yes, but not consciously. The dead woman," Ann said. "The actress. You want to know who killed her."

"Of course."

"Why?" she asked.

"Closure," I said.

She said nothing, just looked at me till I said, "The closure I can't find with my wife's death. You think the reason I take on these searches for people, why I'm a process server is to find people responsible for things they know or have done wrong? You think I do it because I don't know who killed . . ."

"Catherine," Ann supplied. "And do you know who killed Mrs. Trasker?" she asked.

"I think so."

"But?"

"Nothing's ever simple about death. Nothing's ever simple about murder."

"We are once again out of time."

I got up and handed her a twenty-dollar bill. She placed it on her desk and rose.

"Remember, tell the jokes to Catherine."

I nodded. I wasn't sure I could do it.

The sky was threatening but no rain was falling. The homeless, shirtless black man who slept in the park right across the street, with traffic whizzing by on Tamiami Trail, was sitting on

the green metal bench on the corner, his arm spread out along
the back of the bench. He was talking to himself. I couldn't make
out what he was saying.

"Hi," I said.

He nodded back.

"Want a cup of coffee?" I said.

He nodded back again. I didn't have to tell him to wait. I
went back to Sarasota News & Books, got him a coffee and a
bran muffin, and went back to the bench.

He took the coffee cup in one hand and the muffin in
another.

"You want to hear some jokes?" I asked.

11

HEAVY BLACK CLOUDS were moving in quickly from the east, pushing the heavy, slower-moving gray clouds out of the way.

Dr. James Obermeyer's office was in a three-building complex on East Street right across from Michael's on East restaurant. I'd been in one of the buildings a few months ago for an eye exam.

The picture on my television had started to look fuzzy, but Dave had come up to take a look at it and pronounced the television healthy and me in need of an eye doctor. I went to his.

The eye doctor examined me, told me I didn't need glasses, and asked me how much television I watched.

"Too much," I had told him. "Mostly movies on tape."

"How much do you watch?"

"A lot, whenever I can."

His advice was simple. Stop watching so many videos, read books, go to the movies, see a baseball game, or bowl. I thanked him, paid him, and ignored what he had told me.

Obermeyer's office was in the building directly across from the ignored ophthalmologist. It was just before ten when I went through his outer office door and faced one of those glass partitions, behind which sat a young woman talking on the phone and nibbling at the ends of her hair.

I stood waiting till she hung up.

"Yes?" she asked with a tired smile.

"You eat your hair."

"What?"

"You eat your hair," I repeated.

"I . . . what're you, a doctor?" she asked without interest.

"You can develop a fur ball just like a cat," I said. "Only you can't cough it up. It gets big enough and you need surgery."

"You want an appointment with the doctor?" she asked with a look that made it clear she thought I needed a psychiatrist, not an internist.

"No," I said. "Jim and I are friends. We were out drinking last night. I was having my eyes checked across the way and I thought I'd stop by and give him my half of the bar tab. I left before he did and just forgot."

"Your name?"

"Lew Fonesca."

"I'll see if he can see you," she said, pushing a button on the phone as she picked it up.

My question was answered. The good doctor was in.

"Yes, Doctor," she said, after giving him my name. "He says he'd like to see you for a second. He owes you money. Okay."

She put one hand over the mouthpiece and said. "The doctor says you can leave the money with me. He's busy now."

Stuart M. Kaminsky

"Can't do that," I said, and took four quick steps to Obermeyer's office door and opened it before the receptionist could stop me.

"Wait a minute," she called from the outer office, as I let the door close behind me and moved past two examining rooms, one on my right and one on my left. I found Obermeyer in his comfortable, carpeted office complete with leather chairs, a leather love seat, prints made by pressing inked dead fish against canvas on two walls, and all of his degrees, titles, and awards framed on the wall behind him.

He looked up from behind his desk. He was wearing a clean, white smock and a hangover.

"I have a very low tolerance for alcohol," he said, sitting up and blinking his eyes as he tried to focus on me.

Then it came to him.

"I remember," he said, pointing a finger at me. "Kevin Hoffmann's. You wanted me to——"

"Help get William Trasker out of that house."

"Mr. Trasker is a very sick man. He should not be moved."

"What would happen to him if he were moved?"

"I wouldn't want to be responsible," he said.

"So he's too sick to be moved?"

"That's my opinion, yes," he said, putting a palm against his forehead to determine if he might need an aspirin.

The phone buzzed. He picked it up, listened for a few seconds, and said, "No, Carla. It's all right. Do not call the police."

He hung up and looked up at me.

"What happens to you if the police find a way to get a couple of specialists to look at Trasker and it turns out that he's sick but there wouldn't be any problem moving him?"

"Professional difference of opinion," he said, looking around for something. "I'd have to stand by my diagnosis."

I pulled my notebook out of my pocket and read, "James

Ryder Obermeyer, B.S. in physiology, North Dakota State University, M.D. from the University of Utah. Certified in internal medicine, practiced in five different towns in North Dakota before you came to Sarasota six years ago. Malpractice suits, seven. Complaints to American Medical Association, sixteen."

"That's not uncommon for a physician in today's litigious world," he said.

"How about six DUI arrests and three accidents while under the influence?" I asked. "In one of those accidents in Ogden, Utah, a teenage girl was injured, lost her left leg. Your malpractice-insurance rate went up to something near the annual budget of the states of North Dakota and Utah combined."

"Are you threatening me?" he asked with indignation.

"Happens to me all the time," I said. "No, my point was that your professional opinion might not hold up particularly well against a cancer surgeon."

"I stand by what I've said," Obermeyer insisted with very little confidence and a distinct beading of perspiration on his upper lip.

"Mrs. Trasker was murdered. Kevin Hoffmann's holding Mr. Trasker against his will. You could wind up as accessory to a murder."

"I think you can leave now, Mr. Fonseca," he said.

"Fonesca. I'll call you later," I said. "Have Trasker ready to leave Hoffmann's house or I throw you to the American Medical Association, the AARP, the Florida Medical Ethics Board, the County Medical—"

"Stop," he said. "You can't intimidate me and you don't frighten me."

"Channel Forty, SNN television, the *Longboat Key Observer*, the *Planet*," I continued. "The . . . You get the idea."

His face had turned red. He looked distinctly intimidated and frightened.

Stuart M. Kaminsky

"You wouldn't do that," he said. "I'd sue you."

"I don't think so but if you did, it would be a waste of your time and money. I don't have anything. I could have ten thousand dollars if I take Kevin Hoffmann's money to be quiet about Trasker and get out of town. I wonder how much he's paying you."

"Do not come back here," he said with a quiver in his voice, "or the police will be called."

I considered pushing him a little further, but I remembered what he had told me about his bad heart.

I left the office, closing the door quietly before he could say anything more. I half hoped he would follow me into the hall and do some bargaining.

Carla the receptionist gave me a glance and then looked down at whatever she had been doing.

I stopped at the Texas Bar and Grill too early for lunch and not hungry. Ames was in his room in back. Ed Fairing was behind the bar, talking to a pair of black men in their fifties who could have been twins.

There were people at a few of the tables, early lunch birds, all-day drinkers with nowhere else they wanted to be, a woman in a sweat suit drinking coffee and reading a book.

"Ames?" I called to Ed, who nodded toward the narrow hallway next to the bar.

"Fonesca," Ed said, stopping me as I started to walk past the bar. "Listen, I'm thinking of making this place a little more upscale. Lot of pressure on me from some of the downtown business people. Jerry Robins, you know him? Know what he said to me? 'Ed,' he said, 'you've got a really funky place.' I said, 'Yes, thanks,' and he said, 'I hate funky.' You understand where I'm going with this?"

"No," I said.

"I don't want to change the Texas," he said. "I'm thinking about it but I don't want to do it. I like it just the way it is."

"Funky," I said.

"I guess," he agreed, "but that's not the way I see it. I see it as authentic. You know people, right?"

"People?"

"You know what I mean," he said confidentially. "People who might be persuaded to get people like Jerry Robins to leave me alone. People like Trasker and Hoffmann. People on the City Council or Board of Commissioners. People who might owe you a favor, might see the Texas as kind of a landmark."

"That kind of person can't be bought for what you could afford to pay, Ed."

Ed touched the corners of his handlebar mustache to be sure they were still there and properly upturned.

"I'm not talking about bribing anybody," he said. "I'm talking about your maybe calling in some markers."

Markers. He sounded like Dean Martin in *Rio Bravo*.

"I'll talk to someone," I said.

"Thanks," said Ed with a small, gentle punch of my arm. "A beer?"

"Maybe later," I said.

I went down the hallway past the ladies and men's rooms and the utility closet and knocked at a door on the right.

"Who is it?" Ames asked.

"Lew. Want me to wait for you at the bar?"

He paused a long pause and said, "Come in."

I had never been in Ames's room before. He liked his privacy, not as much as I loved my isolation, but enough to be respected, and his privacy was intruded on far less than my isolation. Ames had the bearing of man whose space and dignity should not be violated. I had the bearing of a man whose isolation seemed to call for intrusion.

His room had mine beat in size, cleanliness, and color. There was a bed against one wall under the only window in the room.

Stuart M. Kaminsky

The view through the window was the alley behind the Texas Bar and Grill. There was a chest of drawers, slightly scratched, against the opposite wall. A heavy, dark wood rocking chair sat in one corner next to a floor lamp. In the middle of the room was a wooden table with heavy dark legs. There were no prints or paintings on the wall, just a small battered wooden crucifix next to a magazine-sized, framed black-and-white photograph of a young woman in an evening dress. The photograph looked as if it had been taken at least half a century ago. Ames McKinney sat at the table in one of the three chairs that faced the door.

In front of him were the parts of what looked like a rifle.

"New?" I asked.

"Hmm," Ames answered as he finished polishing a black metal bolt about six inches long. "Marlin, New Model 1895 Cowboy," he said, looking up at me, blue eyes, leathery face. "Ed just bought it. I'm checking it out."

He began to put the rifle back together.

"Good feel," he said as he worked. "Old Western-styled 45/70 with a twenty-six-inch tapered octagonal barrel with deep-cut Ballard-type rifling, nine-shot tubular magazine, adjustable Marble semibuckhorn rear and Marble carbine front sight."

I sat across from Ames and watched quietly while he finished, put a cap on the oil can in front of him, wiped his hands on an oily piece of dark soft leather, and lay the gun gently down in front of him.

"Here about the dead lady?" he asked.

"Maybe. Probably. I want to take a look at Midnight Pass. Like to see it?"

"Want me to carry?"

"Don't think it'll be necessary but it can't hurt to bring something small."

He stood up and showed me that he was wearing his belt with the built-in pistol.

"That should do it," I said.

Ames nodded, picked up the rifle, and left the room, closing the door behind him. When he came back a few minutes later, he was wearing his yellow slicker.

"Looks like it might rain some more," he said.

I looked at the window. It was definitely getting darker.

"Then let's go," I said.

The rain started when we were no more than five minutes out of downtown. It stayed light and steady but the wind began to pick up when we made the turn on Stickney Point Road, turned left on Midnight Pass and headed down the two-lane road.

It still wasn't heavy when I made a right turn into Sarasand-bay Cove, a private, spaced-out quintet of huge houses facing the water. I had been here before, serving papers on a plastic surgeon named Amos Peet, who was being sued for malpractice. Women who didn't like the way things had turned out were constantly suing plastic surgeons. Usually the insurance companies settled, knowing that if it got to a jury, the plaintiff would walk away with a very large check. So, insurance for a plastic surgeon's practice was higher than the annual salary of a Sarasota fireman. So the plastic surgeons charged more and more. It costs about two thousand dollars to get eight hours of cardiac-bypass surgery and six months of follow-up, and four thousand dollars to get an hour of plastic surgery. I had served papers to Dr. Peet on behalf of one of Tycinker, Oliver, and Schwartz's dissatisfied clients.

Amos Peet had been a gentleman about it. He had been through it all before. He did not blame the messenger. He offered the messenger a cup of coffee.

I remembered him telling me that he was about two hundred yards from Midnight Pass. I wasn't interested at the time. This time I was. I parked next to a short, thickly leafed clutch of trees.

Ames and I got out of the car. It still wasn't raining hard, but it was getting darker and the threat of something more was out there. I didn't mind being soaked. I liked going back to my office, getting out of my clothes, toweling down, and getting in bed in a fresh pair of boxer shorts and a T-shirt.

A little distant thunder, a slight increase in the rain, and a noon as dark as night. We went behind Amos Peet's house and headed in the direction of Midnight Pass. Ames led the way through the miniature rain forest. My sneakers were muddy long before we got to the clearing and the open stretch of rocks and shrubs.

"You think this is it?" I said.

"Don't seem like much," Ames said. "Can't even build on it."

"It's worth millions," I said. "Maybe a lot of millions."

A trio of small crawfish scuttled behind a rock on the gravel to my left, and the wind picked up. The rain was steady and getting stronger and the sky was almost night black. Lightning crackled out across the Gulf. Neither wind nor rain made it any cooler. It was humid and hot. A steamy mist was forming close to the ground.

I couldn't see Kevin Hoffmann's house from where we stood, but I imagined it surrounded by fog. Inside that house lay William Trasker, and I didn't seem to be getting very far in earning the money the Reverend Wilkens had given me.

There was nothing much else to see. It didn't look like it would take millions of dollars to study the narrow strip of land to determine if it could be dredged. I didn't know why it would take millions more to keep the Pass open once it was dredged.

"They could just put in a canal," I said, kneeling and picking up a handful of stones and cracked seashells.

"Not that easy," Ames said.

Ames had a degree in engineering. I didn't know what kind of engineering but I was sure he knew more than I did.

"Erosion, pressure from drifting land, storms, level differences to be considered," he said. "Not that easy."

"Maybe this storm will turn into a hurricane and God will part Midnight Pass and everyone will rise up in jubilation," I said.

Ames didn't say anything. In fact, he was no longer standing next to me. I turned and saw him about fifteen yards away, looking toward the thick bushes and heavy-leafed trees swaying and rustling noisily in the wind.

Then the shot came. I wasn't sure it was a shot at first, just another cracking sound that could have been an old rotted tree weighted down with water and breaking at the trunk. It was the second shot that convinced me, partly because I saw the spray of mud, wet leaves, and pebbles fly up about ten yards in front of me.

I went down on my stomach and heard a third shot, but this one sounded different, a lot different. I looked up and Ames was holding a sawed-off shotgun. It was aimed at the bushes in the direction from which we had come.

Ames fired off a second blast. Leaves exploded. Standing upright in his yellow slicker, Ames cracked open the shotgun and was reloading it with shells taken from his pocket.

I expected another shot from the dense blowing trees and bushes. I was a good target. No shot came from whoever seemed to be trying to kill me, but Ames was advancing slowly toward the direction of the shooter. Ames fired another blast, stepped to the edge of the thicket, and fired again.

Maybe I heard something or someone moving in front of Ames. Maybe a frightened animal. Maybe nothing but more sounds of wind and rain.

"He's gone," Ames said over his shoulder, reloading again.

I got up, mud-covered and brushing debris and something that looked like a centipede hanging from my chest.

"We going after him?" Ames asked.

"Yes," I said. "We're going after him."

Shotgun held with barrel forward in his right hand, Ames hurried back the same way we had come. I was right behind him. Ahead of us a car started.

Something crawled up my leg. I swatted at it.

Mud crept into my shoes and squished with each step. I couldn't do anything about it.

We moved faster. When we were in sight of my car, we could hear the shooter's car turn a corner and kick up gravel.

I was going to have to explain to Fred and Alan why the front seat of the rental car was covered with moldy, junglelike decay. Maybe I could clean it up a little myself before I returned it.

When Ames had closed his door and was sitting with shotgun in hand, I turned the car around and went in into thunder, lightning, and rain in search of the person who had shot at me. I hit Midnight Pass Drive no more than fifteen seconds later.

Ames looked right. I looked left. Not a car in sight.

"He pulled into one of the driveways," I said.

"Looks that way," Ames agreed.

"Which one and in which direction?"

"We can start trying 'em," Ames said.

We started toward the left, the logical direction if he was trying to get off the key and not get trapped at the dead end to the right at the end of the key. We found some cars parked on paved paths, found driveways leading into developed communities like the one the plastic surgeon lived in, found homes with high walls.

There were some cars parked in many of the places we looked, but no one sitting in them. He could have been hunched down or leaning over. We could have gotten out and started checking and feeling the car hoods to see if they were warm. And as much faith as I had in Ames, there was always the possibility that the shooter would be waiting for us behind a tree, a rock, a wall, or an SUV.

"No point, is there?" I said, after we did stop to check out a Jaguar and a Ford Explorer parked side by side in a driveway.

"No," said Ames.

The curtains of the window of the house in whose driveway we were standing parted and an old woman looked at us, horror in her eyes. Before her in the rain stood a tall old man in a yellow slicker cradling a shotgun in his arms and next to him stood a shorter, thinner version of the Swamp Thing.

The curtains closed.

Ames and I got back in the car and headed for home.

"You all right?" Ames asked, tucking the shotgun in a deep pocket he had created inside his slicker.

"He missed," I said.

"Question was, are you all right?"

"Yes," I said.

For a supposedly suicidal man, I was doing a remarkable job of surviving.

I dropped Ames at the Texas Bar and Grill and told him I'd be back later, that we had something to do. Ames didn't ask what it was. He never did.

The rain was no better when I pulled into the DQ parking lot. There were no customers. The girl at the orders window had her head in her hands, her elbows propped up on the counter. She was watching traffic slosh by.

When I got to my office and opened the door, I kicked off my muddy shoes, took off my shirt, pants, underwear, and socks and dropped them in a heap along with my drenched Cubs cap. I padded carefully to my room, picked up my last clean towel, wrapped it around myself, and grabbed my soap.

I pushed my wet clothes out of the way with my foot, left

the door unlocked, and went outside on the landing. No one was there. It didn't matter.

No one was in the rest room either. It looked clean and smelled good. Marvin Uliaks had done his daily cleanup. I locked the door and ran both faucets of the sink full blast, cupped my hands, and covered myself with water. I repeated this four or five times before I started using soap, lots of soap. Then I rinsed twice more with cupped hands and began drying myself.

I was clean. The rest room floor wasn't.

While I was drying, I saw myself in the mirror. Someone had tried to kill the man in the mirror, the unremarkable man in the mirror.

It hit me. If he or she had succeeded, there would have been some kind of funeral, probably paid for by Flo, and people would actually come to the funeral—Ames, Flo, Adele with her baby, Ann, her husband, Sally, Dave, John Gutcheon, maybe Billy the bartender at the Crisp Dollar Bill, Marvin if he could get a ride, and maybe even Digger, though I doubted that. Then, if someone tried to find them, some of my family in Chicago would show up. My father would insist on an Episcopalian minister.

Maybe it wouldn't be so bad.

I finished drying and wrapped the wet towel around my waist, took my soap, and headed back to my office. My plan was to write a will saying I wanted to be cremated and have my ashes buried next to my wife in Illinois.

When I got back to my office and opened it, the lights were on and the window air conditioner that Ames had put in about a year earlier was humming.

Detective Etienne Viviase was standing in front of the small Stig Dalstrom painting on the wall. He turned his head to look at me.

"Wanna get dressed?" he asked.

I went into my room, threw the towel over my chair, and found something dry to put on while Viviase talked from the other room.

"Called the FBI," he said. "Told them about Kevin Hoffmann's Social Security–number theft, suggested he might be covering up a crime."

"And?" I said, tucking a gray cotton shirt into my worn jeans.

"Nothing much yet, but they did find out his real name."

I hopped around, putting on my socks.

"His name is Alvin York Dutcher," Viviase said. "He's fifty-five, born in Mill Valley, California. One older sister. Parents long gone. Young Alvin York spent two years in the army. Sniper in Vietnam. When he came back, he picked up an arrest record. Small stuff. No convictions. Then . . ."

"Then?" sitting on my cot and tying my shoes.

"House was robbed a few miles from where Alvin lived," said Viviase. "Very rich retiree who owned jewelry stores all over the country, South America, Europe. Victor Sage."

"I know the name," I said, brushing back what was left of my hair with both hands.

"Two men in masks. Got Sage to open his safe. Sage's wife was asleep upstairs. Got away with millions in cash and jewelry."

I stepped back into my office. Viviase was still looking at the Dalstrom painting.

"Reminds me of you," he said.

"People tell me," I said. "Alvin York?"

"Alvin York Dutcher left home a week after the Sage robbery. Kevin Hoffmann came back to life in Atlanta, Georgia, about two months after that."

Viviase turned toward me. He could have told me this on the phone. He could have not told me at all. I waited.

"You went to see Dr. Obermeyer this morning," he said.

Stuart M. Kaminsky

"Dr. Obermeyer called in with a complaint. I caught it on the morning list. He says you're harassing him."

Since Obermeyer was right, I said nothing.

"He says you threatened to have someone break his hands if he didn't let Trasker out of Hoffmann's house."

"I never threatened to break his hands, head, legs, or heart," I said. "You might want to check the doctor's record. He loses a lot of indignation when he's reminded of it."

"I need a statement," he said. "Obermeyer and his receptionist have already given theirs."

"Your office or . . ."

"Just write it out," he said. "You know the drill."

"Anything else?"

"No," he said, putting his notebook away. "You?"

"Someone just tried to kill me," I said.

"Where?"

"Midnight Pass. Shot at me three times. I got away."

"You think Obermeyer tried to kill you because you threatened him?" asked Viviase.

"Unlikely," I said. "What about Hoffmann's man Stanley?"

Viviase pulled out his notebook again and flipped through the pages. When he stopped, he read, "Stanley LaPrince. Born in . . . He's thirty-six. Born Baton Rouge, Louisiana. Finished high school, two years at Louisiana State, joined the army, Desert Storm action, bunch of medals. Discharged after he shot three unarmed Iraqi soldiers. Made the mistake of doing it in view of a Reuters reporter. Hooked up with Hoffmann about three years ago, maybe more."

"So, are you taking me in?" I asked.

"No," he said. "I'll tell Obermeyer there's not enough evidence to charge you, which is not quite true. I don't like Obermeyer. I don't like Hoffmann."

"And me?"

"I don't much like you either, but I'm getting used to you. You're pissing someone off, Fonesca, and we both know who. My advice? Midnight Pass vote is tonight. Spend the rest of the day watching movies and go to bed early."

Viviase left and I picked up the phone. Dixie was back at work at the coffeehouse. She told me Harvey, my regular hacker, was back in town and at work. Since there was no cost for Harvey's services, I thanked Dixie.

"Anytime," she said. "Got to run. Cappuccino machine is making weird sounds."

I called the law offices of Tycinker, Oliver, and Schwartz on Palm Avenue and got connected to Harvey.

"Harvey here," he said flatly.

Harvey would have been movie-star handsome if he didn't have his recurrent love affairs with alcohol. He was still a handsome man with blond hair. He was a little on the pudgy side. He had developed an intense addiction to the Internet. He had a small office at the law firm where he did work, both legal and questionable, for the partners and work for me as part of my retainer.

"How are you?" I asked.

"All the parts still seem to be connected," he said. "I'm filled with iced green tea and staying busy. What can I do for you?"

I told him. Part of what I asked him to do was to confirm something I'd already found out. The other part was something new. He said he would call me back, probably in less than half an hour.

"Oh, Tycinker says he's been trying to reach you."

"I know why," I said. "Talk to you later." I had papers to serve on Mickey Donophin and one day to serve them. There was no point in calling Tycinker and telling him my troubles. He wouldn't want to hear them. If I backed out, I'd have to turn the papers over to Dick Provner at the Freewell Agency and Tycinker would be less inclined to use me the next time he needed papers served, and less inclined to continue our arrangement, which included the services of Harvey the Hacker.

I took my wallet, keys, notebook, and pen out of my wet pants pocket, picked up the pile of soggy clothes, and dumped them in a white plastic garbage bag from the box Ames had placed in one of the bottom drawers of my desk. I put my red, mud-covered shoes in a corner. I'd deal with them later.

The rain had stopped. The sun was out. The phone started to ring. I let it. Then I heard Hoffmann's voice on the answering machine saying, "Fonesca, if you're there, pick up."

I picked up the phone and said, "I'm here."

"Turn off the answering machine," he said.

I turned it off.

"It's off?"

"It's off," I said.

"I don't trust you," he said.

"I'm not asking you to," I said. "You called me."

"I have a business offer," he said. "You've been bothering Dr. Obermeyer. He has a weak heart. I think he may have gone to the police. I can convince him to withdraw any complaints he may have made."

He definitely sounded much different from the fun-loving baseball collectable man who had threatened to beat my head in with a bat and may have just taken three shots at me. He sounded different from the man in the Double Tiger Productions T-shirt who had offered me ten thousand dollars to spend a weekend in New Orleans. He sounded like a kinder, gentler, and maybe more nervous Kevin Hoffmann.

"Another business offer," I said.

"Consultation on security for me and my business interests," he said.

"Consultation?"

"Much of my work is confidential," he said. "There's a lot of industrial espionage, corporate espionage, particularly in the land business. You'd advise me on how to deal with it."

"I'm a process server," I said.

"I think you'd be perfect for the job," Hoffmann said. "Twenty thousand dollars as a signing bonus, payable this afternoon. Four thousand dollars a month. I can have contracts ready this afternoon."

"This afternoon," I repeated.

"There is one condition," Hoffmann said. "Standard clause. Nondisclosure. You can't talk to anyone about my business or private transactions."

"Retroactive?"

"Of course," he said nervously.

I sat in my desk chair and pretended I was thinking.

"I don't think so," I finally said.

"Five thousand," Hoffmann said, a touch of desperation in his voice. "Twenty-five thousand up front. Two-year, no, three-year guaranteed contract."

"So, you'd give me four thousand dollars a month," I said. "In exchange for which I would do . . ."

"Nothing. And say nothing," he added.

"If the offer's still open after the commission meeting, I'll think about it, Mr. Dutcher," I said.

This time the pause was his and even longer than mine had been.

"We've got to talk," he said.

"Fine," I said. "I'll come out to your place with a couple of my friends. They'll take William Trasker out of your house and then you and I will talk."

"That won't happen," he said.

"Then we don't have anything to talk about," I said.

I hung up the phone. I got up and picked up the white plastic

Stuart M. Kaminsky

bag filled with my dirty clothes. I added a few items that were on the floor of my room. The phone rang. I answered. It was Hoffmann again.

"Fonesca, I didn't kill Roberta Trasker."

"And you didn't try to kill me?"

"You? What the hell are you talking about?"

"I've got to get to the Laundromat," I said, and hung up again.

I called Kenneth Severtson's office. His secretary put me through to him.

"Severtson, are we still on for tomorrow at ten at the First Watch on Main?"

"Yes," he said.

"Are you back with your wife?"

"We're talking about it."

"Have her with you," I said. "Tell her I said it was important."

"Fonesca," he said with what may have been a sob. "You don't know how grateful I am to you for all you've done. I'm bringing a bonus tomorrow morning. I want you to take it without arguing."

Someone else was offering me money. I was about to say no when I changed my mind.

"Make it cash," I said. "I know someone who can use it."

"Cash," he said. "Ten o'clock."

"Stay dry," I said.

"I will," he answered.

We both hung up.

I was out the door with my plastic bag full of laundry when I heard the phone ringing again. I kept walking.

The rain had stopped.

12

THE LAUNDROMAT WAS on Bahia Vista just east of Tamiami Trail. I got my load in, inserted detergent and quarters, and went to Leon's kosher deli a few doors down for a kosher corned-beef and chopped-liver sandwich. I got a Diet Coke from the machine in the Laundromat and sat listening to the washers and dryers while I ate and thought.

There were other customers, running washers and dryers, folding clothes and putting them in baskets, talking to each other, reading old magazines, telling their kids to "stay away from there," or simply watching the circular windows beyond which shirts, underwear, pants, and socks spun in a kaleidoscope of ever-changing patterns. I was one of the dryer watchers.

I ate and thought.

A thin, tired-looking woman in a sacklike navy blue dress with little yellow flowers was at the machines next to mine. She had a little girl with her, about five, who looked like a miniature version of her mother. The little girl was clutching something that looked like a one-eyed green monster.

The mother took her load of laundry out of a once-white laundry bag with a few small tears in it, threw the laundry in the washing machine, and added the bag. She poured some All into the machine and then fished into her pocket. She came up with a handful of quarters and counted them carefully.

The little girl was looking at my sandwich now.

The mother saw her looking at my sandwich and told the kid she shouldn't stare at people.

My sandwich had been cut in half. I had half a sandwich left.

"Does she like corned beef and chopped liver?" I asked the mother, who looked at me while she fed quarters into the machine.

"She's never had 'em," the woman said. "I don't think I have either."

"Can I give her half a sandwich? I can't finish mine."

The woman looked at her daughter and then at me, trying to decide if I was trying to pick her up, was a pervert, or might even be among those few who wanted nothing more than to be nice to a hungry kid.

I guess I looked harmless.

"I suppose," the woman said, pushing the coins in and starting the machine.

I handed the half sandwich and a napkin to the little girl, who shifted the one-eyed monster under her arm. The monster's large single eye lit up.

"What do you say, baby?" the woman asked.

"Thank you, mister," the girl said.

I didn't want conversation, but the haggard woman seemed to feel that she now owed me at least a few words.

"I see you in here before?" she asked, dropping onto an uncomfortable plastic chair.

"Maybe," I said.

She closed her eyes.

"Want to hear some jokes?" I asked.

"You a comedian?" she asked with suspicion. "Like over at McCurdy's, the comedy place?"

"I'm working on an act," I said.

The first joke went flat but she smiled politely. She gave a bigger smile with the second and a real laugh, albeit a small one, with the third. She was shaking her head and smiling when I told the fourth joke, and I decided to stop while I was ahead.

"You have a funny way of telling a joke," she said. "Like it's not a joke."

I wasn't sure whether or not it was a compliment so I said nothing. The little girl was working slowly on the sandwich and my clothes were still washing.

"My name's Dreamer," she said, holding out her right hand. "Francie Dreamer."

"Any relation to Bubbles?" I asked.

"You know Bubbles?" she asked. "She's my mom."

"My name's Fonesca. Your mother punched me in the face about five months ago when I tried to serve some papers on her. I'm a process server."

"The divorce?" she asked.

"Yes," I said, as my washing machine stopped spinning. "How is she?"

"Still in the mobile home," said Francie. "She's better off. You did her a favor."

I wasn't sure how, but I nodded.

"Small town," she said, as I tugged my clothes out of the washer and chucked them in the dryer.

"Sometimes," I said.

I had moved my clothes from the washer to the dryer and was just closing the door when the circular window exploded, spraying me with glass. I had a vision of Shaquille O'Neal hanging on the rim and shattering the backboard.

I turned to Francie, who was looking at me with wide open eyes. Her little girl stood startled, mouth partly open, cheek stuffed with sandwich.

"On the floor," I shouted, as I grabbed Francie and the girl and pushed them down as the second shot came and screeched over the top of the Formica table above me.

People were screaming now, screaming, running, diving. I could have used Ames. I lay there on top of Francie and her little girl. No more shots. Lots of crying and screaming.

I got up slowly and found myself facing an Asian woman with her hands to her cheeks.

"Did you see the shooter?" I asked.

Her mouth was wide open and she nodded yes.

"Where?" I asked.

She pointed toward the back door of Laundromat.

Something filled me, something I hadn't felt in a long time, so long that I wasn't sure I recognized it at first. I moved toward the rear of the Laundromat toward the partially open rear door. I was angry. I was shaking. It hadn't been like this when I was shot at Midnight Pass, but this time the shooter had come close to hitting the woman called Francie and maybe even the little girl.

There was no one in the alleyway behind the Laundromat. There was a parking lot about half full of cars. At the rear of the parking lot was The Melting Pot, a fondue restaurant. There were no people around. I ran a few feet toward my right, where there was a driveway to Bahia Vista, and then I realized that I was chasing someone with a gun who wanted to kill me and that I had no gun of my own.

I went back into the Laundromat.

"I called the police," a lumpy man with thick white hair called out.

"What did he look like?" I asked the Asian woman.

She shook her head, shocked.

"A man, right?"

She shook her head yes.

"You'd recognize him again if you saw him?"

"No," she said. "I just saw the long metal part and a head behind it with some kind of hat. Then I—"

"He was white?"

She shook her head yes.

Francie was sitting on the floor with the little girl on her lap. The kid was still clutching her monster and eating her sandwich.

"You all right?" I asked.

"Yes," Francie said. "How many people did he . . . ?"

"No one," I said. "He was only after me."

"Why does he want to kill you?" she asked.

"It's a long story," I said, looking at the little girl and asking, "What's your name?"

"Alaska," she said. "Alaska Dreamer."

The girl took another bite of sandwich.

"Pretty name," I said.

"My mom's name. Dreamer. My grandmom's too. Not my dad's. He's in Carserated."

Francie put an arm around her daughter, who smiled up at her, cheeks full of corned beef and chopped liver.

A police siren outside, coming fast. I looked at my laundry and decided to just forget it. My maternal grandmother would have said it was cursed. It had been with me both times I'd been shot at today. It was covered in shards of glass and the promise of a bad memory.

Some people had fled the Laundromat. One solitary man had gone back to smoking his cigar and waiting for his load to dry.

Stuart M. Kaminsky

Then there were two uniformed policemen with rifles in their hands at front of the Laundromat and another two at the back.

"Hands, showing, up," called one of the cops at the front door.

We showed our hands.

"Doesn't look like a hostage situation," the cop who had shouted said to his partner. "Anyone hurt?"

There was a mixed chorus of no's.

The cops came in slowly, carefully looking for places a raging maniac might hide.

Alaska was almost finished with the sandwich now, but she didn't stop eating. Her eyes moved between the two pairs of armed cops.

"Don't be afraid," Francie said softly to the girl.

"It's like television," Alaska said.

"Yes," her mother said. "It's like television."

About ten minutes later I was seated in the office of Detective Etienne Viviase.

"We know one of two things about this guy," Viviase said. "Either he can't shoot worth a shit or he's trying to scare you out of Sarasota County."

"Looks that way," I said.

"Hoffmann?"

"He tried to bribe me twice to get me to stop trying to get Trasker out of his house."

"He's trying to kill you because of Trasker?"

"Maybe."

"And he killed Roberta Trasker to keep her from helping you get her husband out of his house?"

"Him or his man Stanley."

"Just to get the Pass open?"

"Big money involved, remember?" I said.

"Big enough to murder? Doesn't sound like Hoffmann. You might want to get out of town for a while."

"If it's Hoffmann, I'll be safe when the vote is over tonight," I said.

"Any suggestions?" he asked, sitting back.

"Doc Obermeyer. But you'll have to get to him fast. Tomorrow will be too late. The vote will be over."

"There's one other way we can go," Viviase said. "Roberta Trasker's dead, but if we can find William Trasker's next of kin and get him or her to—"

"Power of attorney," I said.

"I'll see what I can do," Viviase said with a sigh.

"Can I go now?"

"With God," he said. "You do that statement about your talk with Obermeyer?"

I went into my pocket and came up with a folded trio of lined yellow sheets of paper. I handed the packet to Viviase, who took it with a look of resignation. He opened the folded sheets and looked at them.

"At least I can read your writing," he said. "I'll have it typed up for you to sign. Wait outside."

I got up and went into the hallway. Viviase moved past me with my report. There was a low wooden bench. I sat as far from the other person on the bench as I could.

It was somewhere over ninety degrees outside and about eighty inside the hall. The man at the end of the bench was wearing a heavy winter coat. He was smiling, a kind of goofy, pleased smile. He looked a little like my Uncle Benny when he was fifty: dark, too much hair, not enough chin, but plenty of nose.

I looked at the wall. There was a photograph of a policeman in dress uniform. The photograph was old. I fixed my eyes on it.

"It's my birthday," the guy at the other end of the bench said.

"Congratulations," I answered, still looking at the cop in the picture.

"Had a big birthday lunch at the Cuban place farther down on Main."

I nodded.

"I've had a birthday lunch at a different foreign restaurant every year for the last five years," he said with an air of accomplishment. "Greek, Italian, Jewish, Chinese. This year was Cuban."

"Yeah?" I said, feeling I had to say something.

"Yeah. I go alone. My family's back in Holland, Michigan," he said. "I used to fix clocks there. Holland, Michigan. They have a big tulip festival in Holland every year."

"I've heard," I said.

"I'm a witness," he said. "Murder. Man got shot in the Cuban restaurant two booths away from me. I was eating my refried beans. There was just me and these two guys and one shot the other one and got up and walked out."

I looked at him, trying to decide if he had seen a murder or had simply wandered into police headquarters, plopped on the bench, and started telling a story to the first person who would listen to him. I didn't say anything.

"Didn't get a good look," he said. "Guy just goes *bloughy* with the gun. *Bloughy*, you know. Twice. Gets up and goes. But I heard the other guy, the guy he shot, say his name. That's why I'm sitting here. I'm trying to remember the name. I'm good with faces, not with names."

He had slid toward me on the bench. I was already sitting on the end.

"Carnahan," he said.

"Nice to meet you," I said, without giving my name.

"No, I think the name of the guy was Carnahan. That's it. Carnahan. Or maybe it was Wisnant."

"I can see how you'd get the two confused," I said.

"No, it was something more like Pergamont," he said. "That's why I'm sitting here, trying to remember. They should have asked me what the guy looked like, the killer. I'm good with faces. Just saw him for a second, but that's enough. I used to fix watches."

"You said."

"Moncreiff," said the man.

"The name of the shooter?"

"No, my name. Simon Moncreiff."

He held out his hand. I took it.

"You told the police that you only saw the shooter for a second."

"Less than a second," he said, hands deep in his pockets, thinking. "You think it would help if I went through the alphabet?"

"Can't hurt," I said. "Give you something to do."

"It won't work," he said. "Terrible with names. Good with faces, people."

"What did the guy look like?" I asked, looking down the hall for Viviase.

"The dead guy?"

"The killer."

"Five-foot-seven or seven and a half, one hundred and sixty or sixty-five pounds, blue suit with a dark stain that looked like the State of Tennessee on the left lapel. Light skin with a little blue mole on his neck, right side. Green eyes. Good teeth except for a lower one on the right. Chipped. Looks a little like a volcano with the top missing. Good wristwatch. Rolex, about five years old. On his right wrist. Means he's left-handed, which was

Stuart M. Kaminsky

the hand he had the gun in. Ring, real gold on his wedding finger, initials J.G. etched on it. Little scar, hardly see it, just under his right nostril, right here."

He pointed under his nose.

"Shoes?"

"Armani, black," he said.

"You tell this to the police?" I asked.

"No," he said. "They asked me what I saw of the shooter and I said I just saw him for a part of a second maybe. Than they got all interested in my hearing his name."

Viviase was coming back now. He handed the statement and a pen to me and looked at Moncreiff while I signed.

"Come up with a name yet?" he asked.

"Might have been Kooperman," the man in the overcoat tried. "Or Salter."

I handed the statement back to Viviase and said, "You might want to ask Mr. Moncreiff what the killer looked like," I said.

"I didn't get a very good look," Moncreiff said.

I got up.

"Ask him," I repeated, and started toward the stairway.

Behind me I could hear Viviase ask patiently, "What did the killer look like?"

I started down the stairs and heard Moncreiff begin with, "Five-foot-seven or seven and a half . . ."

I went back to my office. There was a call waiting from Harvey the Hacker. One of the things he told me almost certainly ended Viviase's plan to get Trasker legally out of Hoffmann's house. The other thing he told me confirmed what I had pretty much figured out about who had been taking shots at me.

I called Ames at the Texas Bar and Grill and told him about the Laundromat.

"Can you ride shotgun for me for a few days?" I asked.

"No problem," he said. "Be right over."

"I'll pick you up."

Ames was waiting outside when I got there. The sky was still overcast, but it wasn't raining and he didn't need his slicker for anything other than covering his shotgun.

He climbed in and sat back. I had brushed off the front seat as much as I could, but I'd still have to answer to Fred and Alan. Ames didn't ask where we were going, which was just as well because it was probable we were headed for the two places Detective Etienne Viviase most wanted me to stay away from.

Stop number one was less than five minutes away, the office of Dr. Obermeyer. This time there were two patients waiting in the reception room, an ancient, little, bent-over woman who tilted her head upward and glared at an equally old man directly across from her, who met her glare for glare.

Neither of them looked up at us when we entered.

Carla the receptionist, hair eater, however, did. Her glare was even better than the old couple.

"I'm calling the police," she said.

"First give Dr. Obermeyer a name," I said. "I don't think he'll want the police coming to talk about it and I don't think he'll be happy with you if you call the police before you give him the name."

She hesitated.

"I'm sorry if I got you in trouble the last time I was here," I said. "You've got your job and you were just trying your best to do it."

She picked up the phone and pushed a button.

"That man with the baseball hat is back," she said. "With another man. He says I should give you a name."

She looked up at me.

"Dutcher," I said.

"Dutcher," she said into the telephone. "Yes."

She hung up.

"He'll be with you in a minute," she said.

I sat. Ames stood. It was less awkward to stand when you had a shotgun in your jacket. We watched the old couple glare at each other across the room for just about a minute. Then the door to Obermeyer's office opened and a well-dressed, slender woman came out. She was probably in her late forties. She was certainly not happy.

"The tests results will be back in three days," Obermeyer said, gently touching the woman's shoulder. "I'll call you immediately. I don't think there's anything to be concerned about. We just want to be careful."

The woman glanced at Ames and me as she went out the door, and Obermeyer said, "Mr. and Mrs. Spoznik, I'll be with you in just a moment."

The glaring couple gave him no sign that he had penetrated their concentration.

Obermeyer nodded at Ames and me and we followed him into his office. He moved behind his desk, a barrier from patients and intruders like me. Ames sat in one chair, right leg not quite bent, and I sat in the other.

"You mentioned a name," Obermeyer said.

"Dutcher," I said. "You know it, don't you?"

"I'm not sure," he said.

"Kevin Hoffmann's real name is Dutcher, Alvin York Dutcher," I said.

"So?" he asked.

"He had a sister, Claire Dutcher," I said.

"Interesting," he said. "But—"

"Fraud, murder," I said. "And you're a party to it."

"Wait," Obermeyer said, quickly standing. "I had nothing to do with any fraud, any murder."

"William Trasker's not too sick to me moved, is he?" I asked.

"In my opinion . . ." Obermeyer began, reverting to his role as confident physician.

"It's all going to come apart in the next few days," I said. "You'll go down with it."

Obermeyer sat down again.

"William Trasker *is* a very sick man," he said. "I've kept him comfortable and sedated. He is dying."

"But if he wasn't sedated," I said, "could he get up, walk, talk?"

"How long has he got, Doc?" Ames asked.

Obermeyer looked at Ames with surprise.

"That's difficult to determine," the doctor said. "As I told Mr. Fonesca, probably a few days."

"If a group of cancer experts looked at him," I said, "what would they say?"

Obermeyer sunk back.

"I don't know," he said with a sigh.

"He can function, move, make decisions?" I asked.

Obermeyer nodded and said, "I told you, he is heavily sedated."

"And you'll tell that to the police?"

"No," he said. "I'll tell the police that I think that Mr. Trasker is in no condition to make decisions for himself, that it should be left to his next of kin, whoever has power of attorney."

"And we both know who that is," I said.

Obermeyer said nothing. I got up. So did Ames.

"There's a small town in North Dakota," Obermeyer said, almost to himself. "No more than six thousand people in the entire county. That's where I came from. They need a doctor. I think I'll go back there. It's simply not worth all this."

He looked up at me as if he needed my permission.

"Sounds like a good idea," I said. "And I won't try to stop you if . . ."

"If what?" Obermeyer said hopefully.

"Is there anything I can give Trasker that would bring him back, anything fast?"

"You want him conscious and functioning?"

"I want him conscious and functioning."

"Yes," he said. "I've got samples."

He got up and we followed him through a door to an examining room with a locked glass cabinet. He opened the cabinet with a key on the ring in his pocket and took out an amber pill bottle.

"Take the bottle," he said. "Three of these with water will work. But no more than three."

"How fast?" I asked.

"Imagine forty cups of coffee in one gulp," he said.

Ames and I left him standing next to his examining table. In the outer office we passed the glaring couple. They seemed to be going for the *Guinness World Records*.

The clouds had thinned out now. I turned on 930 on the radio and listened to Neil Bortz while I drove down the trail. Fifteen minutes later we were at the gate to Kevin Hoffmann's estate.

We got out and I pushed the button on the stone wall. No one answered. I pushed the button again. This time Stanley came out of the house, adjusted his glasses, and walked down the path to face us through the fence.

"Fonesca," he said. "I've made some calls about you. There are people who think you're not very interested in living."

"LaPrince," I said. "There are people in Louisiana who remember you."

He paused and shook his head.

"You sure you want to go that way?" he asked, looking at Ames with amusement.

"Tell Hoffmann we're here," I said.

"Suit yourself," Stanley said with a shrug, and went back to the house, leaving the door open behind him. There was a click and the gate opened.

Ames and I went up the cobbled path and through the door. Kevin Hoffmann stood just inside the door. There were no lights on. He stood in a patch of sun that came from a window on his right.

He was wearing white designer jeans, a black silk shirt, and a two-day growth of gray stubble. He did not look good. He was in no mood for New York Yankees attire.

"Dutcher," I said.

Stanley stood back to Hoffmann's left, facing Ames, who stood facing Stanley. Stanley's right hand was in his pocket. The pocket looked heavy.

"That is the name I was born with," Hoffmann said. "How does that change things?"

"Alvin York Dutcher," I said.

"My parents were very patriotic," he said. "My father loved this country, loved Lindbergh, Sergeant York, Franklin Roosevelt, Enos Slaughter, and anything about baseball. Are you here to accept my offer?"

Kevin Hoffmann was smiling, but the smile had the hint of a twitch and his words a touch of nervous amusement.

"Your sister love baseball too?"

The smile was gone now.

"My sister's dead," he said.

"I know. She was shot two days ago. Claire Elizabeth Dutcher, who changed her name to Claire Collins when she became an actress, who changed her name to Roberta Trasker when she married the man lying upstairs."

"Yes," said Hoffmann. "Bill is my brother-in-law. And I have power of attorney. Which, according to my lawyer, means that since he is unable to make decisions on his own because of his illness, I can make all decisions for him."

"Your sister leave a will?" I asked.

"A . . . I'm sure she . . . You think I killed Claire for Bill's money?"

"It's a possibility," I said.

"Bill and Claire have children, grandchildren," he said. "It's none of your business but I loved my sister."

"Who died before I could convince her to get her husband out of here so he could vote on the Midnight Pass issue, which will make you even richer than you are."

"Time to leave, Fonesca," he said, taking a step forward.

"Going to make quite a story on television and in the newspapers," I said. "Ann Rule might even come back here and write a book about this."

"Stanley," he said, and Stanley stepped forward.

Stanley and Ames were a few feet apart now, an amused smile on Stanley's lips, nothing showing on Ames's face.

"Let's go," I said.

Hoffmann turned and walked back into the shadows. Stanley opened the door for us and the three of us marched quietly down the paved driveway while the gate swung open.

Ames and I stepped out.

" 'The meanest thrives the most, where dignity, true personal dignity, abideth not,' " Stanley said through the bars of the gate. He was smiling. " 'A light and cruel world, cut off from all the natural inlets of just sentiment, from lowly sympathy, and chastening truth, where good and evil never have that name.' Wordsworth."

He turned and started back toward the house.

"That's a pair of crazy men," Ames said.

"Or something like it," I said, getting in the car.

Ames got in the passenger seat and buckled up.

"So, what do we do?"

"We find a way to get William Trasker out of there before the commission meeting tonight," I said, shifting into drive and stepping on the gas.

13

THERE IS ENOUGH ROOM in Heaven for every God-loving Christian and all the saints that have been or ever will be," said Reverend Fernando Wilkens from the pulpit of the Fourth Baptist Church on Tenth Street just off of Orange. "God's Heaven and bounty show no bounds."

The walls were brick painted white, with stained-glass windows along both sides of the room depicting stations of the cross.

Directly in front of the pulpit, a simple wooden casket with bronze handles rested on what looked like two sawhorses covered in dark blue velvet.

Ames and I, hats in hand, stood in the back of the air-conditioned church, nearly filled with black men and women and a small sprinkling of whites. I guessed about one hundred fifty people sat listening to the hum of the air conditioner and the deep, confident voice of Reverend Wilkens, dressed in a dark suit and somber tie, his hands on the pulpit, his eyes seeking those below him. Those eyes had met mine when Ames and I entered, but the meeting had only been fleeting.

"Notice," Wilkens said, holding up his right hand. "I said 'God-loving', not 'God-fearing,' for the good need never fear God. The problem is that we never think we are good enough. Beware the man or woman who thinks he or she is good enough to enter Heaven. That is self-righteous vanity. We strive to do good. We know the words and commandments of the Lord. We know which we have disobeyed and which we have violated. We know, in fact, my friends, what the right thing to do is. We know that when we transgress we can always ask for forgiveness. We know our Lord is willing to forgive those who truly repent. I said 'truly' for the Lord can look into your heart. Your idea of true repentance may be that you are sorry for what you did because it means you won't be getting into Heaven. No, the only sorry that counts is when you wish you had not hurt another human being. We can but hope and follow the path of righteousness which is in our hearts and souls."

A woman in the audience said, "Amen."

"And there is always a price to pay for our sins," Wilkens went on. "A stab of pain in our conscience for the small indiscretion, a jab of ice to our heart for the large ones."

"And I know it to be true," came the woman's voice again.

"We are here," Wilkens said, and looked around the gathering in the seats before him. "We are here to bid farewell to the soul of Joseph Lawrence Hopkins. His body we will bury, but his soul has or soon will be taken by the hand of an angel, and may that angel lead him to the land of eternal glory. And to that we say amen."

The congregation, including Ames and me, said, "Amen."

Wilkens eyes met mine now and held fast. A few heads turned to see what or who the reverend was looking at.

　　　　　　　　　　Stuart M. Kaminsky

"Grief is the price we pay for loving and losing," he said. "Grief is a holy gift which we hold tenderly and then let free. Grief must find its way into our very souls and let us go on living, performing God's will, making us better human beings for its sake."

His eyes left mine and turned down to the casket.

"I'm not going to lie to you," he said. "Have you ever known me to lie to you?"

"No," came the chorus of answers.

"I would be a liar and a hypocrite if I were to tell you Joseph Lawrence Hopkins was a good man. He was, at the age of sixteen, not even a man at all. His was and is a troubled soul, one that made his good mother Marie weep. But he was also a troubled soul who clearly cared for his two sisters and regretted the pain he caused his mother."

Wilkens lifted both hands, palms up.

"The Lord will weigh the good and the bad, the right and the wrong, the body and soul."

The right hand moved down slowly and then the left and then both hands came up with the palms of the Reverend Fernando Wilkens facing the congregation.

"And the Lord will do what is best. Let us all rise and sing 'Faith of Our Fathers,' and as those chosen carefully carry the casket to the waiting hearse, follow them, continuing our song. We will meet at the graveside for internment. Let us rise."

Everyone rose with a minimum of shuffling as six men, four young and two past the age of fifty, all but one black, came forward and lifted the casket.

Ames and I moved out of the way. The bearers bore their burden through the door, with people following them and singing.

We stood waiting for the crowd to clear the church. Wilkens remained at the pulpit.

"Life is filled with contradictions and enigmas," Wilkens said, his voice now echoing in the empty hall. "That boy died of a heart attack during a basketball game. The temperature in that gym was almost one hundred degrees. There wasn't enough money to fix the air-conditioning and he quite literally played his heart out to avoid the temptation of drugs. You have something to tell me about William Trasker?"

"I'm not sure this is the right place to tell it," I said, looking around.

Wilkens followed my eyes to a stained-glass image of Christ on his knees with the cross on his shoulder.

"There is nothing that cannot be said here," Wilkens said. "He would hear us even in a steel tomb. In spite of what you may think or the newspapers may suggest, I am not a hypocrite. I believe in my God and I will do what I feel I must to carry out His wishes."

I told him about the incidents at Midnight Pass and the Laundromat. I told him about Obermeyer, Stanley, and Hoffmann. I told him Hoffmann was Roberta Trasker's brother. I told him that I was going to try to get William Trasker to that commission meeting tonight if he were alive, willing, and able.

Wilkens nodded and got out from behind the pulpit. He stood before us now and looked at Ames, me, and at a stained-glass Christ on a stained-glass cross.

"I've got a small, well-educated, and sometimes angry group of parishioners who want to change these windows," he said. "They don't want a white savior. They claim that Christ was not white but a Jew, a dark Semite, a very dark Semite, certainly not the golden-tressed young man with the well-trimmed beard and sad eyes whose image surrounds us."

He had a point to make. I had time to listen.

"And they are probably right and I probably agree, but to change the probably fictional image of the Savior would be seen

Stuart M. Kaminsky

as an alienating challenge to other Christians, both white and black."

"So you can live with it," I said.

"Are you a Christian, Mr. Fonesca? I believe you told me you were raised as an Episcopalian."

"I was. I'm not anything now."

I was going to add that I wasn't planning on changing until God appeared before me or sent an emissary with a convincing explanation for what had happened to my wife and my life.

"You're a man in torment," Wilkens said. "Bringing William Trasker to the commission table to do something decent will ease your torment, if only a little."

I said nothing.

"And you?" he asked Ames.

"Methodist till I die," said Ames. "And I don't care what color you make the good Lord out of pieces of glass. He is what he is."

"I've got to get to the cemetery," Wilkens said.

Wilkens touched my shoulder and Ames's as he passed us and left the church, closing the doors behind him. I hadn't told him that what I planned to do was illegal. I didn't think he'd want to know. I wondered what he thought someone should do when the law and God didn't agree.

Ames and I stood alone in the church.

"Methodist pie," he said, looking around the room. "Think I'll go to church Sunday."

I drove Ames back to the Texas Bar and Grill and told him what I wanted him to do.

"What I need is someone who knows how to get into a house, a big house with walls and a couple of men inside who have guns."

I didn't have to tell Ames which house.

He said he would see what he could do, told me to take care

of myself, and got out of the car. When he opened the door, I smelled grilling beef and onions. I was hungry.

I went into the Texas, had the grande bowl of Ed's Authentic Juarez Chili with crackers and a beer, felt a little better, and went back into the daylight after Ames, who had joined me for both the chili and beer, said, "Sure you don't want me to stay with you?"

"I'll be fine," I said.

"Watch your track and your back and don't go back home till we get this taken care of."

"I won't," I said. "I'll be back in a few hours."

Mickey's Collectibles was about half a mile south of Clark on Macintosh in a mall of five stores. One of the stores sold plumbing supplies "wholesale to the public." A second store dealt in Sperdoni Herbal Products, which, according to the signs in the window, "strengthened the immune system" and provided good carbohydrates instead of evil ones.

Mickey's was in the middle. On the other side of him was a store for rent and the last store was the Welcome Auto Insurance Agency.

There were five cars parked in front of the shops. One was directly in front of Mickey's. I pulled in, got out, and paused to look at Mickey's window.

It was cluttered but neat. *Star Wars* figures, cups and glasses with pictures of Tweety, Minnie Mouse, the Cisco Kid and Pancho, the Creature from the Black Lagoon, and John Wayne were lined up neatly next to each other. Comic books were neatly overlapped like an open hand of cards, just enough so you could make out enough of the covers to know what they were: *Famous Funnies, Daredevil, Submariner, Sad Sack, Justice League of America.*

Stuart M. Kaminsky

I went in. Shelves on both sides filled with cereal boxes, *X-Men* figures, tin lunch boxes, and a whole shelf of Betty Boop items—Betty Boop at a piano with her dog on top, Betty Boop sitting on a Coke machine, a fully gowned Betty Boop in a black-and-white dress with a white corsage inside a box marked "Collectable Fashion Doll."

A chunky man in his late twenties or early thirties sat on a stool behind the glass counter. His hair needed combing. He wore a blue T-shirt with the Superman insignia in the middle.

"Can I help you?" he asked. "Looking for anything special?"

"Nice place," I said.

He gave a tiny shake of his head.

"Nice place, maybe. Bad location. I don't have the money to advertise and I'm not downtown on Main Street or in some big mall where I'd get walk-in trade. And I'm not near a school where kids could drop in."

"Why not move?" I asked.

A shrug this time.

"Can't afford to," he said. "Can't stay. Can't move. I've got a few good customers, but not enough and I don't have the cash to buy much at the flea markets. Vicious circle."

"Cycle," I corrected. "Vicious cycle."

"Yeah," he said. "You interested in early television? I've got a Howdy Doody puppet in perfect shape, in the box, 1950. I'd let it go for two hundred."

"I'm not a Howdy Doody guy," I said. "You Michael Donophin?"

"Mickey," he said warily. "Legal name is Mickey."

I took the folded papers out of my pocket and handed them to him. He took them without a word and placed them on the counter next to a tiny figure of Emmett Kelly sitting on a white ball with a gold star.

"Used to have a lot of circus stuff," he said, ignoring the

papers I had served. "Still have some. Mostly got it from old circus performers who still live around here. My big day was just about a year ago when a lady, no more than this big . . ."

He put his hand out about three feet above the floor to show me how small she had been.

"This lady, real old," he said, brightening just a bit at the memory, "bought all the circus stuff I had. Everything. Three thousand dollars even, no bargaining. Asked her if she'd been in the circus. Said she had but she didn't want to talk about it. I put everything in boxes real careful and got it in her car. Never heard from her again."

"Why the papers?"

"Foreclosure," he said. "I'm fighting it. I'm gonna lose. The Donophins always lose. The Donophins always come back. Don't know anyone who might want to buy me out fast and cheap do you?"

"No," I said.

"That's okay. I guess I shouldn't fight it. I guess I should just pack everything up, put it in my father's garage, and get a job at Winn-Dixie. That's where my father works."

There was a large round bowl of assorted buttons, mostly political, on the counter. I touched a red, white, and blue one with a young Teddy Kennedy's photograph on it with the words "Kennedy for President" in black letters.

"You might try the Internet," I said. "Get a Web site. Sell out of your father's garage. There's even something called eBay."

"Maybe," Mickey said with no great interest. "I like talking to people. It's not just the selling. It's the talking about, you know?"

"Yes."

"Say, you like old music? I mean like really old? I've got old seventy-eights, some of them one-sided, good condition, even got an old Victrola I could let go cheap. Works fine. I've got Paul

Stuart M. Kaminsky

Whiteman, Eddie Condon, Bing Crosby, Tony Martin, Sophie Tucker. Couple of hundred maybe. Want to take a look?"

"I'm trying to get away from the past," I said.

"And I'm trying to keep it alive," he said, looking around his shop. "You know all this stuff is important to people. The way I see it there're two different histories. There's the one we learn in school, the Magna Carta, the Crusades, the Civil War, George Washington, you know?"

"I know," I said.

"I was never good at that stuff. But there's another history, more important," Mickey said, excited now. "There's the history of each of our own lives, filled with little stuff that stays with us, you know? Like watching *Leave It to Beaver* with your older brother. Remember when the Beaver got stuck in that giant coffee cup?"

I did remember, but I didn't have to tell Mickey. He didn't really need an answer.

"That's our lives. That's Nostalgia with a big 'N,'" he said. "Comic books, movies, television, Mickey Mantle, Frankie Avalon, mom baking fish every Friday night, and my Uncle Walt always coming over for it wearing a tie."

"Nostalgia," I said.

"The history of each of our lives," said Mickey.

"You're a philosopher, Mickey," I said

"Take a button. On the house," he said, nodding at the bowl between us.

I went through the buttons and found one I wanted. Then I bought more items Mickey Donophin was happy to show me.

I left Mickey carrying a large, full paper bag and headed for Flo's house. It was after four.

Adele answered the door, baby in her arms, smile on her face. Adele had lost all of her baby fat but not the memory of what she had been through. Adele was tough. Mother murdered by her father. Father who molested her and sold her to a pimp, also murdered, betrayed and made pregnant by a man she trusted. And there was Adele, pretty, blond, baby in her arms, smiling.

"Lew," she said. "Come in."

I followed her inside and closed the door.

"Just finished feeding Catherine," she said, holding up the baby named for my wife. "Want to hold her?"

It was less a question than an order. I put down the bag I had brought in and she handed me the baby.

"Diet Dr Pepper all right?" Adele asked.

"Sure," I said, moving into the living room with the baby in my arms.

Catherine looked up at my face, eyes wide, scanning, tiny wrinkled fingers fidgeting.

"Burp her," Adele called from the kitchen.

I put the baby on my shoulder and patted her back. Flo had shown me how to do it. It took three pats before I heard the small burp and felt a minute twinge of triumph.

"Flo's out," Adele said. "Got her license back, thanks to you. She's shopping."

She put a coaster and a glass of Diet Dr Pepper with ice on the coffee table in front of me. Then she took the baby.

"School?" I asked.

"Easy," she said, holding the baby to her chest and crossing her legs on the sofa.

I sometimes found it hard to remember that Adele was only sixteen.

"Got something," I said, getting the bag I had brought in and placing it next to my bubbling glass of Dr Pepper.

I fished into the bag and came up with a rattle. It was purple and white plastic. I handed it to Adele, who looked at the picture on it and said, "Who's Clarabelle?"

"A clown," I said. "From an old television show for kids."

"Weird looking, isn't she?"

"Clarabelle was a man," I said.

"That is weird."

"Sorry."

"Sometimes I like weird," she said, placing the handle of the rattle in Catherine's right hand. Small pink fingers clutched it tightly and accidentally shook it. The little pellets inside gently clacked. Catherine's eyes turned toward the rattle.

"Something for you too," I said, going back into the bag.

I handed her the foot-long cylinder. She turned it over in her hand and read the words on the side next to the picture of the rocket ship.

"*Tom, Corbett, Space Cadet?*" she asked.

"Another old television show. It's a kaleidoscope."

"I gotta say you come up with some weird stuff."

She held the kaleidoscope up toward the window, closed one eye, and looked into the small round circle. She twisted it a few times and put it down with a smile.

"I like it," she said. "You are a strange man, Lewis Fonesca. You get something for Flo, too?"

I went back into my bag and came up with a 33⅓ album cover. I showed the cover to her. It was black-and-white with the photograph of a plain-looking man playing a guitar. The only words on it were "Hank Williams."

"Hank Williams?" Adele said.

Catherine shook the rattle again.

"Flo will understand. The record's in perfect condition. I've got to go."

"Coming back later? Flo's bringing back barbecue from that shack she knows on Martin Luther King."

"Not tonight," I said. "I've got to rescue a man from a castle."

"Just another day's work," she said.

"Another day," I said.

"Take care of yourself, Lewis," she said, getting up as I did and moving close to kiss my cheek. "Notice anything?"

"What?"

"My language," she said. "Flo and I have cleaned up together. Take care of yourself."

She smiled and looked at Catherine, who was trying to focus on the rattle.

"How are things really going?" I asked.

"Hard," she said. "I don't really fit in. It's not the baby. I'm just not a kid like the rest of them. I pretend. I get along and everyone knows about Catherine and they're cool with it. See, I can even say words like 'cool' when I remember. But I don't have any real friends but you and Flo. I'm not complaining. That's fine with me, but it's not easy. You understand?"

"What about that boy you were seeing? The one who worked at Burger King?"

"He graduated," she said. "He's at the University of Florida. He calls me when he's back here, but Lew, he's still a boy. Maybe things will be different when I go to college, but that's two years away."

"Where are you thinking of going?"

"Lewis," she said. "I've got a baby. The University of North Carolina isn't going to let me go to classes with a two-year-old. Flo said she'd come with us wherever we went if I wanted her or she'd pay for a nanny."

"You don't have to think about it for a while," I said.

"I do," Adele said, touching the baby's cheek. "You see, for fifteen years I didn't have a future. Now that I've got one, I want to think about it."

And I, I thought, had a future for almost forty years and now had only a past and a present.

"I've got to go," I said.

"Kids to help, bad guys to catch?" she asked.

"Something like that," I said.

"Say, how about you come over Sunday," she said. "We'll grill stuff. Bring Ames, your friend Sally, and her kids. Flo'll love it."

"I'll get back to you," I said.

I had vaguely planned, if I lived to Sunday, to sleep it away. It had been almost two days since I had slept, and Sundays were the hardest days for me. They held more memories than other days.

I was back at the Texas Bar and Grill twenty minutes later.

The Texas was busy. The buffalo and steer heads on the wall looked content. Johnny Cash sang out that he was walking the line and keeping his eyes wide open, and Ames was talking to someone on the telephone at the bar.

"Your lucky day, Lewis," said Ames, as he put the phone down but didn't hang it up. "Got a fella on the phone, Snickers. Got a sweet tooth. Says he broke into the Hoffmann place two years back, doesn't want to talk about it. But he says he'll get you in and out if the price is right."

I put my hand over the mouthpiece of the phone and asked Ames, "How much should I offer him?"

"Snickers owes Ed," Ames said, looking at Ed Fairing, who was leaning over a table across the room and laughing along with two customers. "A couple of hundred if you can get it," said Ames. "But he'll take less. He owes Ed."

"Two hundred," I told Ames.

Ames picked up the phone and said, "Man I was telling you about says two hundred."

Pause. Ames covered the mouthpiece and said, "Two hundred and twelve and the bar bill."

"Two hundred and twelve?"

"Doesn't want it to seem like he comes cheap on the first offer."

"How big is his bar bill?"

Ames asked and put the phone aside again.

"Forty-six dollars and change."

"Deal," I said.

Ames relayed my message and handed me the phone.

"Snickers?"

"It is."

"Meet us across the street from Hoffmann's gate at nine tonight. Don't be late. Cash comes half when you get there, half when we get out."

"Fair," Snickers said. "That's fair. Okay if I pick up a few things when we're inside?"

"No," I said.

"See you at nine," Snickers said, and hung up.

I called Reverend Fernando Wilkens's office and spoke to three people before he came on.

"Yes?" he said hopefully.

"If things go right," I said. "I'll have Trasker at that meeting by ten or a little after. Stall."

"Won't be that hard unless the others know the way Trasker plans to vote. They want him there, too."

"I can have someone call and say Trasker is being held up by a flat tire," I said.

"Not necessary. Just bring him, Fonesca."

"I'm pumping as fast as I can," I said. "One more thing. If this works, I'll need more money for someone who's helping me."

"How much?"

"Two hundred and fifty-eight dollars."

"Done," Wilkens said.

I had Wilkens call the mayor, one-third of the solid three. He patched me in so I could hear the conversation.

The mayor was a woman. She was all business and thought that Democrats were a little lower than University of Florida

Stuart M. Kaminsky

alumni. The mayor was a proud grad of Florida State University. Only the people in Florida and those who followed college football knew that there was a difference.

"Beatrice?" Wilkens said, sounding remarkably sober. "This is Fernando. Just got a call from Bill Trasker. He told me to call you and say he's on his way, but he'll be very late for the meeting. He said to tell you he knows the vote is important and he'll be there if he has to hijack an eighteen-wheeler."

"Why didn't he call me?" she asked suspiciously. "You two are hardly the best of friends."

"Perhaps he couldn't reach you," Wilkens said. "You can ask him tonight. I have to go now."

Wilkens hung up before the mayor could ask any more questions.

I called Sally at her office and asked her if she could meet me for pizza with the kids at Honey Crust in about an hour. First she said she didn't think so. Then she said, "Lewis, I've made a discovery. I'm tired and I can't save the world."

"You knew that already."

"Yes," she said. "I knew it, but somehow I wake up in the morning, providing I've been able to sleep, and manage to convince myself that maybe, just maybe I can keep one kid's raft afloat for another day. Okay. We'll be there in an hour."

"What about the one with the gun?" Ames said when I hung up. "Might take another shot at you."

"Want to come with us for pizza?"

"No, but I can stay outside the place."

"I know who it is, Ames," I said, hoping I sounded more confident than I felt. "I know who shot at me at Midnight Pass and the Laundromat. I don't think they'll take another chance. I'll be fine. A little before nine about fifty yards down from Hoffmann's gate."

He nodded.

"Suit yourself," he said, and started to turn toward the back of the bar.

"Wait," I said, reaching into the bag I was carrying and handing him a small desk clock with a picture of John Wayne on the face. The Duke was wearing a red vest, a battered brown cowboy hat, and over his shoulder, a shotgun not unlike the one Ames liked to hide under his slicker when weaponry was called for.

"Hondo," Ames said, picking up the clock.

"I noticed you didn't have a clock in your room," I said. "This one works on batteries. Even has an alarm."

Ames touched the face of the clock with the long knobby fingers of his right hand and said, "Thank you, Lewis," he said. "I'll set it for eight-thirty."

"One more thing," I said. "Flo's having a barbecue Sunday. Adele said she wanted you to come."

I got along well with Adele, but it was Ames she had bonded with and he with her. They hardly ever said a word to each other when they were together, but it was there.

"Tell me when. I'll be there."

I left.

I drove around for twenty minutes through subdivisions just off of Lockwood Ridge to be sure no one was following me. No one was. I got to Honey Crust a little before Sally and the kids arrived. There was the usual evening crowd and the smell of onions, garlic, and oregano.

Sally sat across from me in the booth. Michael sat next to me. Susan sat next to her mother. We ordered a large deep-dish with onions, pepperoni, and sausage with extra cheese. We got a pitcher of Diet Coke and a large salad to share while we waited.

"You have that statement for me?" Sally asked.

She meant the one she wanted to put in her file about the Severtsons, the one in which I told her what had happened in Orlando.

"Here," I said, pulling it from the paper bag between Michael and me.

"It's all true, right, Lew?" Sally said, taking it.

"What's there is true," I said. "What's there is not all. It's the best I can do right now."

She nodded and placed the folded sheets neatly into her purse.

"What's this?" Michael asked, looking down at the paper bag.

I reached into it and came up with an Elvis Presley statue about five inches high. He was standing on a square black box. Elvis was wearing a black-and-white horizontal shirt and pants. He was holding a guitar. I handed it to Sally.

"There's a button on his back," I said, showing her where it was. "Push it."

She did.

"Someone threw a party at the county jail," Elvis sang. His voice was small and tinny but it was Elvis. That was all he sang.

"Fonesca," she said, looking at it. "Sometimes I worry about you."

"You have enough to worry about. You like it?"

"It's great," she said, leaning over the table to kiss my cheek. "I'll keep it on my desk at work."

"I assume you have something equally nuts for us," said Susan.

"I do," I said, reaching into the bag and pulling out a *Buffy the Vampire Slayer* doll. It was still in the box.

"It's old," she said.

"Susan," Sally warned.

"And it's not Sarah Michelle Gellar," Susan said, looking at the doll's face.

"It's Kristy Swanson," I said. "She was in the movie. She was the first Buffy."

"No way," Susan said.

"Definitely way," said Michael, leaning over to see what there was for him.

It was a piece of thick folded paper. The white was showing. I handed it to Michael and he started to unfold it. When he had it down to the last fold, he stood up and let the poster flop open.

" 'Star Wars: Episode Two,' " he said. "Nice copy."

"It's original," I said. "It's signed by Carrie Fisher."

He turned the poster around and examined the white dress of Princess Leia. There was the signature.

"It's real?" he said.

"It's real," I said.

"Mom," Michael said, folding the poster carefully. "Marry this man."

"He's . . ." Susan started, and looked at her Buffy doll. "I don't know."

"You don't marry people because they buy you things," Sally said.

"It doesn't hurt," Michael said, sitting down, poster in his lap. "And lots of people do marry other people because they give them things."

"But they don't stay happy with just things," Susan said. "Right?"

She was looking at Sally, who was smiling at Elvis.

"Right," Sally said, putting Elvis on the table.

We finished a pitcher of Diet Coke and our salad and the pizza came. Susan ate the most. Michael was second. Sally third, and I had a single slice.

"Is this like the real way pizza's supposed to be?" Susan asked me.

"Tastes fine to me," I said.

"You're Italian," Susan said. "You should know. Didn't your mother make pizza?"

"No."

"Your grandmother?"

"No."

"How can you be Italian? My mom makes matzo ball soup."

"So did my mom," I said.

"But you're Italian, not Jewish."

"We liked matzoball soup," I said.

"You know," Susan said. "I can never tell when you're serious and when you're trying to be funny."

"It's a curse," I said. "I'm working with a doctor to find the charm that'll free me."

We finished the pizza and I paid the check. Sally left the tip. It was what we had agreed to do whenever I invited them out.

I walked them to their Honda, each carrying the gift I'd given them from Mickey's Collectibles.

"Come over for dinner Sunday," Sally said.

She looked tired but she was smiling. Her skin was clear, and in the red, white, and yellow lights of the stores in the mall she reminded me of Ava Gardner in *The Barefoot Contessa*.

"Adele invited us to come to Flo's for a barbecue," I said. "You, the kids, me, Ames."

"What time?" she asked.

I don't know," I said. "I'll call you tomorrow."

Michael and Susan waved to me as Sally drove off. I checked my watch. If I didn't drive too fast, I'd be in front of Hoffmann's at least fifteen minutes before nine.

14

I WAS ACROSS FROM Kevin Hoffmann's impressive iron gate and high brick walls at ten minutes to nine. I didn't stop. I drove around the neighborhood and came back. There were no other cars on the street of big houses, all with big driveways and big garages.

Then I heard Ames's motor scooter coming. It was like a call to the curious. When he stopped behind me and turned the bike off, I was sure we had only minutes before we were surrounded by police.

A very thin, very small, very nervous black man wearing a pair of dark pants, a navy-colored T-shirt, a bulky-looking brown leather jacket, and a battered fedora that would have been the envy of Indiana Jones got off the back of Ames's bike. I got out of the car.

"Snickers," said Ames.

I shook Snickers's hand and handed him a hundred-dollar

bill, a twenty, and a ten. He kissed each one and said, "The trunk."

We moved behind the car and I opened the trunk. Since it was a rental, it was empty.

Snickers pointed at Ames's scooter.

"Inside," he said, standing back and looking both ways down the street, constantly adjusting his battered fedora.

Ames and I managed to get the scooter in the trunk. Half of it hung out. Ames pulled a bungee cord from the little pouch on his scooter and expertly tied the scooter down.

"Back in the car," Snickers whispered.

We all got back in. From the backseat, leaning over my shoulder, Snickers, who could have used a healthy dose of Scope, guided me slowly to a driveway two estates over from the Hoffmann place.

"They ain't home," said Snickers. "Go right over the lawn. Lights out. Park near the pool on the grass. Cops can't see a car from the street and they don't do a house-by-house until a little after midnight or one depending on which cop is working. Tonight's Friday. It'll be the fat old white guy, off-duty North Port cop. He came by about half an hour ago. He'll hit this stretch at one, maybe a few minutes past, then again at three-thirty."

I nodded and got out of the car, following Snickers, who disappeared through a clump of bushes.

"Wall's not hard to get up," Snickers said, stopping when we got to the barrier. "But up top it's got a jolt that'll send you flying and lucky to land on your ass and they'll know inside something's been climbing or landing."

The moon was almost full but not bright enough to show us what Snickers's flashlight, produced from the inside of his leather jacket, put into a white pool of light.

"Dead birds, gulls, raccoons on the ground all along here," he said. "All zapped. Probably won't kill a man though I don't know, a skinny one like me or you even or an old one like old Ames here wouldn't want to test it out."

"So what do we do?" I asked.

"We wade in the water," Snickers said, snapping off his flashlight. "Like the old song says. 'I'm gonna wade in the water.' "

We followed him along the wall to the narrow beach where the wall ended, but a metal fence about twelve feet high extended into the water about ten yards.

Hoffmann's house was clear from where we stood. It sat back, three stories, lights on in almost every window. I didn't see anyone looking out of a window at the white-moon ripples on the waves.

"We're gonna get wet to the ankles," Snickers said, taking off his shoes and socks, rolling up his cuffs, and motioning for Ames and me to do the same. We did, tucking the socks into the shoes. "Tide's low, real low. We get around the fence. You do just what I do, right behind me, know what I'm sayin'?"

I wasn't sure that an answer was called for, but I said, "Yes."

"And remember, don't touch the fence," Snickers said, shoes tucked under his arms. "I repeat, do not touch the fence."

The water was cool but not cold, bare feet on finely ground shells and then firm sand as we followed Snickers.

The water was up to my calves when we moved around the fence. Something slithered against my foot. I tried not to think of what it might be.

The wooden dock I had seen from inside the house stood high out of the water, with a small cabin boat tied to it and bobbing.

Snickers motioned to us and, heads together, he whispered. "Dock is wired. Boat's wired too. Likewise about ten feet of the beach from fence we came around to fence on the other side. Some scared people in there with something to hide. A challenge. Anthony Bussy likes a challenge."

"Anthony Bussy?" I asked.

"Me," he said with irritation. "You don't think my momma named me Snickers do you? We ain't no comedy team, Snickers, Cowboy, and the Wop. We're Ocean's Three and the head man is me."

Anthony "Snickers" Bussy was high on something. I hoped it was sugar.

We waded single file to the dock but didn't touch it. Snickers moved toward the beach and motioned underneath the boards of the boat dock where small waves were lapping. He bent over and duck-walked under the dock, still ankle-deep in the water. On the far side, he turned and held up his right hand. Then he reached up and took hold of a two-by-four that jutted out and with both hands swung himself up on the deck. Then he turned and held out his hands, motioning for me to reach up to him.

For a skinny little man on a sugar high, Snickers was strong. He pulled me up and balanced me with one hand to keep my feet next to his. Then the two of us helped Ames follow us. This was a little trickier, since Ames was taller and weighed down by whatever armor he carried under his slicker, but he made it.

"There's a wood plank under the sand," Snickers whispered. "About as wide as J. Lo's behind. Walk behind me real tight-ass and you'll feel it with your toes."

Snickers led the way, with Ames behind me probably wondering who Jay Lowe was and how wide a behind he had. We must have looked like three Alzheimer patients playing Follow the Leader.

After about a dozen steps Snickers stopped.

"Safe here," Snickers said. "No dogs. Let's move."

When we reached the shadow of the house, Snickers put his back to the wall, wiped the bottoms of his feet to get rid of the sand, and motioned for us to do the same. Ames and I brushed our feet and put on our socks and shoes.

I had made a rough two-page drawing of the inside of the house, but Snickers had said he didn't need it. He had been here before. All he needed was to know which room we were going for.

"Windows are wired," Snickers whispered. "There's a door back here, back of the garage, and a big door to the house. We go in back here."

The back door was on a broad, covered porch with wooden deck chairs padded with plush turquoise down pillows. The windows off the door were dark. Snickers moved to one of them and looked in. Satisfied, he reached under his leather jacket and came up with two six-inch-long needle-thin rods of metal.

"Spend maybe a hundred and fifty thousand juicing this place and the lock on the back door ain't worth fire-ant shit."

He inserted both pieces of metal in the lock, played with them for a few seconds, and heard something over the waves that Ames and I didn't hear.

"Black jack, quinine, a bit of dose," he said, putting the pieces of metal away and coming out from under his coat with a ribbon-thin strip of dark metal and a pliers, the thinnest pliers I had ever seen, with long pincers.

"Dead bolts," he whispered, going to work. "Two of them. Got a real quiet little handsaw with diamond blades I can rent from a supplier in Tampa, but I didn't have the cash and you didn't have the time. This worked last time. If they didn't change to something better, it'll work again."

Snickers went to work, slowly, quietly.

"You're working cheap," I said, seeing beads of sweat beginning to form on his nose.

"Love of the game," he said. "Here comes our only sure noise. Cowboy?"

Ames reached under his slicker and came out with his shotgun.

There was a metallic double click, not loud but not quiet either. Snickers tucked his tools away, opened the door, and walked in, with Ames and me behind him.

We were in the kitchen. There was enough light coming from the next room to show us that. We stood waiting, Ames's shotgun aimed at the passageway between the kitchen and what looked like a family room or den.

There were voices far away, deep in the house. We followed Snickers through the next door and found ourselves in a room filled with overstuffed dark chairs and shelves of books and videotapes. A large television set with a monster screen stood at the end of the room.

There was a single floor lamp on. Between the shelves of books and tapes were huge paintings of baseball players in full uniform, four of them altogether. In one, Willie Mays stood with his bat back, waiting for the pitch. In another, a pitcher, hands up, ball protected, looking over his shoulder at a man on second base, was frozen forever deciding whether to throw a fastball or curve. I thought it was Robin Roberts. I wasn't sure.

The third painting looked as if it had been copied from an old baseball card, a very old baseball card judging from the player's uniform, mustache, and the part down the center of his hair. I guessed Honus Wagner.

The fourth painting was someone I didn't recognize at first. The Yankees uniform, the confident smile, the bat over his shoulder, the cap tilted back. It was Kevin Hoffmann, an idealized Kevin Hoffmann, a Kevin Hoffmann at least thirty years younger than the man I had met, but definitely Kevin Hoffmann who, I knew, had never played for the Yankees.

"Come on," Snickers whispered to wake me from Hoffmann's dream.

Snickers first, me second, and Ames last, we moved past a door to our right to a second door at the end of the room. Snickers opened it slowly and we heard a man's voice, clear, distinct, several rooms away.

"He's gonna have some trouble living that one down," the man said.

"He's been through it before. We all were. They'll be cheering him with the next home run."

The voices were coming from a radio or television. We moved slowly through a hardwood-floored dining room to an open door. The sound of the baseball announcers came from our right. There was a spiral staircase just to our left. Up we went. When we were almost at the top, I looked down into the room where the voice from the television set said, "A hit here could tie it up."

I could see Kevin Hoffmann below, sitting with his back to me. He was wearing a pair of tan shorts and a baggy short-sleeved shirt with black-and-white vertical stripes. In his left hand was a glass of dark liquid. On his lap was a large pistol. I nudged Ames, who looked where I was pointing and he nodded.

Stanley was around somewhere but either out of sight in the room where Hoffmann sat, reading a book of poetry in the room next to the one where William Trasker lay, or roaming the house with a gun in his hands.

There was a small landing, not big enough for all three of us, at the top of the staircase. And there was a closed door. Snickers opened it slowly. The hinges made no sound. Light flooded in from the hallway beyond.

We moved through the door, Ames with shotgun held at hip level, aimed down the hallway. The door to Stanley's room was open. The light was on. I moved forward and led the way to the room where I had seen Trasker. That door was closed. I opened it very slowly and stepped into darkness, with Snickers behind me and Ames turning his gun toward the now partially open door.

　　　　　　　　　　　　　Stuart M. Kaminsky

Snickers's flashlight came on, circled the room, and hit the bed.

The covers were pulled down and rumpled. There was an indentation where someone's head had been, but there was no William Trasker.

The overhead light suddenly came on and Stanley, in the doorway, a very large Magnum in his right hand, stood looking at us with an amused smile. He adjusted his glasses with his free hand and concentrated on Ames.

"We play gunfight in the streets of Laredo or do we go downstairs and pretend we're civilized? I'm up for either," Stanley said. "Old Wyatt Earp goes first and if he doesn't put me down hard, you're next. Fonesca?"

"Put the gun away, Ames," I said.

"I can do him," Ames said.

"We'd be murdering him in his own house," I said.

"And you didn't come to kill," said Stanley. "You came for William Trasker. I'll take you to him."

Stanley stepped forward carefully, right hand out.

"Turn it around," he said amiably.

Ames turned the shotgun holding it by the barrel. Stanley took it and motioned for us to walk ahead of him out the door. We did.

"Sorry," I said to Snickers as Stanley marched us to the stairway and we started down.

"Not your fault," Snickers said. "Not the money. The challenge got me. Know what I'm sayin'?"

"I know."

Stanley marched us into the baseball collection room where Kevin Hoffmann sat drinking with a pistol in his lap. I could tell now he was wearing a New York Yankees shirt.

A color television sat on a shelf between two trophy cases.

Someone was sliding into second base trying to steal. He was out by a yard.

Hoffmann pushed a button on the remote and the game disappeared.

Below the television set, in an armchair, sat a haggard man in a blue robe dotted with little white fleurs-de-lis. There was a blue terry cloth sash around William Trasker's robe and he was wearing blue leather slippers. His skin was dead pale white. His eyes were dead blue. His mouth was partly open and his hair flopped over his forehead, probably getting in the way of his vision.

The good news was that he was alive and somewhat awake. The bad news was that he looked like he was going to fall over.

"You know what we're going to do?" Hoffmann asked pleasantly, turning his head toward me and motioning to chairs in the room in front of him with the glass in his hand. "We're going to sit here, maybe talk a little, maybe watch a little baseball, White Sox and Yankees, maybe have a drink until we're sure the commission meeting is over. Then you are going to leave and Bill is going back to bed. Maybe Stanley has an appropriate poetic quotation for the occasion."

" 'In the groin of the natural doorway I crouched like a tailor sewing a shroud for a journey,' " Stanley said.

"Shakespeare?" Hoffmann guessed, a distinctly slightly alcoholic smile on his face.

"Dylan Thomas," said Stanley, gun in hand, standing next to the dazed Trasker.

"I can give you the best of Casey Stengel, Bill Veeck, and Yogi Berra, and tell you the real ones from the ones the reporters made up, but poetry and literature . . . Stanley can't be beat. Right, Stanley?"

Stanley didn't answer. Hoffmann drank.

Stuart M. Kaminsky

"Any of this getting through to you, Bill?" Hoffmann asked his brother-in-law.

"You know, after tonight and a few more little bases on balls, Stanley is going to be very rich. Not as rich as you and me, Bill, not as rich as me particularly when you quietly pass away and I inherit your total earthly assets."

Hoffmann turned his head toward me.

"You understand what I'm telling you, Fonesca? You're reasonably smart. Dumb too, but reasonably smart."

"No," I said. "Mr. Trasker here dies and his money which would go to his wife if she were alive goes to his kids."

"My nieces and nephews," Hoffmann concurred. "Not a ballplayer in the lot. They don't even like the game. Bill and my sister believed their children have been ungrateful and should make it on their own. They made me the beneficiary of the Trasker millions, about twenty-two million including the house here and the apartment in New York. In fairness, I made them the beneficiary of my not inconsiderable holdings," said Hoffmann.

"You got anything to eat?" asked Snickers.

"Baby Ruth candy bars, the little ones they give out on Halloween along with little packets of Cracker Jacks," said Hoffmann. "In the bowl over there. Stanley?"

Stanley reached for the bowl and passed it to Snickers.

Bill Trasker blinked his eyes and tried not to keel over. He said something I couldn't make out.

"Sorry?" I said.

"He killed Roberta," Trasker said, more clearly looking at his brother-in-law.

"No," said Hoffmann, taking another drink. "I did not. Bill, I did not kill my sister. I loved only three people in the world. My sister, Lou Gehrig, and Joe DiMaggio. I wouldn't kill them.

Disease got Gehrig. Age got Joe and Stanley's greed got my sister. He was afraid she would give Fonesca here permission to bring in a doctor to look at you. And knowing my sister, if she decided to go that way, she'd bring in Drs. Shelbourne and Kauffman who would have you out of here in two heartbeats. A Shelbourne and a Kauffman are good for a double play when the batter is an alcoholic quack like Jim Obermeyer."

"He speaks highly of you too," I said. "He says you have no backstroke."

"Backhand," Hoffmann corrected. "Baseball's my game, not tennis."

"So you told Stanley to kill her," Trasker managed with a cough.

"No," said Hoffmann, finishing his drink. "I expressly told him not to touch her. Killing her was his idea. He's a very good shot. I didn't ask for details but I'll bet he shot her between the eyes. I, on the other hand, am only a fair shot, so to be safe I'd fire at the stomach and chest from a close distance like this."

Hoffmann raised the gun in his lap toward Trasker, who didn't seem to notice.

Ames sat forward, hand moving quickly toward his belt. Stanley turned his weapon toward Ames as Hoffmann fired.

The first bullet tore into Stanley's chest. The second hit him low in the stomach. Stanley's gun dropped to the floor. Stanley went to his knees and fell forward on his face. Hoffmann fired twice more. The first shot missed and broke the glass on a trophy case. A baseball came rolling out along the floor. The next shot went into the top of Stanley's head.

Snickers sat frozen with a tiny candy bar in his hand.

Trasker blinked down at the body.

Ames was up, a small pistol in his hand aimed at Hoffmann.

I was a spectator.

Stuart M. Kaminsky

Before Ames could issue a warning or fire, Hoffmann dropped his gun to the floor.

"Can I pick up the gun again?" he asked me. "I forgot to shoot myself."

"No," I said, getting up on shaky legs and moving forward to kick the weapon across the room out of his reach.

The baseball that had come out of the broken trophy case rolled past Stanley's bloody body, over shards of glass, and stopped a few feet in front of Hoffmann.

Ames kept his gun leveled at Hoffmann while I moved to Trasker. I handed him the three pills Obermeyer had given me.

"Can you swallow these?" I asked.

"Need water," he mumbled.

"Water," Snickers said, running toward the kitchen.

Hoffmann reached over to pick up the baseball.

"Bobby Shantz," he said looking at the ball. "Little man could pitch. Remember him, Bill?"

Trasker tried to focus.

"Shove all your baseballs up your ass with your goddamned Babe Ruth bat for a battering ram," Trasker managed. "I'll be happy to help you find the hole."

There was hope for Trasker. I checked the clock. It was a little before ten. Snickers was back with a glass of water.

Trasker downed the pills with the water and coughed.

"Watch him," I told Snickers, and ran up the stairs to the room where Trasker had been held.

I found neatly pressed dark slacks, a slightly starched white shirt, and a pair of Bally woven leather loafers on the floor. In the drawer of the dresser I found dark socks and underwear. There was also a wallet and a ring of keys. I put the wallet in the pants pocket along with the keys and hurried them down to the trophy room, where Hoffmann was still looking at his Bobby Shantz ball. I helped Trasker out of his robe and slippers. He looked as if he had spent a couple of years in a Turkish prison. Dressing him was hard. He tried to help.

"Ready," I said.

"What about him?" Ames asked, nodding at Hoffmann.

"Leave him," said Trasker. "Let him blow his goddamn brains out or wait for me to tell the police what happened. Either way I don't give a shit."

The eyes of the two men met. I'd say that they were about even in awareness of the world about now, but that wasn't saying much.

There was a phone on the desk behind Hoffmann. I picked it up and dialed 911. Then I handed the phone to Hoffmann.

"It's the police," I said.

"There's been an accident," Hoffmann said. "No, not an accident. I just shot an employee of mine who was about to kill me. My name? I've got so many. Let me . . . Hoffmann, Kevin Hoffmann."

He handed the phone back to me and I hung it up.

We went out through the front door. Snickers and I held Trasker's arms to help him walk. Ames backed away behind us, shotgun back in his hands, aimed at the door in case Hoffmann changed his mind and opted for assisted suicide.

We made it through the gate, leaving it open, and got Trasker into the front seat of my car. Snickers and Ames sat in back. Snickers had a handful of candy bars and was munching one furiously.

"If he talks his way out of this, I think I'm gonna have the son of a bitch killed," said Trasker.

"Hey, I know a guy . . ." Snickers began.

"Forget it," I said. "No hits. No runs. No errors."

Trasker needed a shave. There was no time.

"How are you doing?" I asked him.

"You mean can I make it through the meeting?" said

Trasker. "I can make it through the meeting and more, but not a hell of a lot more. I'm dying."

"I know. We all are."

"I'm just doing it a lot faster than you," Trasker said, with a touch of bite in his words that made me think Obermeyer's pills were kicking in.

There was silence as we drove except for Snickers munching. About a block from the town hall, I let Snickers and Ames out. We got the scooter from the trunk.

"You get him in on your own?" Ames asked.

"I can walk in on my own," Trasker said, standing next to the car. The scooter started without trouble and Ames and Snickers got on.

"I still got money coming," Snickers said.

"You do," I agreed and went for my wallet.

"Hold it," said Trasker.

He reached into his back pocket and came out with his wallet. He opened it with shaking fingers and pulled out a handful of bills. He gave them to me. I counted eight hundred and twenty dollars, eight hundreds and one twenty.

"He earned it," said Trasker.

I handed the bills to Snickers who tucked them into his shirt pocket and tilted his hat back on his head.

"I'll call you tomorrow," I said to Ames.

Ames nodded and he and Snickers wheeled off into the night, Snickers clinging to the waist of the tall old man.

When I got into the hearing room, where almost all the faces in the audience were black and many of them vaguely familiar from the funeral service at Fernando Wilken's church, it was nearly midnight. Reverend Wilkens saw me and came to meet me at the back of the hall while a well-dressed young black man addressed the bored commission members on the need for a library in Newtown.

One of the few white faces in the crowd belonged to John Rubin of the *Herald-Tribune*. He looked at me, at his watch, and back at me, a question in his eyes.

"You found him?" whispered Wilkens.

Heads were turned toward us.

I said, "He's in the hall."

"Bring him through that door in three minutes. Three minutes exactly," Wilkens said, checking his watch. I checked mine.

Three minutes later, still in need of a shave but wearing the white shirt and slacks and walking on his own, William Trasker shuffled down the carpeted center aisle and into his seat at the table.

The room went silent as they watched Trasker, many, I was sure, wondering if he would drop dead from the effort.

"I think we need an ambulance," said Mayor Beatrice McElveny.

The speaker rose and returned to his seat. I stood at the rear of the room with Wilkens and Trasker. A uniformed officer with arms folded stood next to us.

"You haul me off in an ambulance, Bea, and I sue your sorry ass," said Trasker. "Let's vote."

A commissioner named Wrightman said, "I propose we hold off the Midnight Pass vote till our next meeting. It's getting late and—"

"I'll be dead by the next meeting," Trasker rattled.

"Do I have a motion to conclude this meeting?" the mayor said.

"I so move," said Wrightman.

"All those in favor, raise your hands," said the mayor.

Her hand and Wrightman's went up.

"Opposed?"

Wilkens, Parenelli, and Trasker all raised their hands.

"I move that no further feasibility study be made about the

issue of opening Midnight Pass," said Wilkens. "And that the issue of Midnight Pass be tabled indefinitely."

"Second the motion," said Parenelli.

"Discussion?" said the chair.

"I still think—" Wrightman said.

"Call the question," said Trasker.

"Bill," Wrightman said, "you don't know what you're doing."

"Call the question," Trasker repeated. "You haven't known what you were doing for the past five years and you've still voted."

"Commissioner Trasker," the mayor said. "Please wait till we've heard discussion on the question. Discussion?"

A less than confident Commissioner Wrightman, amid grumbling from the crowd, stood and said, "Logic, plain simple logic says that a hasty decision now could cause environmental damage, long-term environmental damage that none of us want. Let's go over the history of this controversy—"

"Point of order," said Wilkens. "I get the distinct impression that my colleague plans to filibuster, to talk until Commissioner Trasker, who is obviously unwell, cannot participate in any debate. I move for cloture."

"You have no reason to think that Commissioner Wrightman plans—" the mayor began.

"Vote cloture," said Trasker. "Now. Follow the goddamn rules, Bea."

Reluctantly, clearly defeated, the mayor called for the vote. Wrightman sat down. Most of the audience applauded.

"Call the question," Parenelli said.

"Call the question," Wilkens added.

"Call the question," most of those in the audience repeated.

"All in favor of tabling the Midnight Pass study, respond by saying 'Aye,'" Beatrice McElveny said reluctantly.

"With all due respect," said Wilkens, "that was not the motion. The motion was to have no study and to keep the Pass closed. That was my motion."

The audience applauded again.

The mayor called for the vote.

There were three ayes and one nay. The mayor chose to abstain rather than suffer defeat.

The crowd went wild. The mayor found her gavel and pounded for quiet.

"Quiet, please," Reverend Wilkens said.

Parenelli the radical was grinning and shaking his head. Wilkens raised his hands. The audience went silent.

"Madame Mayor," said Parenelli, "I believe we just passed a motion."

The mayor looked confused.

"You hit the gavel," said the old man. "And then you say, 'The motion carries.' You've been doing that for almost a year. It shouldn't be that hard."

The mayor tapped the gavel and, voice breaking, said, "The motion carries."

There was handshaking all around, but a small cluster of well-dressed men and women gathered in the corner with Commissioner Wrightman. Someone called the mayor to join the group. She gathered her papers and bypassed the gathering.

"Bea knows which side her ballot is buttered on," Parenelli said.

"It's not over," said Wilkens. "William, are you all right?"

"No, but thanks to you, I'm conscious and I got to do something for the right reasons for a change. Not enough to get me into heaven, if there is one, but maybe I'll get a cushy job in hell making cold stale coffee when the damned come off of their one-minute break every millennium."

"Mr. Fonesca," Wilkens said, taking my hand, "thank you. If there is ever anything . . ."

"You know Jerry Robins?"

"Downtown Association, yes," said Wilkens.

"You know the Texas Bar and Grill on Second?"

"Yes," he said. "There's a connection?"

"Robins and some others want the Texas to go upscale or move out," I said. "A friend of mine owns it, another friend who helped me get Trasker here tonight lives and works there."

"And you want me to . . ."

"Talk to Robins," I said.

"He doesn't necessarily represent the feelings of the majority of members of the association," Wilkens said. "I'll discuss it with him. I'm sure reason will prevail."

"Thank you," I said.

"You'll have to excuse me now," Wilkens said, touching my shoulder.

John Rubin was at my side, notepad out.

"What happened here tonight?" he said. "I mean, what really happened?"

"Someone's been shot at Kevin Hoffmann's house."

"Who?" Rubin asked.

"A man named Stanley LaPrince," I said.

"Is he dead?"

"He's dead," I said.

"This have something to do with the vote here?"

"Might," I said.

"Details?" asked Rubin.

"Ask the police," I said.

"Thanks, Fonesca."

He tapped his notebook with his pen, looked at Wilkens and Trasker, and I could see that he had decided that a murder in the home of a rich citizen was more important news than the aftermath of the outcome of a commission vote. Besides, he had his notes. He'd probably be up the rest of the night.

It was almost one in the morning when I got back to my office. The sky had cleared. The moon was full.

I had a breakfast in the morning I wasn't looking forward to.

15

SPANISH OMELET HERE is great," said Kenneth Severtson Sr., digging into the Saturday morning special at First Watch.

The place was bright, crowded, and noisy.

I had bacon and eggs. Janice Severtson, sitting next to her husband, was working on a ham-and-cheese omelet. All three of us had coffee.

Janice's hand rested on the table. Her husband touched it.

"How are the kids?" I asked, pouring myself a second cup of coffee.

"Fine," Janice said with a solemn smile. "My sister flew down from Charleston yesterday to help out. She's watching them."

"How do we thank you, Mr. Fonesca?" Severtson asked.

"You said you had a bonus," I said.

"Name it," said Severtson.

"One thousand, cash," I said. "You have it with you?"

"One thou— No, but I think I have about four hundred. I stopped at the bank yesterday. Janice, you have any cash?"

She reached for her purse on the bench next to her, found her wallet, and came up with almost two hundred. Between the two of them they came up with a little over six hundred dollars.

"I'll settle for that," I said, accepting Ken and Janice's money across the table.

"I can get the rest on Monday or from an ATM if you really need it soon," Severtson said.

"No," I said, pocketing the cash. "This will do it."

"Is there anything else we can do for you? We owe you so much," Janice said, squeezing her husband's hand.

"Three things," I said, drinking some more coffee.

"Name them," said Ken.

"First, stop shooting at me."

No one spoke. A woman at the table behind us said to whoever was sitting with her, "Who knows about Virginia? She blows hot and cold. Today's a cold day. Don't ask."

"What?" asked Severtson.

"Stop shooting at me," I said. "Trying to kill me. You know. Midnight Pass. The Laundromat."

"You're crazy," said Severtson.

"Extremely depressed," I said. "Close to suicidal a few times, but my therapist assures me I'm not psychotic. Dealing with people like you can bring me close to the line, but then there are people who can pull me back."

"Why would I want to kill you?" asked Ken Severtson with a laugh, looking at his wife, who wasn't laughing.

"Because you know I've been asking questions about you and Stark, that I'd found out he has a two-million-dollar insurance policy with you as beneficiary and that the business, which

Stuart M. Kaminsky

grossed over a million and a half last year, is all yours now. It wasn't hard to find."

"This is crazy," Severtson said.

I wasn't looking at him anymore. I was looking at his wife. She wouldn't meet my eyes.

"When you knocked at my door in Orlando," I said. "You told me you knew who I was because you called some friends in Sarasota who knew me. Then you said your husband must have hired me."

Janice Severtson didn't look up.

"Who did you call at three in the morning who knows me?" I asked.

She didn't answer.

"And I told you I was in Orlando with my wife and kids," I went on. "When you came into my room you didn't look around for anyone else. You didn't ask where my wife and kids were."

"I was . . . I didn't know what I was doing."

"You did know," I said. "You knew."

I turned to her husband.

"There was a little girl in that Laundromat," I told him. "She was standing a few feet away from me. Her name is Alaska Dreamer. She's got a toy monster with a big eye that lights up. She could have been killed."

Janice Severtson's eyes looked at her unfinished omelet.

"Wait, I don't get anything if Stark committed suicide," Kenneth Severtson said.

"No, but you do when your wife admits to killing him to protect your daughter from being molested. You set me up, Severtson. You both did. Stark didn't seduce your wife. She seduced him. He never touched your kids, did he?"

Neither of them answered this time.

"How long were you going to wait before Janice supposedly

got conscience-stricken and called the Orlando police? Monday? Then they'd call me and you'd tell me to tell the truth. It wouldn't take much of a lawyer to get her to walk, but you can afford a good lawyer now."

"But why kill you?" he asked. "You're our witness."

"You found out I had checked on your business and Stark's insurance. It wasn't hard. You just called your office and they told you about my coming there. Once I knew about the insurance and your getting control of the business, you'd be better off without me testifying to anything. Maybe you even wondered how long it would take me to ask myself who your wife had called at three in the morning from Orlando and she'd remember that she hadn't asked about the family I supposedly had on vacation. In fact, you couldn't afford to have me tell the Orlando police what I know."

"This is crazy," he said.

"You already said that twice. You didn't miss me on purpose. You're just a lousy shot. The only other person who might have wanted me dead was a man named Stanley who wouldn't have missed."

"You haven't any proof," Janice said.

"I know. That's why I wrote a letter last night and mailed it to a cop in Orlando. If I get killed now, I don't think he's going to buy your story and I don't think you'll stand a chance in hell or on earth of collecting your money. Maybe I'm wrong. Maybe a good lawyer can make me look bad on the stand. Probably can. Maybe you can get away with it. Probably not. The insurance company won't give up. They'll take you to civil court and your business is going to go to hell fast. Great headline: 'Wife Seduces and Murders Husband's Partner in Insurance Plot.' "

"You broke the law," Janice reminded me. "You advised me to say it was suicide."

"And you made the mistake of going along with it," I said. "You thought fast. You'd go along with my suicide story and then break down and tell the police you had killed Stark to protect your children."

"It was self-defense," she said, her voice shaking. "He hit me, said he was going to kill me and the children. I believed him."

Ken Severtson was shaking his head yes. That was going to be their story.

"It's got big holes, especially me, but stick with that. It's probably the best you can do.

"I think my testimony will keep me from being charged for obstruction. I may be wrong. I've got a good law firm to represent me. You know Tycinker, Oliver, and Schwartz?"

They didn't answer.

The waitress brought the bill.

"I'll take it," I said.

"Don't do this to our children," Janice pleaded.

"With parents like you? I think I'm doing it *for* them."

"Look, Fonesca," Severtson said, leaning toward me. "We can —"

"No," I said. "We can't."

They got up and left without another word. I hoped Janice's sister was a decent human being. I hoped she'd take Kenny Jr. and Sydney. I hoped they wouldn't wind up on the desk of Sally Porovsky or someone in her office.

"Hey, Lew," someone said, as I played with a strip of bacon.

I looked up.

Dave from the Dairy Queen sat down across from me with a mug of coffee in his hand.

"Got the kids over there," he said, nodding toward a table across the room where his two children sat across from each other, drinking large glasses of chocolate milk.

He lifted his mug.

"Nice-looking couple you were having breakfast with," he said.

"Nice-looking," I agreed.

"So, tomorrow I take the kids to Disney World."

"I was there the other day," I said.

"You?"

"Yeah."

"Have fun?" Dave asked.

"I'll never forget it," I said.

Dave smiled, glanced at his children. His eyes went moist with a vision of happy kids and magical rides and singing dwarves. Or maybe I imagined it.

I went back to my room and erased the four messages on my machine without listening to them. Then I called Ann Horowitz's answering machine at work.

I hoped she wouldn't answer on a Saturday. She didn't. Her machine said I could leave a short message and she would get back to me quickly or I could call her emergency number if I had an emergency. I didn't have an emergency. What I had to tell her would take a while.

There was a knock at the door. I didn't want a knock on the door unless it was a special delivery from a God I no longer believed in telling me that the last three years of my life had only been a dream.

"Come in," I said.

Digger came in. He was smiling sadly. He needed a shave.

"How was last night?" I asked.

"Perfect. You should have seen me. Tripping the light fantastic. What does that mean, 'tripping the light fantastic'?"

"I don't know," I said.

Stuart M. Kaminsky

"Well, I did it. I charmed old ladies, didn't eat too much from the buffet if you know what I mean, and got paid in cash and asked to come back on Monday to maybe talk about teaching dance lessons part-time."

"Congratulations," I said.

"I'll try it," he said, sitting in the chair across from my desk. "But I don't know if I can handle real life."

"I know what you mean," I said.

"How was your night?" he asked.

I could have said, Digger, I saw a man shot to death, got up this morning and had breakfast with two murderers, but I said, "Fine."

"You look tired."

"I am."

"I was going to offer to buy you breakfast at Gwen's."

"Another time, Digger."

He got up to leave.

"Wait," I said. "I've got something for you."

I dug into the brown paper bag on my desk, the one from Mickey's, and came up with a button. I handed it to him.

On the button was a photograph of Dick Van Dyke on a rooftop in *Mary Poppins*. In quotes above Van Dyke's head were the words "Steps in Time."

Digger grinned at the button and carefully pinned it to the buttonhole on his pocket so he wouldn't make a hole in his shirt.

"I'm a working man," Digger said with a deep sigh, and left the office, closing the door quietly as he left. I hadn't slept much the night before. I pulled down the shades, climbed into bed around two, and turned on a tape of *The Treasure of the Sierra Madre*. I watched Walter Huston do his dance on the mountain and call Curtain and Dobbs damned fools for not knowing they were standing on top of gold. I watched Emilio Fernandez say, "Badges, badges, we don't need no stinkin' badges." I said it along with him.

I made it to the end of the tape and immediately fell asleep.

I had closed the door between my room and the office but I was vaguely aware that the phone rang while I slept. The second time it rang something in the dim female voice got through to me. It rang more times. I slept. Then one of the rings got through to me in the middle of a dream I lost when I opened my eyes. I checked my watch. I had slept three hours.

I staggered to the phone and played the messages back. All of them were from Detective Etienne Viviase. All of them said I should call him as soon as I got in. He left his office and cell phone number.

I tried the office. He didn't answer. I tried the cell phone.

"Yeah," he said.

"Fonesca,"

"I talk, you listen," he said. "Understand?"

"I understand."

"Kevin Hoffmann shot Stanley LaPrince last night. He told the officers who were dispatched by 911 that Stanley had killed Roberta Trasker and was about to shoot him. He also told them that you and two other people saw it all and that you had left the house with Trasker. When I got there, Hoffmann was tossing an autographed baseball in the air and watching a Yankees game. He wouldn't talk to me. He wanted his lawyer. Questions. Were you there?"

"Yes."

"Did Stanley admit he killed Roberta Trasker?"

"Hoffmann said he did. Stanley didn't deny it."

"And Stanley was going to shoot Hoffmann?"

"Looked that way," I said.

"Who were the other two witnesses?" he asked.

I didn't answer.

"McKinney?"

I didn't answer.

"Who was the black guy?"

I didn't answer.

"You took Trasker," Viviase said.

"He went with me willingly," I said. "You can ask him."

"I heard about the commission vote," he said. "I will ask him. I want you to come in and sign a statement. Today. You understand?"

"Perfectly," I said, and hung up.

The phone rang before I could take my hand from it. I picked it up and listened to the voice on the other end. Then I hung up and called Sally.

Fifteen minutes later I had parked in the emergency-room lot at Sarasota Memorial Hospital and was taken to the little room where I now sat.

Sally walked in.

"How does it look, Lew?"

She took my right hand in both of hers.

"He's going," I said. "Doctor says it's a miracle he made it through last night. Obermeyer was probably right."

We looked at William Trasker, his eyes closed, mouth open, tube in his nose, tendons in his neck blue against white skin.

"What I don't understand," I said to Sally, looking down at the dying man, "is why he asked for me."

"Maybe because he knew his children couldn't get here in time," she said.

"Wilkens then," I said.

"You know why," came Trasker's faint voice from the bed. His eyes fluttered open. "Unless you're a dumber son of a bitch than I thought you were. If I had the time, I'd call my lawyer and have him change my will. I'd make you a rich little wop bastard, but you wouldn't want it, would you?"

"No," I said.

"No," he said, eyes trying to focus now, voice failing. "I didn't think so. Trying to do the right things before I die, but there are too many."

"Maybe you'll get better long enough to do a few more," Sally said.

"You a nurse?" he whispered.

"No," she said. "A friend."

"Whose?"

"Lew's," she said. "Now yours."

"Is there anyone we can call for you?" she asked.

Before he could answer, two people in blues, one man and one woman, came in the room and said they had to take him now. They were in a hurry.

"You can wait here or in the waiting room," the man said.

Sally and I got cups of coffee from the vending machine and went into the lobby. It was Saturday but it was early and the weekend horror had slowed down until night came, but there were still people waiting.

"A kid named Alaska Dreamer ever make her way across your desk?" I asked.

"Alaska Dreamer? No, I'd remember, but I'll ask around. Why?"

"I've got a present for her in the car."

"Lew, are you all right?"

"Getting better all the time," I said.

Sally drank some coffee.

"Maybe this is a bad time," she said. "But remember the woman who was in my office the last time you came? Son named—"

"Darrell," I said.

"She's trying hard, Lew. How'd you like to be a Big Brother?"

"I wouldn't," I said.

"Think about it? You're good with kids, Lew. You're good with my kids."

"I . . ."

The nurse in blue who had wheeled Bill Trasker out of the Emergency Room came through the sliding doors and approached us.

"I'm sorry," he said. "He's gone. Dr. Spence will talk to you, if you like. We're getting in touch with Mr. Trasker's children."

"Thanks," I said.

"I'm sorry," the nurse said again, and walked solemnly back toward the emergency-room sliding doors.

"Let's go, Lew," Sally said.

I wondered if the Traskers' kids would come. They could make it a double funeral. Mother and father. After all this time, almost strangers. I knew I would not be going.

We dropped our coffee cups in the parking-lot trash can and faced each other.

"Big Brother?" I asked.

"Darrell's not easy," Sally said. "Lew, if you do it, I wouldn't hope for a lot from him."

"I never hope for a lot," I said.

"Anything you'd like to do today?" Sally asked, holding my hand.

"I've got to go to Viviase's office and make a statement."

"After that?"

"I don't know. I wonder if Flo and Adele need anything for the barbecue tomorrow."

"Let's find out."

Sally tracked down Francie and Alaska Dreamer on Monday.

I went to their apartment in Bradenton. Bubbles was there, filling the door. When she recognized me, she stepped out of the way and let me in. Francie was in a small kitchen off of a small living room with a small television.

It was late in the morning. Francie was sitting at the table with a cup of coffee.

"How's your laundry?" she said when she saw me.

"Full of holes," I said. "Is Alaska here?"

"No," she said. "And much as I'd like to talk to you, I've got to gulp this down and get to work at Wendy's. How did you find me?"

"I'm a process server," I reminded her.

Bubbles behind me confirmed, "He's a process server."

"What can I do for you?" asked Francie. "You want a quick cup of coffee? A little chat about old times with Mom when I leave."

"No, no thanks," I said. "Is Alaska all right?"

"She's fine," Francie said. "At school. Kindergarten. Mom picks her up. Alaska's hooked on that chopped-liver stuff now since you gave her the sandwich. If you're worried about what all that shooting and the cops with guns did to her, it's okay. She liked it. Told her friends. They didn't believe her. I had to tell them it really happened. Alaska was a kindergarten celebrity for a few days."

"Brought you something," I said, taking an envelope out of my pocket and putting it in front of her on the table.

"You're serving papers on my kid?" Bubbles said, angrily stepping in front of me, looming over me.

"No," I said, ready for a punch this time if one was coming. "Look inside."

Francie opened the envelope and counted the money.

"Six hundred dollars," she said.

"A man and woman with two kids and plenty of money gave that to me to give to you when they heard about what happened at the Laundromat. They felt responsible."

"Why? I mean, why did they feel responsible?"

"Long story. Do me a favor and take it. No strings. I'm out the door and out of your life."

"I'm not turning down six hundred dollars," Francie said with a smile. "You find any more people with bad consciences and money they don't need, we'll be here."

"Sorry," said Bubbles. "Thanks."

"It's okay."

"I mean, I'm sorry I hit you that time."

"Me, too."

When I left the Dreamers, I returned the Nissan to Fred and Alan.

"Who was in the front seat of this car?" Alan asked, wiping his hands after inspecting the interior. "A pair of water buffalo after an afternoon of wallowing in the mud?"

"It's Florida," Fred said. "What do you expect?"

"We should add on a cleaning charge," Alan grumbled.

"Al, come on. It's almost halfway to Christmas," Fred said, putting a calming hand on his partner's shoulder. "We've got a good customer here. We don't want to lose him."

"All right," Alan said, and then added to me, "How about a cup of coffee?"

"Sure," I said, sitting down.

This time Alan went for the coffee.

"So," said Fred, leaning back against his desk and folding his arms. "How'd the week go?"

"Fine," I said. "Three murders, lots of threats, a couple of tries at killing me."

"The usual," Fred said with a big grin, as Alan returned with the coffee.

"Cream and sweetener, right?" Alan said, handing me the cup.

"Lew should be a finance officer in some big dealership in town. Can look you right in the eye and say someone's trying to kill him and you almost believe him."

"Lew's got a sense of humor all right," Alan said, handing his partner a cup of coffee.

"Someday I'll give you the stand-up comedy routine I'm working on," I said.

They both laughed.

I got my bike and drove to the Y on Main. I did my usual workout using all the machines and the steps. I had a good sweat going, finished in forty-five minutes, took a shower, and pedaled back.

Dave and his kids were at a DQ table. I said hi, parked my bike, and went up to my office. No calls. No papers to serve.

I went to pull down my window shade. I could see the dance studio across the street. Through the large floor-to-ceiling windows of the studio, I could see a man all alone, arms held as if he were dancing with an invisible woman. The man's eyes were closed. He had a smile on his face.

I watched Digger dance for a few minutes and then pulled down the shade.

All I had to do now was memorize my jokes. I went to bed instead.

The barbecue at Flo's started at eleven and went on till about seven. Ames, who had come unarmed, spent most of the time listening politely to whomever wanted to make small talk with him, but he devoted his really serious time on the screened deck at the back of the house listening to Adele and holding Catherine.

Flo kept the volume on the stereo system down, but not so low that we wouldn't know we were being serenaded by a never-repeating concert of bluegrass, cowboy, country-and-western, and mountain music.

"That's the soundtrack of *O Brother, Where Art Thou?*," Flo told me at one point. "You'd like the movie, Lewis."

Flo saw to it that everyone kept eating.

"No beer. No wine," she had announced to each guest as

Stuart M. Kaminsky

they arrived. "I'm driving now and I'm taking no chances. I should be facing the devil, but every time I've done that in the past, the bastard won."

Sally's Susan ate the most, helped Flo with the grilling, and waved at her mother, who stayed close to me, saying things from time to time like, "Hang in there, Lewis. You can be happy for a few more hours."

Michael, with a huge platter of ribs, coleslaw, and potato salad and an oversize glass of Coke, had settled himself, with his mother's permission, in front of the television in what used to be Flo's husband, Gus's, office. He spent most of the day watching movies and reporting the score of the Cubs doubleheader with San Diego. The Cubs split. Sammy hit one home run.

Everyone looked happy. Everyone thanked Adele and Flo and said nice things about Catherine.

"I'll help with the cleanup," Sally said.

"I've already got a volunteer," Flo said, looking at Ames. "I'll drive him home later."

"Call me, Lew," Sally said in the driveway, touching my cheek.

"I will," I said.

And I did.

EPILOGUE

JANICE AND KENNETH Severtson got a good lawyer, but not good enough. I had a lawyer, Tycinker himself, who cut a deal with the Orlando prosecutor. I testified. I walked with no charges. The Severtsons made a deal and pleaded to conspiracy to commit murder. Kenneth Jr. and Sydney went to Charleston with Janice's sister.

With Trasker dead and my statement, Viviase didn't go after Hoffmann. When enough newspapers and mail had piled up at Hoffmann's gate, a neighbor called the police. They came. Hoffmann couldn't be found, nothing seemed to be missing except for the baseball collection.

No one in Sarasota has seen or heard from Kevin Hoffmann, wherever or whoever he might be now.

Three months later there was a hotly contested special election to fill the place of the deceased William Trasker on the commission. One of the biggest voter turnouts in Sarasota history. A Hispanic named Gomez who owned a big auto-repair business was elected. There was talk of another vote on Midnight Pass.

I did my stand-up act for Ann Horowitz on a Wednesday morning.

"You're funny," she said.

"I'm not trying to be."

"That is precisely why you are. Comedy, like life much of the time, depends on timing and delivery. In your case, you are afflicted with Cassandra's curse, doomed to say funny things, which you do not find funny. We'll work on that."

Later that morning, after I had discussed it with Ann, I called Sally and told her I'd be Darrell Caton's Big Brother.

Life went on.